CH00665866

UNDER THE RADAR

by

David R Ewens

Grosvenor House
Publishing Limited

The right of David R Ewens to be identified as the author of this
work has been asserted by him in accordance with Section 78
of the Copyright, Designs and Patents Act 1988

The book cover picture is copyright to Kim Jackson

This book is published by
Grosvenor House Publishing Ltd
28-30 High Street, Guildford, Surrey, GU1 3EL.
www.grosvenorhousepublishing.co.uk

A CIP record for this book
is available from the British Library

ISBN 978-1-78148-623-8

About the author

David R Ewens worked for many years in the further and adult education sector. He lives and writes in Kent.

Also by David R Ewens
in the 'Frank Sterling' series

The Flanders Case
Rotten
Fifth Column

Chapter 1

Count Dracula

When the phone rang, Frank Sterling almost fell off his chair. His feet were up on the desk and he had been balancing precariously, with the back of the chair angled as close to the horizontal as it would go. He recovered quickly, slipping the lever so the back returned almost upright, propelling him towards the phone on the right of his desk. He had tried to give up the slouching habit, but boredom often prevailed. He couldn't remember when he last got a call. Yesterday? Last week?

'Frank Sterling Investigations,' he said into the phone.

'Hold for an operator-assisted call from a text-phone user,' said a robotic voice.

Sterling almost hung up. Cold callers used endless ploys to start conversations. He hadn't come across this one before. But he had not worked on a case for over a week and perhaps there was sport to be had from declining an offer of cut-price double glazing or the sure-fire certainty of stock market riches via a boiler-room on the Costa Brava.

An operator replaced the robot. 'You have a message from a deaf person. Have you taken one of these calls before?'

This was intriguing. 'No,' said Sterling.

'OK, this is how it works. As we are speaking now, the deaf person is waiting for me to explain 'Text Relay', which is what this is. You will be able to hear his voice when he speaks to you, but because he can't hear, I type what you say to him and it appears on a screen. When you finish your bit of the conversation, say "go ahead", and he'll start speaking. Got that?'

'I think so,' said Sterling.

'Right, we're starting. Is that Frank Sterling Investigations?'

'Yes,' said Sterling, trying to get into the spirit of it. He'd already said that. Was there going to be endless repetition? Nothing happened for a few moments. He wondered if he had lost the call. As things were going, he didn't much care.

'You have to say "go ahead",' said the operator. 'Otherwise I don't know if you've finished your bit of the conversation.'

For God's sake, thought Sterling. He noted the operator's Scouse accent, but surely that had nothing to do with it. 'Go ahead,' he said.

'Bloody hell,' came another voice. 'Are you always this slow on the uptake? It doesn't bode well if I'm going to engage you. Go ahead.'

Sterling resisted the urge to tell the caller to get lost. He couldn't afford it. 'Sorry. I'm not used to this system. What's the problem? Go ahead.'

'I'm not talking about it on the telephone. Are you in your office this afternoon? About two o'clock? Go ahead.'

'That should be fine.' Sterling looked at his watch without knowing why. His diary was empty and he was going nowhere. It was five to 12. 'Two o'clock will be fine. Can I take your name and phone number?' It was a second or two before he remembered to say "go ahead"'.

'Nicholas Jameson. 18002 for text relay. Then 01304 773218. Got that? You're in Market Street, Sandley. Will you be easy to find? Go ahead.'

'There's a sign at my window, which is on the first floor upstairs. I share the entrance downstairs with Sandley library. Go ahead.'

'Right. See you there at two. Thanks, operator. Goodbye to everyone. SK.'

'Just a second. Can I ask what it's about so I can....?'

'The caller said SK,' said the operator. 'That means "stop keying". He's gone now. Goodbye from me.'

Now only the dialling tone buzzed in Sterling's ear. What a performance that was. He put the handset back in the cradle but kept his hand over it, thinking some more. There had been a few cases since he started out privately last September, notably one that had taken him on a dangerous outing to Belgium and a couple of attempted insurance scams, but times were hard. It was April now, and winter's grip had been harsh. Maybe his luck was on the turn.

The name Nicholas Jameson was familiar. Sterling thought it was local. He had been keeping up with the local news. It had been quiet enough for him to go down to the library and read the Kent newspapers. He went to the BBC Kent website on the computer next to his telephone and Googled Nicholas Jameson. There he was – son of Daphne Jameson, resident of Hamworth Place, an elderly woman bludgeoned to death in 'mysterious circumstances' last month. The inquest had said 'Murder by person or persons unknown' and the report indicated that 'police investigations are continuing', meaning, from Sterling's personal and professional experience, that the police were foxed. There was talk of a burglary gone wrong, but few other details.

Sterling wondered why Nicholas Jameson was interested in speaking to him. He would be able to add nothing to the police investigation except, almost certainly, resentment. He couldn't do much more now. He would wait till two o'clock. His clattering steps echoed on the narrow wooden staircase down from his office, which occupied a small upstairs portion of Sandley library's premises. Instead of going out of the front door, he turned right into the library itself. Angela Wilson, his friend the librarian, was at the Issues and Returns desk.

Sterling watched her slender dark fingers dance over her keyboard as her slim frame leaned towards the computer monitor. He still had no idea why she had deserted her metropolitan life for a librarian's job in the sticks, but he certainly wasn't complaining. They had met on his last job in the Kent police – investigating a burglary of the house she'd just moved into in a modern terraced block, coincidentally just a few doors down from his own. They'd had coffee after the court case, when the young housebreaker had been sent down for six months, and Sterling had spoken up for the district. 'You were unlucky. It's actually peaceful and pretty down here. I'll show you', he had said, and it was the start of a warm friendship – just what he had needed in his own time of lonely turmoil.

He was the tourist guide. She was the educator, filling in the gaps in his inattentive schooling with witty and wide-ranging discourses and unearthing in him a talent for puzzles and crosswords. Angela had alerted him to the empty office he now rented above and conjoined to the library and, if she had not encouraged him, then she had at least supported him in his escape from the bureaucratic hierarchy of the police.

Quite how a first class double honours degree in German and Modern History was necessary for her current post would be hard for anyone to fathom. Quite apart from her qualifications, it was as if a scion of West African royalty, via a later lineage from Trinidad and Tobago and south London, was doing work experience in east Kent.

'Angela, I'm going to Spar for a sandwich. Do you want one?'

'I've brought my own, thanks, Frank. You should do that yourself. It's not as if you're so inundated with work you haven't got time to slice a bit of bread and put some cheese in it of a morning.'

'Yeah, yeah,' said Sterling, flapping his hand. 'Put the kettle on. I won't be long.'

A few moments later, they were sitting in her small office behind the desk with a cup of tea each and their sandwiches. It was quiet in the library. Easter had been and gone. The schools were back and Wednesday in Sandley, with no market and half-day closing, meant that most of Angela's regulars would be indoors – likely reading or viewing what they had borrowed.

'Nicholas Jameson,' said Sterling, swallowing a bite of cheese and chutney sandwich and washing it down with some tea. That was the only way to eat supermarket sandwiches successfully, especially if, like his, they had reached their 'sell-by' date and were reduced. Then they tasted even more of cardboard.

'Why do you ask?' said Angela. 'I assume there is a question in there somewhere.'

'He's coming to see me at two o'clock this afternoon. After that Ypres thing last year, I'm trying to do my research the right way round.'

'Ah yes, beetling off to Belgium on a wild goose chase and then getting all the background afterwards. Good to know that you have learned your lesson.' She nodded and smiled at the memory. 'Still, you got away with it in the end.'

Sterling noticed a crumb at the corner of Angela's mouth. The brown contrasted with her red lipstick but was more camouflaged against her dark skin. 'Crumb,' he said, putting his finger up to the corner of his own mouth.

Angela was immaculate in everything. She ducked her head and brushed at her mouth, but on the wrong side.

'Other side,' said Sterling. 'You've got it now.' She had a tendency to tease him that she generally held in check. Pointing out the crumb redressed the balance between them in an indefinable way.

'Nicholas Jameson,' said Angela. 'Property developer, local philanthropist, occasional campaigner. He lives at Hamworth Place, which is a very elegant Georgian pile in the centre of the village. His mother lived there with him, and some other family. I think his wife died, and I seem to remember reading somewhere that it was in childbirth. She's not on the scene anymore, anyway. You heard that the mother was found dead three weeks ago. The police are treating it as murder, but haven't got very far. Jameson must have had a solid alibi because he wasn't ever arrested – and nor was anyone else connected with the family. I know all this from the papers. I'm probably just reminding you. I imagine Andy Nolan could tell you more, if he's still speaking to you.'

Andy Nolan, always known and addressed by his full name and now a detective sergeant, was about Sterling's only firm friend in the police, but that friendship had been tested during the Belgian adventure.

Sterling pretended to bridle. 'Andy Nolan and I are OK. He knew that my interests and police interests didn't always converge. The police got their convictions. I didn't obstruct them. They would have been nowhere without me.'

'OK, Frank,' said Angela, holding her palms up towards him. 'He's your mate.'

'Maybe he was a bit cross at the time. I told the truth and nothing but the truth, just not all of it. But you don't undo the friendship forged on night shifts in patrol cars over five long years when things go a bit astray in one private case. I'll contact him after my appointment. Speaking of which, I think I'd better go back upstairs and get ready.'

Just before two o'clock, Sterling was looking out of his office window over the square. Freddy Henderson, the grocer a few doors down from Spar, glanced up from stacking potatoes outside his door. His eyes were hidden by the pebbles that passed for lenses in his tortoiseshell spectacles and he raised his hand in salute. Even though it was April, he still needed his fingerless gloves. A brisk wind rustled around the square, and a patter of rain squalled against the window. It was dark for a few moments, but it was the kind of weather that would mean sunshine again almost immediately. A middle-aged man emerged quickly out of No Name Street, probably having parked in the Cattle Market beyond the Guildhall. He was wearing a long, dark cashmere overcoat, not yet put away after winter, with the collar turned up. He looked up at the sign and ducked through the door below. As Sterling lost contact with his eyes, he found it again with his ears as the man, obviously Nicholas Jameson, bounded up the steps, by the sound of it taking them two at a time.

Sometimes Sterling's clients clambered laboriously, worn out by disappointment or illness. Sometimes the clatter signified urgency or anxiety. There was energy and brusqueness in this nimble movement.

There was no time to call out 'come in'. The door sprang open and hit the doorstop, vibrating slightly. It was a cheap, thin door to a cheap, spartan office. The man who entered had a pale complexion, except for a hint of colour in his cheeks, a short, straight nose in a face of generally regular thin features, spiky, short white hair and an ascetic air. With the collar of his dark greatcoat turned up, he looked not unlike an early silver screen Count Dracula, but without the fangs.

'May I?' he said, removing the coat and hanging it on the peg on the door, which had eased back and which he closed. Without the coat, the Dracula effect completely disappeared. Sterling, made alert by the bustle and energy, sat upright in his chair and angled the computer monitor so that there would be uninterrupted eye contact between him and his potential customer. Jameson settled quickly in the chair opposite the desk and tossed a small notepad and pen onto the desk in front of him. Sterling noticed that the pen was inscribed 'Tower Bridge Hilton'. If he had a case, there would surely be no problem with his fees.

'Nicholas Jameson,' stated Sterling.

'Frank Sterling,' countered Jameson.

Both men nodded in unison, as if they were listening to the same piece of music.

'Well, are you Frank and are you Sterling?' said Jameson. Sterling was beginning to grasp who was running the interview.

'Yes. I thought we'd just done introductions.'

'I mean, are you what it says on the tin?'

'What it says on the… Oh, right. That. Maybe. It was my father's little joke, or maybe not so little. He couldn't resist it, and my mother was in no position to interfere. He read a lot of *Boy's Own Papers* when he was a kid. Perhaps he thought there'd be a bit of self-fulfilling prophecy about it as well. Anyway, I'm honest, as you'd expect, and genuine enough. I'm not sure it's for me to judge. The name's done me no harm. It's not as if I was a boy named Sue.'

'A toy named Boo?' An irritable, puzzled look flashed across Jameson's face.

'A Boy named Sue'. The Johnny Cash song.' Sterling started singing the last verse. It was part of his father's generation of music, from which he himself had never moved on.

Jameson put up his hand. 'Spare me, Mr Sterling,' he said, turning his head each way to show a hearing aid in each ear. 'I haven't been able to hear music for years. All I've got is a kind of music memory bank. Music's just a tedious clackety clack these days. 'A Boy named Sue,' he murmured. 'It was wonderful though.' He looked up and left towards the ceiling and sighed.

'Right,' he said, refocusing. 'Preliminaries over. I think we can do business. I'm deaf but it's relatively late onset, or rather, I've always been deaf, but it's got a lot worse lately. So I don't use sign language and I haven't bothered to learn. I live in the hearing world, so who would I communicate with by signing? I do lip-read to a degree. Put it like this: I hear better with my contact lenses in. So we'll have to adapt, or rather, you'll have to adapt. If I can't hear you, we use the pad and you write out what you want to say.'

'Fair enough,' said Sterling.

'You must enunciate clearly, Mr Sterling. I knew what you said because of the context, but what it actually sounded like to me was 'Fairy snuff.' There's another problem looming. You're framed against the window and the sun has just come out. I'm not seeing your face properly. We're going to have to swap around so I can lip-read better.'

Hell's bells, thought Sterling as he took his far less comfortable client's chair. Who's the detective and who's the client here? And when are we going to cut to the chase? The interview had developed an unsettling topsy-turvy air.

'That's better,' said Jameson. 'This chair's more comfortable too. Obviously, I suppose.' He nudged the computer mouse as he settled. 'You've done a bit of research, I see,' indicating the web page about his mother's death. 'Good. Enterprising.'

'If it's about that, Mr Jameson, I've got my doubts,' said Sterling.

'Forget that – or rather, put it to one side. That's not why I've come to see you this afternoon.'

Sterling waited.

'My mother is dead, Mr Sterling, and I can't do anything about that. The police are competent enough, given the circumstances, to investigate that. A Detective Inspector Smithson and a Detective Sergeant Murphy are leading. You might know them, given your line of business.'

'I know Murphy,' said Sterling, 'and he is competent. I don't know Smithson.'

Jameson flapped his hand, as if dismissing that whole issue. 'My concern is with the living, and particularly my daughter, Emma. She's gone missing.'

'Right,' said Sterling. 'I'm going to need my own notepad and pen.' He got up and went around to his own side of the desk and took the equipment from the top right hand drawer. Another MISPER, he thought, just like the Flanders case a few months ago. I wonder if I can remember the missing persons procedure. I might have to wing it.

Chapter 2

Missing

If in doubt, think murder. That was the main thing Frank Sterling recalled from his MISPER training in the Kent police. Remembering that helped him remember other things, and he needed to improvise less than he feared. He kept the slogan to himself.

'Before I agree to take this on, and before we get to photos and paperwork and all that, I need to know more. Tell me about your daughter, Mr Jameson.'

'She's 22. Her name's Emma. Emma Jameson. She's blonde. Naturally blonde, but with a pink stripe she dyed in. You know what young people are like. Pretty, in my opinion, but then I'm probably biased. She lives at home with me – her grandmother lived there, too, when she was alive. They were close. This whole business has affected her deeply. She went off to university over a year ago, but she didn't stay. She couldn't adapt to university life, she said, and the course was all wrong. She was doing history, but the wrong sort of history, according to her. She might have been better off with the social sciences – sociology or possibly history with a strong social history orientation. When she came back from university, she spent a lot of time with her grandmother. She hasn't got a job.'

Sterling noticed that after the first time, Jameson wasn't able to describe his daughter as 'missing', or 'disappeared'. He jotted down some notes. As Jameson talked, and as his notepad passed back and forth for words he could not hear, Sterling's training came back to him. The act of going missing is not the whole event. It indicates something else. There are push factors and pull factors. He made a particular note of that, but he would have to be careful not to get ahead of himself.

'I may need to bring us back to some of those details. But tell me when she first went missing.'

'It was yesterday morning at about a quarter to ten. I watched her waiting for a bus at the stop opposite the house. She had a going away bag.'

Another phrase popped into Sterling's head. Risk assessment. What were the three categories – high, medium, low? It didn't matter really. He was getting the hang of it.

'So your 22-year-old adult daughter caught a bus, with a going away bag,' Sterling looked at his watch and calculated, 'about 28 hours ago. I wouldn't describe her as a vulnerable adult from what you've said so far. She doesn't have what the agencies describe as learning difficulties. Is she depressed? Is she forgetful, anything like that?' He searched for another phrase. 'Is she…mentally unstable?'

'No to all those,' said Jameson. He laughed, a harsh and abrupt sound. 'That last one. If you knew her, it's not a question you'd think of asking. All in all, I'd describe her as almost militantly sane. As you'll find out when you meet her.'

'OK,' said Sterling. He thought of push factors and questions Jameson wouldn't like. If he'd still been in the police he would have plunged in, but he softened it. His prospective client would be paying a fee. 'Are there any reasons that might have pushed Emma to leave, Mr Jameson? In cases like this, the police, if they were involved, would be considering, well, signs of abuse.' He swallowed. 'Sexual abuse. Domestic abuse.'

Jameson stared back. 'I know you've got to ask. Better you than the police. It wasn't an easy household, the three of us and then the two of us. But there was nothing like that. Why would I come to you if there was? She was working on some project with her grandmother before her grandmother's...death. They never shared any of that with me. Sometimes there was a female solidarity in the house that excluded me. But I don't think there was anything in it to make her up sticks and go and catch a bus yesterday.'

Sterling made another note. Pull factors. 'What about a boyfriend, Mr Jameson? Or even a close friend or friends she goes to see. She's 22, isn't she? Not really an age when you have to account for your movements to a parent.'

'There's no boyfriend to my knowledge,' Jameson said. 'I checked with some of her friends this morning when she didn't come home last night. If Emma was meeting someone local, she'd go out later – to the pub or something. If she was going further afield, she would tell me. She just got on that bus and hasn't come back.'

'How were you getting on with her? Her grandmother is dead. Everything is up in the air. It's a miserable time. Were you having rows? Arguing?'

'We've always had what I'd call a robust relationship, Mr Sterling. We both called a spade a spade. Yesterday wasn't any different from usual. She's 22 and impatient, like many young people. I'm deaf, and impatient myself, as you've discovered. But just to up and leave without even talking to me is not in character.'

'Which direction was she heading in when you last saw her?'

'I didn't see her get on the bus, but it was towards Sandley.'

'How do you know it was Sandley, Mr Jameson?'

He stared again at Sterling for a long moment. A look, as if from a headache that was just starting, shadowed his temple, which he rubbed with his fingers. 'She was on the Sandley side of the road.'

'Right,' said Sterling. 'Obvious. Sorry. Let's see if I can summarise again. Your daughter caught a bus towards Sandley yesterday morning at about 9.45. She has no mental health issues and is not prone to blackouts or forgetfulness. She had a bag with her when she left. You had not had a row before she went and your relationship is 'robust' but sound. She was very affected by the death of her grandmother but not to an excessive or intolerable degree. They were close and working on a project together. As far as you have been able to establish, she did not spend last night staying with friends and to your knowledge she does not have a boyfriend. Accurate so far?'

Sterling was using the notepad more and more. He could see that his client was tiring and struggling to hear. Jameson had turned 'accurate so far' into 'a curate's snow car'. 'I wonder if we should have a break, Mr Jameson. I can make us a cup of tea.'

Jameson nodded. As Sterling put the kettle on and set out the crockery, his client got up from his chair, went over to the window and looked out over the square. He took the cup and saucer and sipped the tea as he continued his survey. Sterling joined him, careful to be silent so that the break was genuine. He was getting used to communicating with a deaf person, and beginning to understand the foibles of his client. Another dark cloud had appeared. Outside, an elderly woman with a heavily made up face wrestled with her shopping bag and a small umbrella. Her patterned dress and coat, and the silver jewellery around her neck and wrists, gave her a Bohemian air. The spokes of the umbrella would not shake loose as the first drops of rain made large, dark stains on the pavement. She rattled the umbrella more and more desperately as she retreated into the shelter of a shop.

The two men gravitated with their cups and saucers back to their places and resumed.

'When the police embark on a missing person investigation, Mr Jameson, they do a risk assessment. If I remember rightly, it's the usual high, medium or low-risk categories. From what you've told me, I'd be putting Emma into a low-risk category at the moment. She's been gone for a day, but everything you've told me indicates a competent, sensible young woman who may have just wanted to get away for a while, given recent circumstances. She didn't hide anything. She caught a bus in broad daylight. It doesn't seem that there was an abductor. What do you think? Is there anything you might have overlooked?'

Sterling had wanted to avoid saying 'anything you haven't told me'. He wasn't a policeman anymore.

'I don't think so,' said Jameson.

'What about my assessment of risk?'

'It seems reasonable so far – I'd expect it to get higher as time passes.'

'Yes, you're right. But ignoring all the procedures and formulas the police use in missing persons investigations, just how worried are you about Emma at the moment? You know her. What's your gut feeling?'

Jameson rocked in the high-backed office chair and swivelled it this way and that. He rested his hands on the table and started wringing them, not aware of what he was doing. 'Emma isn't a spontaneous girl, Mr Sterling. She generally thinks things through. With my mother's death, things have certainly been turned upside down. But something else has happened. I don't know what, but it triggered her going. You say "low risk". I'm convinced there is high risk. Maybe not immediate high risk, but moving into high risk. I am seriously worried. Find her, Mr Sterling.'

Sterling reviewed his caseload. It didn't take long. He had no current commitments. 'Right,' he said, 'I will take it on. As I said, the way I work is what I've done here – to get some background first to establish if I can be of any help. I think I can. You need to know about the practicalities.' He told Jameson his daily rate. 'Plus expenses, of course, and my minimum engagement period is three days. The payment for those days has to be up front, with extra payments agreed and made as we go. After that we can do regular reviews and you can make decisions on the basis of those reviews. I'll need to visit you at home to get a feel of Emma's surroundings and for any other additional information. Is that all satisfactory?'

'Yes, yes,' said Jameson. 'We're wasting time. You need to get on with it.' He got a chequebook from the inside pocket of his jacket and began writing.

'I'll need an up to date photo of your daughter,' said Sterling. 'Did you bring one with you?'

Jameson stopped writing for a moment and went to the side pocket of his jacket. He took out a standard-size photo and pushed it across the desk. Sterling thought he'd been thorough and professional. He had conducted a decent, transparent interview. He had been realistic, making no promises until he was sure that he had a chance of solving the case. But he was still taken aback by the inadequacy of his preliminary work. The girl in the photo was as Jameson had described. In the sunlight of a garden she had the even features of her father in a way that confirmed his judgement that she was pretty. Her shoulder-length hair looked naturally blonde and there was the pink stripe across the longer side of her parting. She was wearing a close-fitting, blue sleeveless T-shirt. Her arms were bare and lightly tanned. Her smile had a hint of challenge. So far, so useful for tracing and identity purposes. What flummoxed Sterling was that Emma Jameson was looking up into the camera lens from a wheelchair.

Chapter 3

Tank Tops for Displacing Peas

Jameson handed over the cheque. The deal was done. He gave no indication that he'd deliberately withheld any case-changing information, or indulged in any equivalent sleight of hand. That his daughter was in a wheelchair did not seem of any significance to him. Sterling made some rapid calculations. What difference did this information make? Surely, none at all to him. In fact, it should make tracing Emma Jameson easier. And sometimes, people were so used to circumstances that were out of the ordinary that they no longer noticed them. Perhaps Jameson had assumed Sterling would know of his daughter's situation. Sterling tried rapidly to come to terms with this new and unexpected information.

'How long has Emma been wheelchair-bound, Mr Jameson?' That would do for an opening gambit on this subject.

Jameson had been slumping in Sterling's chair, his original energy and brusqueness dissipated. His chin was dipping into his chest. The handwringing was continuing. Now he sat up. 'She's not wheelchair-bound,' he said.

Sterling cocked his head and put his forefinger on the photo. 'Sorry, but....' he said.

'She's a wheelchair-user, Mr Sterling. There is a world of difference. We don't chain her to the damned thing. She fell off a horse when she was 13. She never walked again.'

'Nine years with a disability,' reflected Sterling.

Now Jameson was agitated. He sprang from the chair and began pacing. 'No, *no*. She hasn't got a disability, Mr Sterling. For God's sake. And she's perfectly independent, even on a daily basis. She has no full-time carer.' Then he returned to the chair and slumped again. 'Never mind. Never mind. None of that matters at the moment. I just need you to find her.'

Sterling did not understand the cycle of flare-ups and despondency. Everything he said in this part of the conversation seemed to trigger a hostile reaction. It was safer to deal with practicalities. 'This is what I'm going to do, Mr Jameson. I'll start making some enquiries about where Emma might have gone.. See if there are any leads in that direction. I'll make some other enquiries as well. I may need to call on you at home and look through Emma's things. I need to explore all her connections, including with your mother. How do we get in touch with each other? There's the special phone number, but what about other ways?'

Jameson took out his wallet and extracted a business card. 'You can use text relay – that was how I telephoned you earlier. As I said before, you have to dial 18002 and then my home number. It's a pain, as you know. Even I think that. But you can text me using the mobile telephone number. That's good for alerts. I check my mobile frequently. For longer messages, use e-mail. All the details are on the card, including my address.'

'Right,' said Sterling, handing over his own business card. 'I don't think we can do much more today. I'll have

a think and come up with further questions, and I'll
start in earnest tomorrow. Thank you for engaging me,
Mr Jameson.'

'Tank tops for displacing peas, missing J-cloths,'
Jameson replied.

'Yes,' said Sterling as they shook hands. For the first
time in the meeting, he sensed a glimmer of light humour.
'Tank tops for displacing peas.'

He listened to his new client, coat over his arm, clatter
down the stairs, though now not two at a time. A moment
later he watched Count Dracula sweep around the corner
of Market Street, cross the road by the church and
disappear from sight, coat billowing and flapping as he
went. Sterling reclaimed his chair, took the upside-down
photo from the other side of the desk and laid it next to
Jameson's card and his own note pad and pen. When
he shifted the mouse, the screensaver on his computer
disappeared and news about Jameson's mother's death
came back up. He glanced through various media stories.
The police seemed to have made little progress on Mrs
Jameson. He looked at the business card. It was embossed
and expensive-looking. Jameson described himself as a
building designer and property developer. He'd be worth
a bob or two.

Sterling started planning the case. What was that
quadrant of choices he used to find so helpful when he
was on the job? It came to him: urgent/important/not
urgent/not important. On the list he developed, only one
thing turned out to be urgent and important: to try and
pick up Emma Jameson's trail from the bus stop outside
her house. He would have to do that tomorrow at the
same time of day as the girl had taken off because there
would be regular travellers who might remember her.

Everything else was important but not so urgent. Bus timetables: he needed to know what time the weekday bus that arrived at Hamworth at 9.45 reached the Guildhall at Sandley. It looked as if Traveline was the site to visit – and there it was – the 9.15 from Deal via Sholden and Hamworth – Sandley Guildhall at 9.55, and then on to Canterbury.

The girl's face in the photo held his eye. 'Where are you, then, Emma?' he murmured. 'Lying low in Sandley, or gone further afield? And why did you take off?' Her look remained challenging, and there was no clue there. Experience told him that Jameson's anxiety was genuine. This was not yet a police matter, but something had happened. At this stage, there might not have been danger or skulduggery, as his police friend Andy Nolan would have put it, but he still couldn't shake off the MISPER mantra from his police training: *if in doubt, think murder.*

At half-past five, he could get no further. He switched off the computer, straightened everything on his desk, took his coat from the peg behind the door, and went down to the library. It was Tuesday, and most weeknights if he was in his office, he and Angela had a quick drink before parting for dinner. Unusually, she had already closed and locked up and was waiting. Outside in Market Street, the late afternoon sun burst through the dark clouds that had deposited the recent heavy shower and bathed the small square in sparkling, dancing light. There was a smell of smoky tarmac from the road and mown grass from St Peter's churchyard. As they crossed to the top of Milk Alley, Freddy Henderson was shifting his stock indoors. He smiled as they passed.

'I might join you for a bit if I'm not too long here,' he said.

Sterling offered Angela his arm as they strolled down the alley. In her shoes, she was taller than him, and when they walked together her elegance enveloped him, smartening him up and straightening his back. From St Peter's Street they walked through Holy Ghost Alley and into the high street. In The Cinque Ports Arms, the snug was empty. They unfolded the crossword and set it out. Mike Strange, publican, friend and troubleshooter, appeared silently with the mandatory pint of Spitfire and glass of gin and tonic and silently disappeared.

'Cheers,' said Angela as they clinked glasses. 'How did it go this afternoon?'

'Well, he's taken me on. He's very deaf. Tetchy. I seemed to keep saying things that irritated him. But his daughter has gone off and he wants me to find her. That is, his daughter in a wheelchair.'

'Interesting. Different. It might make things easier, Frank, the wheelchair bit.' Angela echoed Sterling's view. 'Do you reckon the girl's going is connected with his mother's death?'

'Maybe. I don't know yet. I'll have to do some digging. I'm thinking I might have to hire a car too. I can't ask Jack. Not after Ypres.' He had been double-crossed by his former friend in that adventure, and the hurt was still raw.

They bent over the crossword. When he had a new case, Sterling had come to be superstitious about the clues. It was like reading the runes, and finding answers in them. But today's crossword had an East Anglian theme, and that didn't seem relevant at all. Angela filled in 'Suffolk Punch' and 'Norfolk jacket'. One clue flummoxed them: Townie (no North) initially makes county show (3, 4, 3, 2, 5). Later on at home, after a microwaved dinner for one supplemented by extra boil-in-the-bag rice and some ready-prepared vegetables, Sterling put on *Johnny Cash at San Quentin*, one of the LPs in the album collection his father had bequeathed him. Nicholas Jameson had been right. "A Boy Named Sue" was a wonderful, funny song, brilliantly rendered. The answer to the crossword clue came to him through the screen credits of a TV programme that came up as he was channel-surfing – *The Only Way Is Essex*. He had read the runes all right, but he'd only realise it much later. Upstairs, he fell asleep full of anticipation about the case ahead. In his dreams a telephone was ringing. 'If I answer this,' his dream-self said, 'my life will change forever', but as soon as he picked it up, he awoke.

Chapter 4

Jobsworth

The pedestrianised area next to Sandley Guildhall was busy when Sterling arrived there at 9.40 the next morning. The turbulence of the previous day's weather had gone. It was still and overcast. Directly opposite, an elderly bareheaded Charlie Chaplin shuffled painfully into the day centre. Through the Guildhall arch, Sterling could see the Park-Brite cleaners in the car park filling their buckets at the standpipe next to the public toilets. The gangmaster, cigarette hanging from the side of his mouth and baseball cap and sunglasses hiding the rest of his face, wandered between the cars touting for business, clipboard and pen in hand. After a brief conversation with a driver, he flipped up one windscreen wiper of her black Jaguar and motioned over one of his team.

The Canterbury bus wasn't due till 9.55 but there was already a knot of would-be passengers waiting to board. He could start his day's work here. There were about eight people, a small enough group for Sterling to address all at once.

'Excuse me everyone. Did any of you catch this same bus the day before yesterday? I'm looking for someone who might have been on it then.' Even before he surveyed the blank and, in one or two cases openly suspicious faces in front of him, he guessed that bus-stop canvassing was not common or necessarily acceptable. He plunged on. He needed to know. 'Anyone?'

'If it was the day before yesterday it wasn't the same bus, was it?' said a woman with a sour, lined mouth.

Sterling recognised the response from his time on the job. Something about police work, and work related to it, encouraged logic chopping and pedantry, as if people had nothing better to do.

'It might have been, Mavis,' said someone else. 'They probably don't change the buses. Unless there's a breakdown. Or a shortage.'

The other thing about canvassing was that it could get out of control. There was a danger of that here. Sterling needed to get things back on track. He didn't need technical or philosophical discussions about whether or not Tuesday's bus was the same as today's.

'Back to my que....'

'Who wants to know?' said another voice. 'You come up to this bus stop asking questions. You could be a terrorist. Or worse, a bus inspector.' A tall man in a tweed jacket faced him, a shock of white hair springing from underneath a cloth cap. The sleeves of the jacket finished almost a third of the way up the man's arms, and the jacket barely reached over his tatty trousers. Even with his stoop he loomed over Sterling, who was already thinking 'God, it's going to be one of those days.' This was the moment when he produced his warrant card and cut out all the nonsense, except he didn't have a warrant card. His professional investigator validation was far less impressive, and so far less influential.

'I'm an investigator,' he said. 'Not the police. It's a private matter.' He flashed his nondescript card at the group. Things weren't going well.

The group digested his words. There was a low-level chuntering, a mixture of curiosity and truculence.

'So, the 9.55 bus the day before yesterday - Tuesday. Was anyone on it?'

Sterling had been wasting his time. There was no one. On the other hand, he'd certainly learn to modify his approach if he was in a similar situation later on.

Then today's bus pulled into the bus stop. Sterling held back as members of the little group aligned themselves to board. When his turn came, he asked the driver if he'd been driving Tuesday's 9.55 bus to Canterbury. The driver, who had a faded old-fashioned blue anchor tattooed on his left forearm, looked boredly at him.

'No, I've just come back off holiday. Where do you want to go?'

Sterling looked down the bus. 'Does anyone catch this bus every day?'

'One or two. I dunno. Maybe. Do you want a ticket or don't you? I can't be late.'

Sterling made a quick decision. If someone was on the bus the day before yesterday, well and good. If not, he'd get off and catch a bus going the other way, back into Sandley. It was all coming out of expenses anyway. 'Yeah, a return to Canterbury please.'

He lurched as the bus pulled out and sat heavily in a side seat at the front. Looking down the gangway, he calculated that there were about six more people to canvas. There would be more as others boarded. Moments later, he thought that it might not be one of those days after all, and that his bus stop canvassing had not been entirely negative. He moved to a seat almost at the back. On a parallel seat across the gangway, a young man sat fidgeting. He had a smooth, bald pate to go with an unlined face, a 25-year-old baby, or, Sterling could not help thinking as he looked at the smooth bulging forehead, the Mekon in the Dan Dare adventures in his father's *Eagle* comics – before the Mekon went bad. He was expecting Sterling's approach.

'Yeah, I'm on this bus most days. What do you want to know?'

'Don't tell him anything, Kenny,' said the tall man in the cloth cap, now sprawled across the back seat where there was room to stretch his legs out.

The woman called Mavis offered Sterling unexpected support. 'Let the man do his job, John.' This time, the chuntering seemed to be in her favour, and therefore Sterling's. John looked out of the window.

Sterling showed the man-boy Kenny the photo of Emma Jameson. 'She left home on Tuesday, Kenny. Her father's worried about her.' He played on Emma Jameson's situation. 'Her being in a wheelchair and that.'

Kenny looked at the photo. 'Yes, she was on here Tuesday. She sat up at the front.' He jerked his head towards the empty space for wheelchairs and buggies. Sterling moved next to Kenny on the seat. This was good. This was promising.

'Where did she get out, Kenny?'

'Canterbury, like me.'

'This is really helpful. Thank you very much.' Sterling sensed that the young man was uncomfortable. 'Is it OK if I ask you one or two more questions? Then I'll leave you in peace.' When he was on the job, he was the hothead and Andy Nolan was calm and reassuring. Sterling was learning to adapt his style.

'Did you notice anything about her? Did she seem alright?'

'She was OK. I didn't really pay any attention. She had earphones in so she might have been listening to music on an iPod or something. Once she got on the bus she just sat quietly. Please,' he said softly. 'That's enough. I can't do long conversations.'

Sterling noticed that it had become quiet at the back of the bus, but for the hum of the engine. 'Thank you again, Kenny.' He withdrew to his own seat, ostentatiously took out his notebook and bent over it with his pen. When he glanced up, Kenny had hunched himself up, his domed forehead pressed against the window. The woman Mavis caught Sterling's eye and smiled, all sourness instantly disappearing. She gave a little nod. 'I helped you with that,' it seemed to say – a complicated mixture of approval, satisfaction and a touch of smugness. He nodded back.

When the bus arrived on schedule in Canterbury 30 minutes later, Sterling shuffled off with all his fellow passengers. He looked over from the bus stand at the hordes of people milling around across the bus station. The man in the tweed jacket sidled up to him, unable, Sterling imagined, to resist some point scoring.

'Now where did she go?' he said, standing next to Sterling and surveying the same mass of people before striding off through the shopping mall abutting the bus station and into the city. He's got a point, thought Sterling. He leaned against the Perspex panel of the shelter and carried on looking. An elderly man in a lumberjack hat tottered by pushing a kind of Zimmer frame on wheels, looking pinched and unwell. A young girl in a pink beret and short blue denim jacket sat on a moulded plastic seat nearby, her mouth chewing gum as her fingers danced over the keypad of her mobile telephone. Finding where Emma Jameson went next would surely have been impossible without the wheelchair. Even with it, Sterling faced a challenge. Then he had an idea.

He cast his eyes around the bus station. There he was – a short, wiry man with an air of bustle and energy in a fluorescent green jacket with *Canterbury Bus Station Supervisor* etched in black on the back. Close up, his beanie was a dirty olive colour above the white stubble of his beard, but his eyes were blue and alert in a lined and weather-beaten face.

'Got a minute?' Sterling called out as he walked over.

'You can't come out here, mate,' said the man, brusquely but not unkindly, clearly used to passengers wandering where they shouldn't and knowing how to be patient about it. As if to confirm that the spot was dangerous, two double deckers roared past in quick succession, the smell of diesel and blue exhaust fumes hanging in the air as they lined up diagonally in adjacent bays in front of the waiting queues. Sterling thought of rockets docking onto space stations. 'Walk over to the office and I'll come to you. Careful as you go.'

A minute later the man hurried over to the hexagonal office building. 'OK, what can I do for you?' As he spoke his glance kept flicking to the wide space in front of him.

The man's edginess transferred itself to Sterling. He knew he did not have much time as more buses came in. He fumbled for Emma Jameson's photograph. 'She came here the day before yesterday - Tuesday. Got off the Sandley bus at about half-past ten in her wheelchair. Did you see her?'

Beanie-man fumbled in his pocket for a pair of half-moon reading glasses. He slipped them on and peered myopically at the photo.

'Who wants to know?' he said, looking up.

'I'm a private investigator,' said Sterling, getting out his identity card. 'She's gone missing, probably temporarily, but her father asked me to look into it.'

'Alright. I did see her.' He rolled his eyes and grinned. 'How could I forget? It was a bit of a performance her getting off the bus. She made the driver line up the exit platform till it was just right. But why not? I expect she gets plenty of that kind of hassle. She went off that way.' He pointed south-east, towards Dane John Gardens. His eyes flicked back to the bus station. Four buses had appeared in the course of a few seconds. 'Gotta go. It's busy.' He strode off back to his work.

'Thanks,' called Sterling to his back, and a hand rose in acknowledgement.

On the other side of the zebra crossing, Sterling looked down the long gravelled vista bisecting the gardens. The path was lined with plane trees like leafy sentinels. He looked around. There seemed no obvious other direction. If he did not pick up the girl's trail, he'd double back and start again. Halfway down the path, as far as he could judge, a wooden-boarded kiosk, painted a darker green than the leaves and grass surrounding it, sold drinks and sandwiches. He felt again for the photo.

'Did you see this girl on Tuesday morning – not yesterday, the day before?' he asked the woman behind the high counter. Her long, dark, straggly hair was streaked with grey, and had a denser white stripe from the widow's peak at her forehead. But for her careworn, gentle face she might have been Cruella De Vil's elder sister. She didn't even ask why Sterling wanted to know.

'Poor little thing. I made her an egg bap. I had to come around the side to give it to her, for obvious reasons. She was by herself. Normally they have someone to help, don't they?' She tut-tutted, as if the system had failed in some way.

'Did you see which direction she went in after she left you?'

'We had a little chat actually. Around here, either it's really quiet or it's really busy. When she came by, there was no one around. Anyway, she said she was going to the station. It sounded like she was on some kind of mission.' The woman sighed. 'I wouldn't mind a mission myself.' She looked around her little domain – the small rickety green cast iron chairs around the little green tables to the side of the kiosk, the blackbirds pecking desultorily in the scabby grass, the little galley and the ice-cream freezer behind her.

Sterling followed her sad gaze. There was nothing much to say about that. Talk of the egg bap made him realise that he was hungry too, so he ordered one, along with tea that came in a Styrofoam cup.

'What else did you talk about?' he said.

'Nothing much. She was cagey. I asked how long it would take and she said no more than five days because that's when her clean underwear ran out. We had a laugh about that.'

'Thanks,' said Sterling at the end of the conversation. A few metres down the path he turned and raised the tea and bap in each hand in a silent toast. The woman was leaning on her elbows on the high counter, chin in hands.

She waved back with two fingers lifted from her face – tired, resigned, the effort exhausting.

At the end of the path, city wall on the left and the handsome white Dane John mansions on the right, Sterling picked up the sign to Canterbury East station. At first, he wondered how Emma Jackson would have managed the steep steps up to the walkway that curved gently over the ring road to the station and student accommodation area on the other side. Then he remembered the slope on the opposite side to the stairs. Even then she'd have struggled, he thought, gradually learning to see things from her perspective. That would have been hard work. The traffic roared in a continuous shining stream beneath the walkway as he approached the zebra crossing in front of the station entrance. Outside the nightclub opposite, a man half-sat, half-sprawled in the sunshine, sipping from a can. When he was on the job, Sterling remembered the occasional visit he'd had to make to the homeless day centre opposite the snooker club on the station approach road. Taking everything into account, he preferred his new occupation.

At this time during the end of the morning, the ticket counters in the station concourse were quiet. There was only one young man, who seemed to be Japanese, negotiating a complicated transaction with the exasperated ticket clerk. Sterling approached the other counter, wiping a smear of egg yolk from his bottom lip. Eating the bap and walking had been complicated. He reached again for the photo.

'I wonder if you can help,' he started cautiously, pushing the photo and his ID through the gap in the screen. Ticket clerks, in his experience, were an unpredictable species. 'This girl has gone missing and her father's asked me to look for her. Did she buy a ticket from you on Tuesday morning?'

The man sat back. His square beard gave his face a long, bottom-heavy look. He folded his arms, not even looking at what had been pushed through the grille. Sterling noticed his sharp blue eyes surrounded by crow's feet and vertical lines chiselled in his cheeks in a surly, disappointed face. Jobsworth, thought Sterling, and he wasn't wrong.

'I can't talk to you about customers – not unless you're the police. Regulations.' He pushed the photo and the ID back through the grille without a glance.

Detective Constable Sterling would have raised his voice and made a scene. He would have accused the clerk of obstructing a missing person inquiry. He would have demanded to see the supervisor.

'Her dad's frantic with worry,' said Private Investigator Sterling. 'She's not just a vulnerable young girl, she's a vulnerable young girl in a wheelchair.'

The clerk's arms stayed folded. His mouth fixed in an obstinate scowl. 'If I give you information about customers, I'll get into trouble. Disciplinary action.'

'It's more than my job's worth,' Sterling mouthed to himself. He stood in front of the counter with the photo and the ID in the little trough on the counter where money was exchanged for tickets. What next? And up to now he'd been doing so well.

'Don't be an arse, Phil. Take down the bloke's details if there's any problem later. It seems legit to me, from what I've heard.'

Sterling looked over towards the other ticket clerk, who had the same type of beard and bottom-heavy look as Phil, but without the surly manner. Was the look part of the uniform? Phil shifted in his seat and rolled his neck in a peculiar, indecisive fashion, as if he was weighing up the pros and cons.

'Go on, mate. I'll see you don't come to any harm at the disciplinary hearing.' He gave Sterling a wink and waggled his RMT tiepin. It clicked with Sterling straight away. He'd needed plenty of help himself from the Police Federation rep during his numerous scrapes in the Kent Police.

Reluctantly, Phil reached back out for the photo and the ID. Sterling knew he was saving face when he wrote down Sterling's details. Jobsworths can't be too careful, he thought.

'She was here. In the morning the day before yesterday if you say so. Around about this time. But I didn't serve her. It was you, Merv.' He passed over the photo.

'Yup, I sold her a ticket.' He passed the photo back to Sterling.

'And,' said Sterling, 'I wonder if you can tell me where she was going.'

'Hmm,' said Merv, glancing sideways at his colleague. 'Not sure I can divulge that information. It might be more than my job's worth.' He laughed. 'Gone missing, you say. OK, well, it was to Woodbridge – Woodbridge in Suffolk. I told her it would be best for her to go over to Canterbury West and go on the high-speed service but she couldn't face wheeling herself across town. So I told her to change at Faversham, get the high-speed service from there and then change at Stratford International. Plucky girl,' he added. 'It was a bit of a trek she was going on. Hope she's OK.'

Sterling thanked the ticket clerks. Phil could not look him in the eye but Merv's eyes twinkled and he gave his colleague a playful punch on his arm.

Chapter 5

Bart's Kneebone

Back on the other side of the walkway, Sterling reflected on a successful morning, successful far beyond expectations. He looked at his watch. It was midday. He couldn't contemplate going to Woodbridge yet. There was much more to do before he was at that stage. Only one thing could make his morning better than it already was. Instead of making his way back to the bus station along the path he'd just come down, he turned right and started out along the city wall that divided Dane John Gardens from the ring road. At the first roundabout on the opposite side was the police station. Perhaps Andy Nolan was in. Perhaps he could be tempted out for a bite of lunch. On the left, the gardens below were quiet and serene. A Labrador nosed among the flowers near the palisaded play area. On the right was a kind of mayhem as drivers tried any kind of ploy to make progress along the snarled up carriageway. In the underpass under the ring road, 'We will never graduate' was graffitied on one of the walls. Sterling remembered that the library of one of Canterbury's universities was close by. You will, he thought. Sooner than you think. And then real life begins.

The police station was all toughened glass and steel, even in the reception area.

A civilian employee with a referral pad appeared. 'I'll go and see if he's in,' she said when Sterling asked for Detective Sergeant Nolan. He was looking over at the fire station when he felt a hand on his arm.

'Frank,' said Andy Nolan. 'What a pleasant surprise to liven up a dull April morning. I'm drowning in a rising tide of paperwork.'

'You'll be ready for a bit of early lunch then, Andy,' said Sterling as they shook hands. 'Remind me what firefighters do apart from that.' He nodded to where a team was washing down a fire engine in the forecourt.

Andy Nolan shrugged. 'Long days and nights of boredom. A bit of moonlighting in the early days, when there's still some energy. Resentfully mulling over paycheques with eye-watering deductions for early retirement. And short periods of intense heat, extreme danger and sights Joe and Joanna Public would never want to see. On balance I prefer our line of business.'

'Without the paperwork.'

'They'll have paperwork of their very own, Frank. Don't you worry about that. Yes, I can do lunch.'

'Not the university though, Andy. All that glass and chrome and learning gets me down a bit. Focuses me on my wrong turnings.' The last time Frank had been here, they had gone to the university library next door.

'OK, we'll go up to the Spread Eagle.'

The two men went through the heavy glass doors onto the busy Old Dover Road. Students drifted past them on the walk from the university's main campus to the library – the glass and chrome pile that Sterling referred to. On the pedestrian crossing, a young girl in a group of three lost her red plimsoll. There was a flutter of laughter and mock panic as she retrieved it while the lights flashed orange and the warning signs beeped.

'What's wrong with this one?' said Sterling as they approached the Chequers.

Andy Nolan shuddered. 'I don't even want to talk about it. I probably wouldn't get out alive.' Across the railings of the pub garden, a 'View Sky Sports' banner flapped listlessly, the top right hand corner was detached from its fittings, and winked at passers-by. It reflected the louche air of the pub. 'The Spread Eagle is much more civilised. Only a little further.'

Andy Nolan was right. The Spread Eagle was set back a little off the main road, its little garden backed against the top of a railway cutting along the Canterbury-Dover track. The black beams and white plaster in the saloon were not real Tudor, but they were clean and neat. A line of blue fairy lights across the bar gave it a cheerful, welcoming air. The publican, a large man with a bird's nest beard, clearly knew Andy Nolan.

'Usual? And a plate of ham and cheese sandwiches?'

'Thanks, Ray. And a pint of Spitfire for my mate. Sometimes there's a college crowd in here,' he said to Sterling. 'I know the Director of Further Education there because of the drugs. Big bloke. Larger than life. Luckily he's not in today or we wouldn't have been able to get down to business. I assume there is business.'

They took their drinks into a corner.

'There always is,' said Sterling. 'But before I get on to that, how are Jacquie and the kids, Andy?'

'They're good. Vickie is enjoying school and George will be starting in September. Jacquie's talking about getting back into the force when they're both at school.

I won't complain. It's been tight these last few years, despite the promotions.'

'Won't be long before I'll be calling you Detective Inspector.'

Andy Nolan smiled. He had a sharp, analytical brain and an excellent way of managing situations and people – colleagues, criminals and ordinary citizens – and the police hierarchy recognised that. Sterling looked into his beer. There was a sorry contrast between them. They'd made a good team, but Andy Nolan had rescued the hothead Sterling more times than either of them could probably remember. Sterling was not sorry to have left the job. Andy Nolan was much better suited to it. But sometimes he missed his friend's steadying influence.

'How about you, Frank? Didn't you see that ARV sergeant a few times?'

'Yeah, Clare. I liked her, but she had a squeaky voice.'

'Easily bored, more like. I thought that might go somewhere.'

'Actually, it wasn't her squeaky voice,' said Sterling. If he couldn't be honest with Andy Nolan, there was no one else. 'And it wasn't me who ended it. She said she didn't want someone who was always holding back. Always restless.'

'Ah, holding back. Same old Frank. What did that counsellor say after your injury from the Tonbridge heist? You're still looking for your mother.' Andy Nolan was one of the few people who knew that Sterling's mother had abandoned him when he was a baby, and his father, and never been seen again.

Sterling took a deep pull from his pint. He wasn't having lunch with Andy Nolan to discuss his personal life. In the silence, the sandwiches arrived.

Andy Nolan backpedalled. 'Sorry, Frank. Maybe it's because my life is a bit, well, dull that I take such an interest in yours. And Jacquie would like to see you settled again.' Jacquie had been close to Sterling's wife, long gone, and they had often gone out together.

'To business,' said Sterling, biting into a ham sandwich. 'Daphne Jameson, deceased. What can you tell me?'

'Whoa. Rules of engagement first, Frank. Quid pro quos to be negotiated. Especially after the Etchingham debacle.'

'That wasn't a debacle. It was a decent result for everyone.'

'In the end. By very dodgy means. I think you should go first this time. It's only fair.'

'How long have we known each other, Andy? About 13, 14 years? Since we were first in a patrol car together after training. We've been in some scrapes, but there was always trust.'

Andy Nolan folded his arms.

'OK, OK,' said Sterling. 'Me first, I suppose.' He gave a complete account of his engagement by Nicholas Jameson to find his missing daughter, his knowledge so far about Daphne Jameson's death and the progress he'd made already during the morning.

Andy Nolan shook his head admiringly. 'You could be a lippy bastard, Frank, when you were on the job. But I haven't met anyone before or since who could get people talking like you can. I can't understand it. People tell you things. That was a good morning's work, and you couldn't even get to look at CCTV. How do you do it?'

'My cheeky face?' said Sterling.

'Possibly,' said Andy Nolan, taking the flippancy seriously. 'Maybe that and other things. If you could bottle it you'd make a fortune. So, the girl's gone to Woodbridge. It certainly doesn't seem like a police matter at the moment, but it's definitely intriguing.'

'Right, Daphne Jameson.'

Andy Nolan sat back. He had a story to tell.

'She was 94, you know. To get to 94, and then be murdered. Terrible. She was battered about the head. One of Smithson and Murphy's lines of enquiry is that it was a burglary gone wrong, that she withheld information about something or other – valuables, money stashed away – and someone had tried to beat it out of her. There was some cash and jewellery missing. But they've got doubts about that. There was no sign of forced entry that we could find, and it was only the old lady's study that was turned over badly, not the rest of the house. There were a couple of drink tumblers washed up on the draining board in the kitchen. There was no forensic on them, but it left a nagging feeling with Smithson. So the burglary might be a red herring. Both those blokes – Smithson and Murphy – are good. They don't do sloppy. And they were struck by the fierceness of the attack. Most burglars wouldn't do that.'

'Obviously they looked closely at Nicholas Jameson and his business. That was the second line. His business is OK. Doing well actually. He was fond of his mother and gutted when she was found. He had a cast-iron alibi for the time of death. Hours and hours at Sandley Bridge Club. Virtually every moment accounted for. There was no way he could have gone out and slipped back. His partner and thirty other people could testify to that. He could have got someone to do it for him, the old 'contract hit' beloved of the papers and TV, but there was no motive. She hadn't changed her will.

She didn't seem to be intending to. There was nothing untoward there.'

'Emma Jameson also had an alibi, but she couldn't have done the bludgeoning from her wheelchair anyway – the angles were all wrong. The old lady was attacked from above as she was sitting. Not horizontally as it were. Not from another chair. Smithson and Murphy are going through all burglars locally and from further afield with any kind of a similar modus operandi. But they're stuck, pretty much. There's little in the way of DNA or other evidence. I'll tell them the girl has gone walkabout, Frank. I expect they'll let you get on with it, but they'll be interested in any progress you make.'

'Of course,' said Sterling. 'They might want to speak to her if and when I find her. What about the old lady's background?'

'She had a relatively unremarkable later life, from what I've heard. She was born in Sandley and always lived locally. She went to the girl's grammar in Ramsgate. The only bit of drama was in the Second World War. Jameson told the lead detectives that she was something in the RAF. Some ill-defined role. She was only 21 when war broke out, but apparently did well and was in demand because she'd done a Modern Languages degree. That was rare in those days and she was apparently fluent in German. Her son said she was competent and efficient and built up the property business he took over. Even at 94 he described her as fit, able, intelligent, lucid. Locally she was respected and liked, but private and self-contained. She never talked about the war. Her husband died early. She brought her son up by herself.' Andy Nolan paused. 'So, what are your plans now, Frank?'

'Well, I don't think there's much point me rushing off down to Woodbridge today – what's left of it. I need to know more. There's a bus back to Sandley in about 20 minutes. I'll get that and see if I can get to the house and look through things there – if Jameson is about so that he can let me in. He's deaf, so communication is a performance.'

'He's got a short fuse too, from what I've been told,' said Andy Nolan.

'Tell me about it.'

Sterling and Andy Nolan drank up, finished the sandwiches and then strolled back towards the police station and the bus station on the city side of the ring road. As they shook hands outside the police station, they had to raise their voices against the roar of the traffic. The air was gritty with pollution.

'Thanks for the briefing, Andy. Love to Jacquie and the kids. Maybe we'll get together as a foursome again soon.'

'Pigs might fly,' said Andy Nolan. 'Oh, before you rush off, there was a small detail about the murder I forgot. When the paramedics arrived, Daphne Jameson was still breathing. She died as they were preparing to carry her to the ambulance. But one of them said she was trying to say something. She told Smithson that it sounded like 'Bored Anna' or 'Bart's Kneebone'. But with all the blood and battery....'

'Thanks Andy. It's all grist to the mill, I guess.'

Chapter 6

Hamworth Place

On the bus it was time for another attempt at communication with the case principal. What was that Text Relay number? He drew out Nicholas Jameson's card and found 18002 and then the number. Sterling muttered to himself. 'Damn case. Typical that I get one with extra complications.'

The Text Relay operator had a Liverpool accent again. 'Have you used Text Relay before?' she said.

'Well, once, when I received a call. I need reminding.'

'OK, when I've connected you and the deaf person you're calling knows what's happening, I tell you when to speak. I type what you say to the deaf person and they reply. You'll hear their voice. They say "go ahead" and you can start speaking again. When you've finished a particular bit, you say "go ahead". Don't forget to say "go ahead" because there's no switch till you do.'

'What a palaver,' muttered Sterling. 'OK,' he said to the operator.

A few moments later, a gruff voice came over the line. 'Yes? Go ahead.'

'Mr Jameson? Frank Sterling here. Go ahead.' There was a pause. Sterling assumed that the operator was typing so that Jameson could see the words on a screen.

'Mr. Sterling. How are you getting on? Have you found Emma? Go ahead.'

'It's early days, Mr Jameson. But I've made some progress. I'm calling because I'm hoping to be able to come to the house. I could do with seeing Emma's room and whether there's anything to help me there. Go ahead.'

'When? Go ahead.' Jameson had used Text Relay often enough not to be troubled by social niceties.

'I could be there in half an hour. I've got some momentum going, so it would be very helpful.' There was a long silence.

'Say "go ahead",' said the Scouse operator. It sounded like a small whine. Sterling cursed under his breath. 'Go ahead.'

'I thought you'd gone,' said Jameson. 'Alright. SK.'

'SK?' said Sterling. But all there was left was a dialling tone.

On the rest of the bus journey, he noticed what he'd become aware of on the way into Canterbury. There was a little bus community. The passengers called the young driver 'Callum' and knew him well. As people got on, they'd say 'Afternoon all' to the assembled company, and as others got off there was often a cheery farewell. There was a rhythm to the journey as the bus wended its way through the Kentish villages. Much later, Sterling came to realise how important and how protective a bus-using community could become.

Getting into the spirit of bus travel, he made his own cheerful farewells to Callum and his fellow passengers when he got off the bus beyond Sandley on the road east to Deal, and as the bus disappeared down the road he looked through the wrought iron gates at the elegant Georgian grey brick house standing before him – Hamworth Place. Nicholas Jameson and his mother before him had done well. The house was large, spacious and clearly well kept. A high brick wall had recently been repointed. Sterling could see where new fillings of white cement had been worked between the bricks. He slipped in through a side gate set in an archway in the wall.

Much of the area in front of the house had been tarmacked and a silver Mercedes was parked in front of the white portico with its two columns and plain triangular top. Within the portico was a heavy double door in Oxford blue, with matching brass doorknobs. Between the portico and the main iron gates was a circular rose bed, with some spring growth. To the right of the house was a newer addition – a double garage, and in front of that, beyond the tarmac, there was a rectangular shrubbery neatly inserted underneath the wall that kept the house, garage and drive separated from the road. A wooden fence joined the garage and the house and continued beyond the house to a sidewall on the left with a door built in. The front area and back garden were clearly segmented. Everything spoke of quiet prosperity, order and comfort.

Sterling's father had been a passionate egalitarian, but he himself was never much exercised by disparities between wealth and poverty. His small house in Sandley was good enough for his purposes, and at least a part of him believed that if you worked hard why shouldn't you have the rewards? But he loved order and tidiness, and there was plenty of that to admire here. The rose bed was so immaculate that he could imagine a daily task of clearing up debris of leaves and petals. The Mercedes was parked square in front of the portico. It was Sterling's kind of set up.

As he took in the surroundings, two blackbirds descended amongst the roses. One was making little darts and jabs at the other, which flapped off for a moment or two and then returned. He watched. Surely blackbirds faced enough dangers without fighting among themselves. He heard chimes within the house from the bell-pull he operated at the door, and wondered if Nicholas Jameson had heard them. Then one of the doors opened and he stepped into an airy foyer, light streaming in from the large sash windows either side of the door. He saw a red light next to the burglar alarm. The bell obviously activated lights as well as sounds. There was a smell of polish. In front of him a wide staircase dominated the middle of the hall, sweeping around upstairs in generous curves into small balconies on the left and right. On the left hand wall was a pantomime cartoon of a turbaned character looking terrified on a raft and oil drum contraption being swept towards shore on the surf. 'Sinbad – The Pantomime – Drury Lane Theatre, December 1958' said the caption.

'I'm busy, Mr Sterling,' said Jameson. 'Tell me what you need.'

'A look around, especially Emma's bedroom. I want to get a sense of her.' Sterling noticed the paraphernalia of the wheelchair user as he spoke. There were strategically placed handles in the hall. A stairlift stretched up on the right hand side around to one of the balconies. At the bottom was a modern-looking wheelchair with sleek black lines and glittering spokes, matched by a similar one Sterling could see through the balustrade.

Jameson saw him taking everything in. 'Emma collected wheelchairs and mobility scooters the way some women collect shoes. The way she put it was that each had a specific purpose.'

A thought occurred to Sterling. 'Mobility scooter. One of those things you see people riding around Sandley. Did she take that when she went off?'

'Of course not. For goodness sake. How would she have got on the bus with that? How would she have charged it? God,' muttered Jameson.

'Just asking. You've got to understand, Mr Jameson, that I'm not used to disability.' Sterling was feeling his hackles rise. The irritability was wearing him down.

'Bus passing,' said Jameson automatically, as if his heart wasn't really in it. 'It's not about disability, as I said in your office – but we've been through this. Where first?'

'Emma's room.' Sterling knew he was missing something, something beyond his experience, but it didn't seem important to the case. He decided to press on.

At the top of the stairs they turned right and went along the short upstairs corridor beyond the balcony.

'In there,' said Jameson, indicating the door on the left to a room at the back of the house. 'I'll be in my study downstairs.' He stumped away.

Sterling pushed the door open and stood in the doorway. He was startled. The room was painted entirely black. The carpet was black and so was the duvet, the sheets, the desk and the dressing table. There was a built-in wardrobe with a short mirror. Sterling eased it open and noted the design, which made access to clothes and shoes easy for the girl. At least not all the clothes were black. In fact there was a splash of colour in the wardrobe that contrasted with the rest of the gloomy room. Sterling glanced out through the black curtains. The garden at the back was as immaculate as the front, but with a larger, more varied array of plants in beds within a verdant lawn. Beyond the side of the house he could see out towards the marshes.

He looked back into the room. It wasn't grubby, but it was untidy. Clothes were strewn on the bed, papers and pens on the desk and potions and make-up on the dresser. He glanced through books stacked untidily on the bookshelves – mainly social history, feminism and a few novels. A cover caught his eye. A man in a wheelchair sat outside a village hall, facing the camera. The expression on his face was inscrutable. Behind him some steep steps led up to the door. Over the doorway was a notice – Polling Station.

Sterling leafed through the papers – mostly notes and jottings. There was no clue here about why Emma Jameson had gone to Woodbridge. There was no chair in the bedroom. Presumably the girl manoeuvred herself from the wheelchair at the bottom of the stairs into the stairlift chair and then transferred to the wheelchair at the top. He returned to the doorway and looked in again. Amidst the light, open, airy orderliness of the house and the neat garden, where there was a place for everything and everything seemed to be in its place, the room was a jarring contrast. Perhaps Emma had much to be gloomy and pessimistic about. Maybe the untidiness was defiance.

Sterling listened. He had heard Jameson go down the stairs but he hadn't heard him come back up. He'd be derelict if he didn't have quick shufti around the rest of the upstairs.

The room opposite Emma's across the corridor was the old lady's. The bedstead was an old iron one. The walls were papered in a red rose design on a cream background. Even the ceiling was papered, like a provincial French *pension*. In front of the window that looked out onto the road at the front was an ornate kind of writing desk with a matching chair that fitted perfectly under the flap. At the window that looked out over the marshes was a dressing table with a few bottles and brushes.

On the walls were a few Impressionist reproductions – Monet's *Water Lilies* and Van Gogh's *Peach Blossom in the Crau*. It was a plain room, simply and conventionally furnished. On the inner wall was a small section of old photos of an attractive and vivacious-looking young girl in military uniform, sometimes by herself and sometimes in a group of other uniformed young women in front of an imposing Victorian house. In one photo, she was between two men who looked like officers. Andy Nolan said Daphne Jameson had been in the RAF. He made a note to confirm it with Jameson. Next to Emma's room, opposite the stairs, was a guest bedroom that doubled as a box room, and next to that, at the back of the house, the bathroom, full of low handles, light and shower cords that went down to wheelchair height and an extended wet room area. There was a hoist over the bath.

Sterling listened again. There was still no sound from downstairs. He eased open the door opposite the bathroom. This must be Jameson's room. It was a monk's quarters. There was no carpet, just parquet flooring. The room was decorated in a kind of off-white. The sliding doors of another built-in wardrobe matched the flooring. There was a chest of drawers and a couple of bedside tables next to a plain structure that looked more like a futon than a bed. Apart from a pile of books on one of the tables and a reading lamp, it was a room for sleeping and getting ready in.

As he went downstairs, Sterling considered what more he had learned. Specific details: none. But it was a house where the complications of the girl's life seemed to be offset by plainness and simplicity, and perhaps he'd got a better idea of the person he was searching for and the circumstances in which she'd gone missing.

'Mr Jameson?' Sterling called loudly. Jameson emerged from a room beside the stairs.

'Find anything?' he said.

'Not really. There was no computer on Emma's desk. That's a bit of a surprise.'

'No, not at all. She had an iPad. She kept everything on that. We got rid of her PC and laptop a long time ago. The iPad went everywhere with her. She kept it in a compartment under the seat of her out-and-about wheelchair. The one she was in when she went away.'

'Right,' said Sterling. 'What about your mother? Did she have a study that I could see?'

'Why do you need to see that? What's that got to do with anything? I hired you to find Emma, not rummage around in my mother's affairs. I wasn't expecting you to be so intrusive.' There was a bitter edge to Jameson's voice.

'I can't put the case into compartments, Mr Jameson,' said Sterling. His training came to him automatically. When the person you are talking with is agitated, soften your voice and speak calmly.

'My aunt shot this rake while fully starkers,' said Jameson. 'You've dropped your voice so I can't hear you.'

Sterling rolled his eyes, a kind of involuntary, reflex movement. You could try, but you couldn't always overcome being a hothead. No amount of training could alter that.

'You can hear when you want to hear,' said Jameson. 'That's what you're thinking, isn't it? You're not concentrating. You're not listening. If you listened, really listened, you wouldn't come out with these nonsense sentences. That's it, isn't it? And maybe I jerked off too much when I was a kid. It makes you deaf, you know. If it doesn't make you blind.'

Sterling raised his voice, and not just to ensure that Jameson could hear. He was angry too. 'Help me out here, Mr Jameson. I don't mean to keep putting my foot in it. You engaged me to find Emma, and that's what I'm trying to do. All this other sh… All this other stuff is confusing me. Now, did your mother have a study?' He wanted to ask about the photographs on her bedroom wall, but did not want to reveal that he'd been snooping around beyond Emma's room, especially after the current exchange.

Jameson stared at him. Then the fire seemed to fade from his eyes. 'This way,' he said. They moved to a side room by the front door. The house was one of contrasts – the teenager's dark bedroom, the monk's quarters, the provincial French hotel room. This new room consolidated the differences. Although its shell looked newly refurbished, with its light parquet floor and white walls, it was as if the old woman had tried to obliterate modernity. Rich red Persian rugs covered the floor. Under the window a square dark desk with inlaid writing surface and blotting paper squatted, the surface scratched and marked from long usage. The drawers on each side had lion heads as handles, expensively carved. Two bookcases flanked the walls on either side.

Next to the door was a straight-backed upholstered armchair in the same shade of red as the rugs. On the desk and on the walls were lamps with frilled lampshades. Beside the desk stood an ancient two-drawer filing cabinet.

Where the walls were not backed by bookcases, framed Oriental embroideries, more dark than light, filled the empty spaces. Sterling noticed an ancient cylindrical electric stand-up heater, certainly older than he was, next to the armchair. He remembered one from his early childhood. The elements at the bottom glowed red and drew air in from underneath. He used to look down through the grille at the top and let the warm, fusty, metallic-tasting air wash over his face and ruffle his hair.

'When Emma came back from university, she was pretty low,' said Jameson. 'She was always very close to her grandmother, as I said before. And my mother was a wise woman. She knew that Emma would need some kind of focus. They used to spend hours in here together. But it was something they did together. They didn't share it with me. You can see the tracks of Emma's wheelchair in that rug.' He pointed to the one nearest the armchair.

Sterling had thought the room was dark, but occupied by Mrs Jameson and her granddaughter it was probably more cosy than gloomy. He pictured them together, the old heater supplementing the warmth from radiators.

'And this is where your mother was...attacked,' said Sterling.

'Yes. We were allowed to clean up after my mother's body was taken away and the forensics people had finished. It was a horrible time.'

'I'm sorry I'm raking over it, Mr Jameson, but if your mother and Emma were doing something together, perhaps it's linked with Emma's going away. My police source says there was no forced entry. Any thoughts on that?'

'Well, maybe she let someone in and gave them a drink. I wouldn't describe her as lonely, but she didn't get many visitors and she was sociable in her way. It wouldn't have been entirely outlandish for her to invite someone in – a salesperson or someone. It's possible she invited someone when she knew for certain that Emma and I would be out. The police found it odd that the tumblers they found on the draining board in the kitchen had been wiped clean of fingerprints. But surely you know much of this already if you've been talking to the police.'

Sterling nodded. 'Yep, I know quite a lot. But a different perspective can be very helpful. Can I look through the filing cabinet?'

Jameson shrugged. 'You can, but the police found nothing. Nothing in the desk either. Anything that my mother and Emma did is probably somewhere on Emma's iPad, and she's taken that with her.'

Sterling opened the top drawer, looking through the file labels in their neat diagonal row stretching to the back of the cabinet from left to right, in strict alphabetical order, exactly as he organised his own affairs – building society, insurance, savings – the whole gamut of an ordinary life. The bottom drawer was exactly the same, and nothing caught his inquisitive eye. He picked out a green file and found letters and documents in perfect order.

'It wasn't like this after she was killed,' said Jameson. 'There were papers everywhere. The place was ransacked and my mother was slumped in the armchair.' He shuddered. 'All that blood. And she was still alive.'

'I'll stop harking back in a minute, Mr Jameson. One last thing. One of the paramedics who attended your mother said that she tried to say something just before she…died. I'm told it was 'Bored Anna' or 'Bart's kneebone' – something like that. Do you have any inkling of what she might have been trying to say?'

'The police asked me that. I honestly don't have a clue. She was retired. She didn't seem to have anything on her mind, apart from the project she was doing with Emma. I don't know of anyone in her circle who was called Anna. The other phrase is nonsense. It could have been anything.'

'OK. Thanks. I don't think there's anything more I can do here. It's probably been helpful, and in my experience it may give clues to something I might find out later on. Something positive for you now. I picked up Emma's trail from the day before yesterday. She went to Canterbury and then she caught a train from Canterbury East station with a ticket to Woodbridge in Suffolk. I found out that she packed for five days away. I'm going to go to Woodbridge early tomorrow to see if I can catch up with her. It's looking pretty positive, but the mystery is the destination. Does anything about Woodbridge ring a bell?'

'Footbridge wishing well,' said Jameson absent-mindedly. 'Not at all. Your guess is as good as mine.' He looked at Sterling. 'You've done well – so far. Make sure you finish the job.'

Chapter 7

Eureka

Sterling, like Emma two days before, waited for a bus back into Sandley. He looked across at the house. He might just have been thanked for his work so far, but he wasn't sure. He wondered if Andy Nolan had told the case detectives about Emma Jameson's disappearance. For Sterling, that could put a different slant on the old lady's murder, but unlike the police, he had no other case to think about, and plenty of time for speculation. He watched Hamworth Place fade from view as the bus bore him away back to Sandley. Now there was the ordeal of preparing to leave his hometown. He hated being away from the familiar streets and alleys, the pub, his house and his friends, few as they were. What was the point of going away if you didn't have to? There was nothing but expense and disruption. He didn't want to be part of the teeming millions restlessly traversing the planet, exhausting its resources. That was why he didn't own a car, and why Sandley was good enough for him.

He found his pre-packed overnight bag and supplemented it with clothes and underwear for two more days. He consoled himself: the sooner he went, the sooner he'd be back.

At Canterbury West station in the early morning, after the bus ride from Sandley, things had changed again since he had last been there. He had the same left-behind feeling as when he had first seen the new university library next to the police station on the other side of the city. He couldn't even remember what the station had looked like before the dark blue and grey facelift before him.

It wasn't just the station. In the old days, when he was on the force, he and Andy Nolan used to catch a slow old slam-door train that wheezed and dragged itself to Charing Cross for Special Branch training at the headquarters in Soho. It took not far off two hours to get there, and it was miraculous if it arrived on time. Now there was a sleek dark blue number with light blue doors – resembling his old school colours – to whisk him up to London in under an hour, in a coach full of students. A boy and girl next to him chattered excitedly into their mobile phones and then switched to games. Their machines glowed and beeped. The lettering on their drinks bottles looked Japanese.

The old slow train did not cross the Thames until it reached London Bridge. The new one emerged full pelt from a long tunnel just before the Dartford Crossing and swept on westward through the Essex marshes. Through the pillars of a roadway elevated over the railway track, a Norman church stood amongst a row of semis in the empty flatness. Further on, Ford's abandoned Dagenham works stretched mile on mile beside the track.

Stratford, in east London, was another shock. A new concrete monolith masquerading as an international station joined a vast new shopping mall called Westfield, through which Sterling had to walk to get to the local station to take him to East Anglia. If Andy Nolan had been with him, he'd be wondering where Sterling had hidden himself to remain so ignorant. In the halls of Mammon, he passed gaggles of shoppers walking the arcades and resting in the cafés that filled the open spaces. In sight of the local station, a toddler lurched from nowhere and wrapped himself around Sterling's leg. 'Sorry,' said the child's young mother as she prised the little boy away. They disappeared into a crowd, mother, pushchair and child.

—◊—

Two hours later, via a change at Ipswich and a gentle ride through rural Essex and Suffolk where little happened except the rhythm of stops and starts at small country towns, Sterling stepped out into a calmer world at the small station of Woodbridge. Later, when it was all over, he would reflect on how easy the outward journey had been compared to the return. Once the train had pulled out and the platform had emptied, Sterling looked around for a member of the station staff – anyone who might have seen a girl with blonde hair and a pink stripe in a wheelchair leave the station at about the same time three days ago. She must have come out here. Where had she gone? But there was no one. Woodbridge station seemed uncannily like Sandley, where there was nothing but a ticket machine that was often broken and a weekly visit from uninterested maintenance staff.

Beyond the platform in the station precinct, Sterling could see three potential sources of information in lieu of station employees: M and R taxi service, Whistlestop Bed and Breakfast, and the Woodbridge and Mid-Suffolk Coast Tourist Centre. They all seemed to be part of the station complex, springing up to take over accommodation from more grandiose times. And as well as helping him track Emma Jameson, he might need transport of his own, somewhere to stay, and information.

The taxi firm was closed. The office was open only in the evenings. When he tried the telephone number, it went to voicemail. During the day, said the voicemail message, taxis were only available for school runs (speciality - students with special needs) or pre-booked journeys. The bed and breakfast place did not even offer a telephone number. It would open at 4 p.m. Could a place be more dead-and-alive? He gravitated to the tourist centre next door. It was 12.40. At least he had twenty minutes before it too closed at lunchtime – plenty of time for what he needed.

In Sterling's extensive experience of tourist information centres there were two main types of assistant – those he'd come to define as the eager enthusiast and the reluctant researcher. At Ypres, when he'd been deep in the Etchingham case, the woman at the museum in the main square had been a reluctant researcher. She'd barely been able to bring herself to point him in the right direction, let alone give him any other help. In the Woodbridge centre, he thought he'd struck lucky. The woman at the counter was surely an eager enthusiast, proud of her county and her district and keen to assist. Her plump face was freckled and open and her eyes an unusual pale green. Her peasant blouse, cotton skirt and sandals gave her a rustic look. A smallholding with chickens and animals, and a couple of acres for vegetables would have been a more obvious setting.

'Good morning.' She glanced at the clock. 'I mean, good afternoon. Welcome to Woodbridge in the beautiful county of Suffolk. How can I help?'

'Hi. Well, first things first. What about a map of the area and a map of Woodbridge? I could do with some information about transport and bus timetables, and places to visit in the area. And accommodation locally, I guess.'

'Right, I can help with all of that. Obviously.'

Sterling let the young woman go through her spiel. The jewel in the district's crown was Suffolk Hoo, where the whole boat of a Saxon king had been found buried. Transport, if you didn't have a car, was tricky. The locality was sparsely populated and buses relatively scarce. He could ride on school buses if they were convenient. There were plenty of bed and breakfast places around. She could phone up for him. The Whistlestop was fine and of course convenient. She picked out maps, bus timetables and addresses.

'Thank you,' said Sterling. That's wonderful.' He felt uneasy now. It wasn't the burial barrow of a long-dead Saxon king and his treasures he wanted to visit, or to look out to sea at Dunwich, where a medieval town had been inundated by the sea four hundred years ago. But admitting that made him look a fraud. 'There's another thing. I should really have started off with it. Not that I didn't need all this information.'

Doubt crept into the young woman's open face.

'Three days ago, on Tuesday, a young woman in a wheelchair had a ticket to this station. I wonder if she called in.'

'You don't really seem like a tourist, to be honest,' said the woman. 'But I'm not really rushed off my feet, so I can't say I mind. But no one in a wheelchair has been in lately while I've been here, and I wasn't in on Tuesday. I'll ask Jean.' She called out towards the office at the back. 'Jean, did we have a wheelchair user – a young girl – come in the day before yesterday? Jean?' She looked at Sterling. He thought she might have made a face. There was a reluctant researcher out back. All the signs were there.

Jean appeared at the doorway, a woman of about 50 in a two-piece grey business suit, in stark contrast to the style of her colleague. There were lines radiating from the moue of her small mouth. 'Who wants to know?' She looked Sterling up and down. His easy charm rarely worked on reluctant researchers, who were engrossed in their work and did not want to be diverted by enquirers off the street. 'Identification? Photograph?'

Sterling produced his card and Emma Jameson's photo, which the woman examined closely. He explained the reason for his search. 'No,' the woman said. 'We've had no wheelchair users. What will you do when you find her?'

Sterling hadn't thought much about that. 'Well, she's an adult. Check that she's safe. Tell her father I've located her. Offer her help to get home if that's what she wants. Ask her to let her father know she's OK if she doesn't.' It was a useful question, but now the reluctant researcher knew about Sterling while he had had little in return. She withdrew back into the office and he felt oddly disadvantaged.

Her colleague made an odd little gesture, screwing up and turning down the corner of her mouth, acknowledging the rudeness. 'Jean can be a bit prickly, but if she said no wheelchair user then there won't have been one.'

'OK, thanks. Sorry to have been a bit misleading. One last query. Where can I get a spot of lunch?'

In the bookshop café in the high street, Sterling laid all the information from the tourist centre out on the table as he sipped his cappuccino and ate his sandwich. If Emma Jameson was going to a private destination then he was stumped, but he sensed that it was more obvious than that. The tourist map was detailed and he scanned it closely. Emma and her grandmother were working together on a project that linked the old lady to this district. He reviewed all that he had found out. In Daphne Jameson's ordinary life one thing stood out: her RAF service in the war years. What was there in this corner of Suffolk that might fit the bill? On the map, he considered Orford Castle, but that was far too old. Nowhere else seemed remotely promising. He considered going back to the Tourist Centre, but it wouldn't yet have reopened. He cursed softly. Why hadn't he looked at things from the other end while he had access to his computer in Sandley – not from the point of view of picking up Emma Jameson's trail but from finding out possible destinations? He would go back to the Tourist Centre if he had to, but as he sipped his coffee, he had a better idea. He was in a bookshop after all.

'Excuse me,' he said to the top of the woman's head. He could see the parting in the tired, mousey hair, but the woman's face was much younger, oval and unlined. Whether she was an eager enthusiast or a reluctant researcher was in the balance. 'I'm wondering if you have a section on local history.'

'Does a bear?' she said, dragging her eyes from her computer screen. 'Or is the pope? We're an independent bookshop, trying to keep the wolf from the door. What would you expect?'

'Yes, I would expect a section. Anything that's likely to sell here, I guess. So where is it?'

She tilted her head. 'Over there. But I have to say there's a lot of, well, rubbish. As you'd expect with legions of amateur historians. Have you got a particular interest?'

'World War II,' said Sterling. He was beginning to get attuned to the bookseller.

'Not another World War II buff. Suffolk had a history long before that. Have you heard of Anne Boleyn? It's said that her heart is buried in one of the churches in the Shotley peninsula. She spent her summer holidays in Ipswich.'

'I'm not a historian. I'm looking for someone. I'm following clues.'

'Hmm. Interesting. Well, the most obvious place is Orford Ness. It was used in both wars and in the fifties and sixties as an Atomic Weapons Research Establishment.' She moved around from behind her desk and took Sterling over to the shelves. 'Here's the modern section. She ran her fingers over a few volumes. Some of these aren't bad. You need to flick through them to get an idea of which are any good. OK if I get back to my spreadsheet?'

'Yes, thanks.' Sterling thought of Angela at Sandley Library. She'd be much quicker. He started to look through various volumes with the enthusiasm of a man who knew it was a long shot. The bookseller was right – there was plenty of dross. He flicked through a fat book on Orford Ness. However you looked at it, the plates showed an already desolate place miles from anywhere made worse by 'The Street' of jerry-built military offices, stores and hangars and a rudimentary grass airfield. It had indeed first been used for military research in World War I – bombs replacing sheep. It was possible that Emma Jameson needed to go there, but not very likely. Normally he got a feeling about something – a hint or intuition, a quickening of the pulse, a feeling in his guts. There was nothing like that here.

He thought he'd have to go back to the station, get a room at the bed and breakfast place and phone the taxi company. There had only been dead ends so far, but he was sure that he had just not found the right people to ask. He put *A History of Orford Ness* (two thousand years of sheep grazing and twenty of bomb testing) back on the shelf and drifted back to the bookseller.

'Find anything?' she said, without taking her eyes from the computer screen.

Sterling marvelled at the ability of retailers to know exactly where their customers are. He was almost tempted to put on a squeaky voice to make her think he was someone else. 'Nothing promising,' he said, 'There's certainly nowhere habitable at Orford Ness. And I have to say, you were right about the dross.'

'The thing is, that dross sells.'

'Well, I don't think Orford Ness is what I'm looking for. It was used in World War I, and then in the 50s and 60s, but not that much in between.

The bookseller suddenly went still. 'Radar. I completely forgot. That's the other big connection with this area. They did some work on it even at Orford in the 1930s – just for a brief while, but then it moved. Hold on a second. I think there's a slim little book tucked away somewhere about that.' She went back to the shelves and rummaged about. 'Here it is, the inspirationally titled *Suffolk Radar Story*. A lot of people came here to work on that. I think some of them and their families still live locally.'

But the bookseller's voice was coming from far away. A moment ago, nothing in Sterling's guts indicated a breakthrough. Now he remembered that you could never underestimate the suddenness or source of a *eureka* moment. He was looking at the subsidiary title on the book's cover. The paramedic listening to the battered, bloody old lady's dying words in Hamworth all those months ago had got it wrong (though who could blame her?) in a way that might have done justice to Nicholas Jameson's rich deaf imagination. No 'bored Anna' or 'Bart's kneebone' obsessed Daphne Jameson as life drained from her. The message to Sterling, and perhaps to Emma Jameson before him, surely couldn't be clearer. He mouthed the words softly: *Bawdsey Manor. The War Secrets of Bawdsey Manor.*

Chapter 8

Reconnoitre

'Hello. Houston to Apollo One,' said the bookseller.

'Copy Houston,' said Sterling, coming out of his reverie. 'Sorry. I just had one of those moments.'

'Seems like it. It looks as if you've found what you wanted though.' The bookseller was pleased. She was going to make a sale.

Sterling handed over the money for the slim volume. He didn't really need it now he'd made the link, but he'd be able to claim it as an expense, and perhaps he'd get some extra background if he found the time and inclination. But he felt a renewed optimism. Things were looking up in terms of a likely destination even if Emma Jameson's trail had gone cold at Woodbridge Station. He decided he needed to go back to the Tourist Information Centre. If Emma had gone to Bawdsey Manor, how would she have got there? And if he wanted to go, how was he going to get there?

'Back again?' said the young woman with the open face. There was no sign of the sour-mouthed Jean.

'Yup. Now I wonder if you can tell me how to get to Bawdsey Manor.'

The woman looked at her watch. The gold effect glittered on her light brown skin. 'The best and cheapest way, and indeed the only way, if you haven't got a car, is the school bus. That leaves from Farlingaye High School in forty minutes. Plenty of time for you to walk up.' She peeled off a map of Woodbridge from a thick pad. Her voice changed as she returned to her spiel. There was a cross for the current location and a cross for the school, and then her biro joined them up. 'The only snag is how you get back.'

'Something usually turns up,' said Sterling. It came out as a bit of bravado.

'Not so likely in the depths of rural Suffolk. Make sure you take the number of the taxi firm.'

—⁂—

At the bus stop, Sterling joined two old men in cloth caps and faded tweed jackets with elbow pads. Their eyes were a startling blue in their dark, leathery faces, bluer than Sterling had ever seen. They were surely retired labourers from farms down Bawdsey way. When the bus arrived, the driver's eyes were the same shade. He took Sterling's money with a calm rural courtesy. Sterling caught a Suffolk burr in his soft voice.

'I wonder…Did you have a girl in a wheelchair on the bus on Tuesday?'

The driver shook his head. It means nothing, thought Sterling. I'm still going down to Bawdsey. The silent serenity lasted only till school was out. Then the bus filled with a cacophony of schoolchildren and the driver set off, the cab a little island of care and concentration as high spirits and horseplay marked the end of the school day. Amongst the children in the bus were some with the same blue eyes. Sterling thought of life around Woodbridge. So long as there was work, it was as it was at Sandley. Why would families think of leaving?

'This is the end of the line,' said the driver to Sterling as the last schoolchildren, two girls about fourteen, possibly sisters or cousins, hopped off the bus, their bags swinging at their sides. Sterling was almost reluctant to move. It was 4.30 and already he was wondering how he'd get back to Woodbridge.

'Thanks,' he said. He looked out over the water beyond the driver. 'What river is this?'

'The Deben,' said the driver. 'It goes back to Woodbridge and beyond.'

'And this is Bawdsey Manor,' said Sterling.

'Strictly speaking, no. We've come around the side of Bawdsey Manor – the long brick wall that was on your left. You might have noticed the back entrance. This is Bawdsey Quay. We went through the actual village a couple of miles back. But the entrance to Bawdsey Manor is over there.' He twisted in his seat and pointed through the back window of the bus, having done a U-turn on the asphalt in front of the quay so that he was pointing the right way for the return journey. 'See that raised building. The Boathouse Café. He looked at his watch. 'It's still open. The coffee's really good.'

'Thanks again,' said Sterling. He watched as the bus lurched away. There was a slight chill in the early evening air. If nothing turned up, it was going to be a long walk back to civilisation. He looked out over the river. The tide was full and boats bobbed at their moorings. In the mud and dunes next to the bus stop, a couple of turnstones picked around industriously for morsels. Sterling walked back across the asphalt and car park area to the front entrance of Bawdsey Manor. Progress did not look promising. Two large wrought iron gates with black bars topped with golden fleurs-de-lis dominated the surrounding area and looked disturbingly like shark jaws. Sterling made out a little wooden gatehouse a few metres inside. The driveway within bent sharply to the left and up a slight hill. The manor itself was completely out of sight. Notices fixed to the gate were hardly welcoming: entrance in use at all times – keep clear; vehicles parked illegally will be towed away; visitors by telephone appointment only; guard dogs loose in grounds; and finally, most unequivocally of all, KEEP OUT.

Sterling knew that there were times to press on and times to hold back. In the old days, it was Andy Nolan who used to hold him back and urge patience. Now he was more aware of his own hot-headed ways. Anyway, he was slowed down by lack of transport and resources. The temptation was to go up to the gates and ring the bell. I'm looking for Emma Jameson, he'd say. Come on in, the gateman would reply. No scenario seemed less promising. Weighing everything up, this was a time for holding back. He'd hang around a little and take it from there. He could start at the cafe fifty metres away, and to reach it he passed through wooden gates far more dilapidated than the ones he had just surveyed. Old dinghies punctuated the yard in various states of disrepair, some hull up and some hull down. The café seemed to rest on a platform of wooden stilts. He went up the wooden staircase and through the entrance at the back. The dilapidation ended outside. The café and its veranda, looking out over the river, were white and pristine, and the red and white checked plastic table covers gleamed. A small, energetic woman bustled behind the counter, her apron the same check as the table covers.

Her dark red hair was also matched by a pair of large spectacle frames that dwarfed her face. Sterling was reminded of a TV quiz presenter with a cruel wit, but only the looks were similar. The café manager's manner was brisk but kindly.

She set down his ham, egg and chips and pot of tea. 'You've got plenty of time, but I'm closing up in half an hour.'

When a young couple came in from the veranda with binoculars, which were clearly part of the café's service, Sterling was the only customer left.

'Do you see much of the people up at the Manor?' asked Sterling.

The woman paused for a moment from drying her hands on a tea towel and looked Sterling up and down, a long, appraising examination. He seemed to pass. 'No,' she said. 'Since that family took over no one from the house has been here, or the goons that "look after" them.' She bracketed the "look after" with imaginary quotation marks with her forefingers. 'They sweep in and out in their fancy cars and pay no attention to the people who live and work here. But...I don't suppose it makes much difference to us in the scheme of things. It's just that this is a friendly place and it lowers the tone.'

'Where are they from?'

'Dunno. They say the bloke in charge owns a company. His father's here with him, and his son. So it's the three of them and a group of employees and assistants. They've been there about a year. But I doubt if anyone's even spoken to them. The bloke at the gatehouse has a go at kids if they come too close. The back of this place is next to the estate. They've put broken glass on the top of the wall. Very neighbourly. Why are you interested?'

'I'm looking for someone. I think she came down here on Tuesday. Did you see her?' Sterling got out his photo. 'She didn't come on the school bus.'

'In a wheelchair,' mused the woman. 'Sorry, I wasn't here. We don't open on Tuesday. Why don't you ring the bell and ask?'

'I'm not quite ready for that yet. She might not be there. And from what you've said, I wouldn't get a very friendly welcome. I need to think things through.'

The woman nodded. 'Well, remember I'm closing up soon. I didn't see your car. Where are you staying?'

'I haven't got a car, but I need to get back to Woodbridge,' said Sterling. He wiped up some egg yolk with his last chip.

'I live that way. I'll take you.'

Something always turns up, thought Sterling. Something turned up in terms of accommodation too. At the Whistlestop Bed and Breakfast, he managed to get the last single room and the facilities were comfortable enough. There was one more thing to do before he went up to the town centre for a late evening snack. The M and R taxi office was now open for the evening's business. Behind the glass counter, a young woman with a beehive sat boredly in front of a mike. He'd watched her walk across the forecourt from his window and open up. She was short and had a slight limp.

'This service is hard to get hold of,' said Sterling. 'There's only voicemail during the day.'

The girl shrugged, as if it was nothing to do with her and she wasn't interested. 'It's all schools and booked work during the day. I only come in for the evenings.'

'OK. Well, I may need to book a taxi for tomorrow morning,' said Sterling through the glass. 'But before

I confirm, do you know if your service gave a lift to a girl in a wheelchair on Tuesday afternoon or evening?'

'Last Tuesday? I'll ask.' She flipped a switch. There was nothing of the jobsworth about her. 'Calling all drivers. Did anyone have a fare from a girl in a wheelchair on Tuesday afternoon or evening?'

There was crackling and static. In a short moment, Sterling became tense and anxious. He realised how much he'd staked on his hunch that Emma Jameson had made her way to Bawdsey. If she hadn't, he was stumped. After a few moments, there was another blast of static.

'Yes, Despatch. Harry Brown here. I gave a girl a lift down to Bawdsey Quay. Tuesday afternoon about two o'clock.'

'Did he bring her back?' mouthed Sterling.

'Harry, did you bring her back?' said the girl.

'No, she told me I needn't wait. I don't think anyone brought her back.'

'OK?' said the girl to Sterling.

'Yeah, thanks. So, can I book that taxi for tomorrow morning to take me to Bawdsey Quay?' said Sterling.

'No problem,' said the girl. 'What time and where from? Are you coming back within the hour? I can do you a package.'

Sterling thought about it. 'Yes, make it a package. Say, 9.30 am from the Whistlestop next door.'

'OK, that's booked.'

'You must get a bit bored of an evening in here.'

'It's a job. There's not a lot around Woodbridge, and I'm not that mobile. I've got my college homework – and magazines.' She motioned to the counter behind the glass. 'Sometimes there's a bit of interest. Who's the girl you're looking for?'

Sterling showed her the photograph. 'She left home in Kent a few days ago. Didn't tell anyone. Gave no reason. Came up here. Her father asked me to find her.'

'Well, if I hear anything....'

'Thanks.' When Sterling looked back, the girl was flipping through her magazine. It was a job, but it certainly looked dull.

Later on, back in his room, Sterling came around to thinking about Emma Jameson's underwear. Not, of course... No, he was calculating that she only had two days' clean clothes left. He wasn't thinking MISPER and murder anymore either. All the signs so far were that Emma Jameson was alive, if not kicking.

Chapter 9

The Lucky Breakdown

Sterling knew things had been going his way. It was lucky that he had located Emma Jameson promptly, with the willing help of a range of people from Kent to Suffolk. More mundanely, at the end of yesterday, he'd even got a lift back from Bawdsey Quay in unpromising circumstances, and the last room at the Whistlestop. He just couldn't decide how much of the luck he had made himself. Now he hoped it would continue. Outside the taxi office at 9.30 the next day, things started well. The taxi turned up exactly on time, and the driver took Sterling in silence back down to the settlement at the mouth of the Deben. They pulled up outside the Boathouse Café.

'I've been told you've got the package,' said the driver in his Suffolk burr. 'I'll wait here till you're ready to come back. School run's over. I can wait for an hour.'

Sterling walked back to the gate guarding Bawdsey Manor. He had thought of telephoning to ask for an appointment, but was sure he'd be fobbed off. It was better to go up to the gate. He'd have to ask about Emma Jameson and if she was staying there, and he'd have to explain his business – commissioned by Nicholas

Jameson to find his daughter. If he were told that the girl wasn't there, he'd have to say that a taxi brought her down from Woodbridge but did not bring her back. He would imply that the police might show an interest if the girl continued to be reported missing. Sometimes a little insinuation could have a powerful effect – not that the police, in his own direct experience, would move as quickly or show as much interest as he would imply.

He felt nervous as he approached. It was all very flimsy. Giving him the brush-off would be easy. Then he heard an engine behind him, and a white van approached the gates. At the same time he heard a clatter and the sound of a curse from within the Bawdsey Manor estate, which seemed to come from just beyond where the drive curved around out of sight beyond the gatehouse. The van was from a supermarket, delivering groceries. The driver, a young woman with spiky blonde hair and dark eyebrows, and in garish luminous green supermarket livery, hopped out of the van and went around to the bell on the wall by the gate. Just as the man in the gatehouse came out, a wheelchair containing a slight figure bustled around the corner. Nicholas Jameson had been right. Sterling knew straight away that it was Emma.

His training kicked in. ADA. Assess. Decide. Act. But a year as a private investigator had taught him wiles he had never needed in the job.

As the gates rumbled open parallel to the walls on either side, he called out, making his voice a mixture of surprise and urgency. 'Emma. It's cousin Michael. Your Dad said you were down here, and I'm touring. Over here.'

The girl looked bewildered for a moment, and something else. She glanced furtively towards the gatekeeper. She's quick on the uptake, thought Sterling, and quick with the wheelchair too.

'Cousin Michael. Lovely surprise. How are you doing?' As she began to roll over the grooves of the electric gate, the gatekeeper stepped in front of her with the clipboard from the van driver.

'Oi. No one in or out without say-so from the house.'

'Excuse me,' said the girl aggressively. 'I'm going to have a chat with my cousin.'

The man, short, fat and wide and in a poorly fitting dark suit, did not move. 'I've got my orders.'

'Half a moment,' said the supermarket driver. There was a look of shock on her face. 'Last I heard, this is a free country.'

The gatekeeper was a gatekeeper for a reason. He was used to following orders from above and managing his undemanding little gateway fiefdom. But all this was out of the ordinary, and taxing his almost non-existent initiative. His cocksure manner was replaced by uncertainty. He stepped aside. 'I need to check,' he muttered, waddling to the gatehouse still clutching the clipboard.

The driver turned to Emma Jameson. Sterling felt the exclusion of female solidarity. 'It's not really allowed, but do you want a lift?'

'I've got a taxi waiting,' said Sterling.

'Thanks,' said Emma to both Sterling and the driver. But the van's no use. The taxi might be better.' She faced the driver. 'Can you stay parked here for a few minutes?'

'Sure. He hasn't signed anything, and I haven't delivered, so I've got to stick around.'

'Come on,' said Emma to Sterling. 'We need to get out of here.' She wheeled off down towards the quay. Sterling found himself jogging behind, struggling to keep up. By the water fifty metres from the gates, Emma did a kind of wheelchair pirouette to face him. 'So,' she said, 'you know who I am, but who the fuck are you? Certainly not my cousin Michael, whoever the hell he might be.'

'I'm a private investigator. Your father wanted me to find you.'

'OK, that will do for the moment. What I need now is to get away.' She looked across the river and saw something that pleased her. 'The taxi's actually no good. Tell the girl at the van to send it away. You'd better give her some money. Chop-chop.'

Sterling did as he was told and hurried back to the van. He was seething. He left the force because he couldn't take orders and now he was being bossed around by a girl in a wheelchair. Only the prospect of mission accomplished and fee paid went a small way to soothing him.

'Can you give this cash to the taxi driver parked in front of the café back there and tell him I won't be needing a lift back?' he said to the van driver.

'OK. Is everything going to be alright?'

'Don't ask me,' said Sterling. 'I'm just the hired help.'

'Not cousin Michael?'

'Long story. Thanks for your help.' He hurried back to the river side.

Emma Jameson was looking over to the other side. 'Look,' she said, and Sterling saw a long boat with a gangway plank tethered to the side puttering across the face of the river. 'We didn't even have to wave the bat.'

'The bat?' said Sterling.

She gestured to her side. Sterling saw the bat in its makeshift holder next to a lifebuoy, like a ping-pong bat or the devices used to direct planes on aircraft carriers. On it was a crude sketch of a matchstick man and the words 'Wave bat for ferry' in clumsy capitals. 'I noticed the bat and the ferry on Tuesday when I arrived.'

The boat pulled up on the shingle, and the boatman let down the gangplank parallel to the side of the boat. That's a neat arrangement, thought Sterling.

'This will be interesting,' said the girl. She wheeled to the edge of the shingle.

It was four metres to the beginning of the gangplank. The boatman, a large man with a weather-beaten brown face and clothes not far from becoming rags, pushed back his tatty sleeves. 'How do we do this?' he called. Sterling noticed that he had no front teeth and a clown's tear of light oil streaking one cheek.

'Impressive,' said Emma softly. She seemed to be doing a little commentary to herself. To the boatman she called, 'He's going to carry me and then load the wheelchair.' To Sterling she said, 'crouch down in front of me. No, no, face the river, not me. Bend your legs, not your back. God,' she sighed impatiently. 'OK, I'm going to flip on to you and put my arms around your neck. I'll be holding a bag. Drag me over to the boat.'

Sterling did as he was told. If he'd had time to think he might have objected. The arms came up and he heard a small grunt. He felt the girl's small body flop against him and staggered off onto the gangplank. Between them, he and the boatman wrestled the girl into the middle of the boat, where she propped herself up.

'Get the wheelchair.'

Sterling examined it quickly. The wheel spokes glinted in the sunshine and the wheels themselves were cambered so that the width between them was narrower at the top than at the base. The hand rims were a rich bright red and matched the colour of the padded chair. At the bottom, low slung behind the chair, was a storage compartment, and between the foldaway handles at the back a bar with hooks. It looked as though the brakes, through connected cables and levers, could be operated by the user as well as a person pushing. It was sleek, light and compact – clearly a Ferrari amongst wheelchairs. But he struggled to find buttons to press and handles to pull so that he could fold it up.

'Christ, what are you doing?' called the girl.

'Trying to fold the wheelchair,' replied Sterling. 'Keep your hair on.'

'It's rigid frame, you idiot. It doesn't fold. Just pick the bloody thing up and put it in the boat.' The girl didn't trouble to hide her exasperation.

The ferryman was smiling a gap-toothed smile. At the gates there seemed to be a flurry of activity. The spiky blonde driver was arguing with someone out of sight.

'Hurry up, for God's sake,' said Emma as Sterling wrestled with the chair and the boatman shook his head. In a few seconds, both the chair and Sterling toppled into the boat, the gangplank was up and the short passage across to the small hamlet on the other bank of the river was underway.

For a few moments, Emma relaxed. She turned her face to the sun in the south. But when she looked back to the north, the top half of her stiffened and her face drained of colour. Sterling followed her gaze across the river. Framed against the shoreline on the shingle was a large man in dark trousers and a dark jacket that his upper torso filled. Black-framed sunglasses covered his eyes and his light brown hair was shaped in a crew cut.

Even halfway across the river, Sterling could see the bull neck jutting from an open-necked shirt. Perhaps he wasn't so large after all, but he was doing more than simply standing on the shingle – he imposed himself on his surroundings. And held aloft, like the Olympic torch or a pagan symbol from beyond the mists of time, was the ferry bat. The dark figure on the shore was not just requesting a ride across the river; he was demanding it.

Much later, Sterling remembered how the river had glittered in the bright spring sunshine. The gaily-painted boats all around had bobbed on their moorings, and a brisk warm breeze had brushed his face under the wide East Anglian sky. In the distance he had seen the squat round shape of a Martello tower, reminding him of his own Kent coastline. This is a picture postcard setting, he had thought. But there had been a stronger, more visceral memory – of his nape-hairs standing out, his stomach lurching, and a prickling that ran in a wave over his skull.

Emma turned to the boatman, who was looking over at the summons. 'How long will it be before you go back over, fetch him and let him off this side?'

'Funny you should ask that.' His Suffolk burr was more pronounced than the taxi driver's. 'Engine's been playing up. Should just get up to the jetty here, but after that…' He flicked a switch and the steady putter was replaced by a series of stutters and then silence. A large plume of blue smoke rose over the water. The boat drifted perfectly up to the short jetty. 'I'll just tether up and let you off, and then I'll have to do some repairs. I'd better lift you out myself, girl, while your mate gets the wheelchair.'

He tottered up the steps like a tipsy bridegroom with Emma in his arms, standing patiently on the jetty while

Sterling wrestled with the wheelchair. When she was settled, the boatman turned to the north shore and started an elaborate mime. He pointed at the outboard and made a slitting gesture with his hand across his throat. He prayed to the heavens, pointed to his watch, held up his finger to indicate an hour and shrugged his shoulders. The man on the other side threw down the bat and stood arms akimbo on the shoreline.

'That should give you a bit of time, girl,' he said to Emma, his back to the river. 'Those bastards, pardon my French, don't own the place. You'll have time to get to Felixstowe. Station is just off the town centre if that's any use.'

'Thanks,' said Emma. 'Really appreciated. OK, Mr PI, let's get going.' She began wheeling at a sharp pace off the jetty and into the hamlet, disappearing behind a shanty and a beautifully kept miniature memorial garden set in an old rowing boat. The village sign at the top of a wooden pole, a trawler and a sailing boat in silhouette against a dark Martello tower, showed that Sterling and Emma were in Felixstowe Ferry.

Sterling found himself running to catch up with the girl in the wheelchair. 'Hold on, hold on. This is madness. What are we doing here? Where are we going? My grip bag is still in the taxi. Haven't you got any luggage?'

Emma did another wheelchair pirouette to face him. 'What's your name, Mr PI?'

'Frank Sterling,' said Sterling. He felt as if he was sulking. He was slouching, hangdog.

'Right, Mr Frank Sterling. My father engaged you to find me. You've done that. Now I need you to help me get out of here. You've seen where I've come from and you've had a little taste of what I'm up against. To be honest I'm scared to buggery. We've got just under an hour, I reckon, to cover our tracks and put some distance from Bawdsey Manor. When we've done that, and when I'm feeling a little less like a rat in a trap, I'll tell you more. Your grip bag,' she said contemptuously, 'is the very least of your worries. Trust me. And if you don't want to help, sod off back to Woodbridge and look for your…grip bag there.'

Sterling thought about the man who flung down the bat. He thought about his bag – it only contained a few clothes and a sponge bag. He thought about Nicholas Jameson, whose irascibility genes his daughter had inherited. He thought principally about his fee.

'OK,' he said. 'Where do you want to go?

Chapter 10

Progress – At a Crawl

'I need a push,' said Emma. She and Sterling had left the hamlet by the river behind and were making their way south towards Felixstowe itself. Occasionally she would crane her neck around to where they'd come from, as if afraid that the giant man in sunglasses would suddenly burst out from behind the small ridge hiding the village. Perspiration glistened on her arms and forehead. The flush in her face darkened her already tanned complexion. 'This is too slow. Felixstowe is a good four miles away.'

'Well, why didn't we just get in the taxi for God's sake?' said Sterling. The sun was beating down and he was getting hot and thirsty.

'I hope I haven't got a whinger. It's been crappy enough already. Remember the deal. When we get to somewhere I think is safe, I'll fill you in. Capisce? In the meantime, why don't you stick your thumb out.' To demonstrate that she could act as well as direct, she stretched out her arm and her thumb at the end of it. The small road wended and twisted its way through a large golf course with greens and fairways either side. A big shot PI was pushing a slight girl in a wheelchair through rural Suffolk. And they were hitchhiking.

The first few cars went by without stopping, often with couples who initially looked startled and then stared straight ahead with glazed unseeing eyes, as if the girl in the wheelchair and the man beside her did not really exist.

'We might as well knuckle down to it and walk the whole way,' said Sterling.

'Don't bloody well give up so easily,' said Emma.

Minutes later, a blue estate car pulled up just beyond them in a narrow dent in the road. It was a Renault with a strange back end. A large woman got half out of the driver's side and twisted back to face them. Her long curly hair was dark chestnut with a hint of auburn and cascaded down her back. She was wearing a complicated, expensive-looking brown sleeveless dress. There were dark freckles on her pale arms and across her nose. Her singsong voice matched her friendly face and warm smile.

'Where are you going?

'Felixstowe,' said Emma. 'Anywhere but here really.'

'OK, that's easy. Let's get you in. The wheelchair can go in the back. Is he the carer?' said the woman directly to Emma.

'Not exactly,' said Sterling. There it was again – that female solidarity. He lifted and manoeuvred Emma into one of the back seats.

'Ouch,' she said. 'Be careful. I'm not a lump of clay. There's plenty of me with nerve endings that still work.'

In the front passenger seat, an older man with a wise face and a Mona Lisa smile looked benignly on, as if he and the woman picked up disabled hitchhikers every day. Sterling noticed the tremble in his hands and the nod-nod-nod of his head.

When they were all settled, the woman turned around to face Sterling and Emma.

'Right. Felixstowe. Anywhere special? We're going to the town centre.'

Emma paused, made a decision and then launched out. 'Some people on the other side of the river are after me and I'd prefer not to be found. We need to get out quickly – so maybe you can drop us at the train station or the bus station.'

The trembling man spoke for the first time, the nod intensifying. 'There's only really one direction out of Felixstowe by car or public transport – west towards Ipswich and beyond. But there's one other way that might work.' He turned to the woman. 'Why don't we take them to Landguard Fort, Esther?'

She looked blank. Then came understanding. 'The ferry to Harwich.' She looked at her watch. 'Plenty of time. Good thinking, Derek.' She turned to Emma and Sterling. 'What about that? It's not obvious, and from Harwich you can go on to Colchester and London.'

Emma looked back towards Felixstowe Ferry a few hundred metres behind. 'Perfect. I don't mean to be rude, especially as you stopped for us, but can we get out of here?'

Sterling watched Felixstowe slip by. The golf club gave way to the elegant detached seafront homes of the northernmost part of the town. A house of the future, all chrome and triple glazing, its wide gallery window looking out across the North Sea, caught his eye. Then came the bungalows and more prosaic dwellings up to the town centre – still genteel but not so grand. Towards the south came the business end – the blocks of takeaways and terraces, the workshops and the lock-ups. It was poorer down here, with all the growing influence of the container port. Then they were on a narrow, more desolate road as human habitation stalled and bird reserves took over. Even then, Sterling noticed the mobile home park between the road and the sea – lines of white corrugation beyond the tall wire fence. Two small boys were having a kickabout just inside the gates – brothers by the look of their light complexions and slight frames, one a little taller than the other.

'Nearly there,' said the woman called Esther, and then they were in the car park by the Landguard Fort. They were surrounded by tall metal palisade fencing, spiked at the top. In the background, loading derricks loomed. On the other side of the car park was the squat fort in all its concrete ugliness. The open gates to the scrubby dunes next to the fort provided a welcome relief to the air of oppression. Sterling struggled to think of a less prepossessing place, but his view softened as he walked to the shoreline and looked out from the shingle beach over the expanse of water towards what he assumed was Harwich.

While the two women went over to the mobile café on the edge of the car park, the man called Derek joined Sterling at the top of the beach. His body shook and trembled, as if activated by the breeze.

'Good of you to stop,' said Sterling. 'Not many people would have done that. Hitchhikers can be dodgy.'

'Yeah. Especially ones in wheelchairs. What could you have done? Mugged us and made a run for it? The girl and her wheelchair in a police line-up – always assuming they could find enough other wheelchair users. She'd claim mistaken identity. Or that the cops were fitting her up. Dodgy? Nah.' He shrugged, overriding the tremor for a moment. 'Anyway, Esther's a rescuer – and it looked as though the girl needed rescuing.'

There was silence between them. Sterling pictured an identity parade of young girls in wheelchairs.

'I only met her shortly before you,' said Sterling, 'but I assure you she can look after herself.'

'Maybe,' said Derek.

'What about you? Would you have driven on?'

'No, I wanted to stop too. I like underdogs.'

'Who says we're underdogs?'

Derek looked out over the estuary. 'I know underdogs when I see them. How come you were walking out of Felixstowe Ferry that time of day? No luggage. No transport.'

'The girl kind of disappeared. Her father asked me to find her. I did. We were at Bawdsey Quay and she wanted to get away from someone. So we jumped on the ferry.'

'Sounds a bit far-fetched. But it's livened up our day. The perfect follow-up to fish and chips at the café. Where do you need to get to?'

'I don't know yet. I assume back to Kent, where we come from. When we've made ourselves scarce enough and the girl feels safe, she's going to bring me up to speed.'

Derek nodded – large nods in addition to the tremors. 'In Harwich, you can walk from the pier where the ferry lands up to the railway station. Trains go to Manningtree and you can change there for London. Or you can get a bus from the station up to Colchester and beyond. The girl's probably got disabled rail and bus passes.' He pointed at a large church whose spire dominated the skyline. That's Harwich.' Then he pointed to a shoreline beyond Harwich to the right. 'That's Shotley Gate. We're at the point where two rivers come together into the North

Sea – the Stour and the Orwell. The Orwell leads back up to Ipswich. The Stour goes up to Manningtree and beyond. It's the border between Suffolk and Essex. The derricks just along the shore are Felixstowe container port – biggest in Britain. Big ferries go out to Scandinavia from Harwich. At Shotley Gate, the navy ran a training establishment, HMS Ganges. There's a marina there now.'

Sterling stared out across the estuary. All the grey water made it seem as though it was a huge vessel filled to the brim. 'You know a lot,' he said.

'I'm retired,' said Derek. 'I've got time to get out and about and explore while Esther's working. I don't drive.' He held his hand out so it was horizontal to the asphalt and they watched it tremble. 'Not safe.' He pointed out towards an orange speck in the middle of the water. 'There's the ferry. It goes between the three points – Harwich, Shotley Gate and Landguard. Esther,' he called, 'the ferry's coming.'

The four of them, three standing and the girl in the wheelchair, watched as the orange speck became a motorboat with canopy at the back, bobbing and ducking through the waves. It was larger than the Deben ferry, but Sterling noticed that it was the same boarding arrangement, with a ramp extending onto the shingle beach.

The boatman looked up across the five metres of shingle, truculent, stony-faced. 'No wheelchairs,' he said. 'It's in the brochure.'

Sterling felt Emma tense beside him. 'What do you mean, no wheelchairs?' she called.

'No wheelchairs. We haven't got the facilities.'

'So how the hell do I, a registered voter, a free, passport-holding British citizen, a fully paid-up member of society, get where I need to go?'

The boatman shrugged. It wasn't his problem.

'Right,' said Emma. She tipped herself forward, upending the wheelchair and sprawling front-first onto the shingle, gasping as the breath was knocked out of her. Then she began a slow crawl down the shingle to the ramp, scrabbling on her elbows, her legs trailing uselessly behind her. Her shocked audience looked on.

'Leave me alone,' she shouted, as Sterling moved to help. Under the eyes of her watchers, she panted and manoeuvred herself in painful bursts up the ramp and collapsed headfirst into the well of the boat.

'Thanks for your help, Esther and Derek,' she called. 'If they won't take the wheelchair, Frank, leave the bloody thing on the beach.'

'Alright, alright,' the ferry master intervened from the cabin. 'We'll make an exception just this once, Jack.' The boatman looked down at the shingle, sheepish.

Sterling manhandled the wheelchair aboard. He was getting adept and it was surprisingly light. He gave the good Samaritans a little wave, unable to avoid rolling his eyes momentarily as Derek looked on. 'Mum's the word,' he said.

'Emma told me,' said Esther. 'Safe journey.'

Sterling noticed Emma still quivering as the ferry backed off from the beach, wheeled around and pointed back towards Harwich. The front of her T-shirt was smeared with detritus from the shingle and the ramp, seaweed and maybe tar. She sat at the bow of the boat, looking out ahead, refusing any contact with the boatmen, her back straight and defiant, the wheelchair standing next to her. Sterling retreated to a bench in the cabin out of the stiff breeze.

As the ferry got further from the shore, the estuary became choppier. A vast cargo ship slipped its moorings and steamed on around the small boat and ahead. Sterling noted the China Containers logo everywhere. It's come to this, he thought, the country in thrall to cheap imports. As the ferry moved into the wake of the leviathan, it rocked and bobbed even more vigorously. Clouds of spray came over the bows and spattered on the girl out in the open.

'Emma, come into the cabin. It's dry in here,' called Sterling. 'Warmer too.' But she stared stonily ahead, not even indicating if she'd heard him. The master and his mate squirmed silently. Halfway over, Sterling went out and sat next to her. When he draped his jacket around her shoulders, she didn't object. They sat together in the spray until the ferry jetty at Harwich loomed into view. Amongst the complex range of emotions he was experiencing, generated by the drama of escape, the fear of pursuit, the kindness of strangers and the more prosaic loss of his grip bag, one seemed to pop up that he wasn't expecting. As he lifted her clumsily into the wheelchair on the pier, he tried to identify what it was. Yes, he noted. Tenderness.

Chapter 11

Sterling Learns the Score

'Those bastards,' said Emma. She had insisted that Sterling pay the fare that the master had offered to waive. 'Let them bloody well feel guilty. I'm not letting them off the hook. Christ, I could do with a coffee. Let's go in the café.'

Sterling pushed her up the ramp to the quayside and into the imaginatively named Harbour Café. An outing of other wheelchair users and their carers was already occupying many of the seats.

'Excellent,' said Emma. 'We've found ourselves a bit of camouflage. If they pick up our trail here and ask about us, people will remember this whole group. Mine's a latte.'

'Mine's a cappuccino,' said Sterling, flopping down. She wanted to be treated the same as everyone else. Let her get the drinks. 'And a piece of fruitcake if they've got it. And when you've got that maybe you can bring me up to date. Like you promised. Tell me who you mean by 'they'.'

Emma looked at him. 'Touché,' she said, 'as my prat of a dad would say. 'You've got a bit of spirit about you, I'll say that. Thank God. I was beginning to wonder.' She wheeled off up to the self-service counter.

She returned with a tray expertly balanced on her knees. 'I need the toilet. Did you see anywhere?'

'There's a disabled toilet over there,' said Sterling, pointing away from the food counter.

'Accessible,' said Emma.

'What?' said Sterling.

'Accessible. It's an accessible toilet, not a disabled toilet.'

'Your father did this. I don't know what you're on about. Haven't we got more pressing matters on the agenda?'

Emma paused and stared. "Accessible' means they're for everyone, not just wheelchair users. Words and meanings are important. Listen. Disabled. Yes, I'm disabled. But I don't have a disability. This is an impairment,' she said, pointing at her legs. 'What disables me is not my impairment, not the fact that I can't use my legs, but the way things are organised to stop me doing what I should be perfectly capable of doing. Stairs disable me. Lifts don't. And let's not forget the disabling potential of people's stupid ignorant bloody attitudes. It's society that disables me, not my useless legs. I'm with my dad on that, and you're just an ignorant arsehole.' She wheeled away.

Sterling leaned forward and scratched his head with both sets of fingers. Little flakes of scurf floated down on to the table and he wiped them away. He tried to think through what Emma had said. How could you be disabled without having a disability? It depended on what was making you disabled. Not her legs then, but places she couldn't reach in her wheelchair, or people being difficult. It made a kind of sense.

When she came back, she seemed to have recovered. 'God, that's so much better. There's nothing like a good piss for improving your mood.' She'd had a go at her T-shirt and her hair as well. 'I'm still a mess, but I'll do for now.'

'Yeah, not bad,' said Sterling. 'So, we can warm up and dry off in here, take stock, decide what to do next. First things first though. You said you'd give me an update.'

Emma took a sip of her coffee. She had bought a sandwich as well, and took a bite of that. 'If my dad engaged you to find me, I expect he told you about my grandmother and stuff.'

'Yes, Emma. I'm sorry about all of that. It can't have been easy for you.'

'Yeah, yeah. Whatever. She was a tough old bird, and she could bear a grudge. She knew how to feud too.' Then her eyes grew softer. 'But she was great to me, my grandmother. My mother died having me, so I never knew her, and Grandma helped to bring me up. In some ways I was closer to her than to Dad, him being such a bloody deaf martyr. It was easier to talk to her. Literally easier, actually. Anyway, I had a miserable time when I went off to university. For a start, there's this massive bureaucratic procedure if you're disabled. You have to go through to get the support you need. You have to be assessed for a Disabled Student Allowance and after that the shenanigans continued. I hated the course, and I hated the isolation. You're meant to make friends at uni, but in the end the only people I was talking to were various carers. So I went back home.

'Grandma knew me pretty well. She knew I liked to be busy and get my teeth into something. So we started this project together. She wasn't getting any younger, so she wanted to sort something out about her war service. 'For posterity', she said. She was a WAAF – Women's

Auxiliary Air Force – and a radar operator during the war. She had letters and photos and loads of other paraphernalia she wanted to organise and classify. We even talked about doing a book together. Dad probably told you some of this.'

Sterling nodded. 'Not in so much detail,' he said. 'He didn't know what you were doing. And of course you didn't tell him where you were going. You just disappeared.'

Emma bristled. 'Well, point (a), Mr PI. My father is not my keeper. I can bloody well come and go as I please and it's none of his business. And point (b), I didn't know I was going into the lion's den, which I'll get to in a minute if you give me a chance.'

Sterling put his hands up in surrender.

'Right,' said Emma. 'Moving on. In the end, Grandma wasn't just a radar operator. She was bright and quick on the uptake. Maybe a bit ambitious too. The war was a time when talented people, even women, could get on. There was no time for any messing about. In the end she ran the office of the superintendent at Bawdsey Manor. What do you know about radar, Mr PI?'

'Radar,' mused Sterling. 'I don't know anything really. Just what I've seen in old war films. Pretty girls in uniform at mission control pushing planes and ships around, like casino croupiers. Young blokes in aeroplane cockpits in leather flying caps saying 'Bandits at five o'clock'. Old blokes with pipes looking at charts. Clipped tones all round. An air of doom and crisis.'

'God,' said Emma. 'All the old clichés. Well, radar was developed in the 1930s. It was credited with saving Britain during the Battle of Britain and taking the sting out of the Blitz. Like with all these things, in some bits of the technology we were ahead of the Germans, and in other bits we were behind. Their engineering was better than ours, and they tended to work through problems, whilst we worked around them. Grandma was no scientist. She was wanted for her languages. But she was in the perfect position to know what was going on. She was at Bawdsey, where the main radar station was set up, throughout the war, and it was there that she met and married my grandfather, Richard Jameson, who was a physicist in the RAF, one of the most brilliant of them, in fact.

'He and his colleagues had to find out about German technology. They did it in three ways: German planes were captured and taken to bits to see what equipment they had and how it worked. There was lots of photo reconnaissance of German tracking arrangements in occupied Europe. That was often backed up by sketches and communications from resistance workers and partisans. Then there were the raids – to capture German radar equipment – and that's how my grandmother lost my grandfather – in a raid, the Cauville Raid, on the French coast in 1943. You can see how I got interested in all this, a mixture of family history and the history of the war, and my interest rekindled Grandma's.'

Sterling broke off a piece of cake. 'This is still going a long way around the houses.'

'I'm getting there. Show a bit more patience.' Emma looked out into the estuary. 'She had loads of stuff – letters, photos, other papers. You don't really need to know all that. The important thing is that one morning, when we were working on the project, something to do with the war really upset her. I'm sure she got a letter about it. And I found a new word in her notes after she died - 'Fang' – written on one sheet. In capitals.

Underlined. I knew she'd made some phone calls after the letter, and they upset her even more.'

'So 'Fang' was connected with, well, what happened to her?'

'You know, Frank, you have the knack of stating the bleedin' obvious. Of course it was. The police's fixation on the idea of a random break-in was crap. But why would they listen to a cripple like me? A young girl cripple. Tossers. So I started a little investigation of my own.'

Sterling doubted that the investigating officers had a fixation with burglary. It was true that most murder motives are banal and not rooted in the past, but he thought about how the combination of a chippy girl and experienced officers might produce a clash. All the chemistry was there. Best keep quiet about that. 'And that took you to Bawdsey,' he said.

'Doh. Clearly.'

'It was a statement, not a question,' said Sterling. Part of him, once he'd got used to it, enjoyed the banter.

'I was always going up there. Grandma told me a little about one of the other wartime radar scientists in the superintendent's office, who was a friend of both my grandparents, Alan Whitman-Wood. He was like Grandma – still alive in his nineties. He had recently moved back there with his son Jimmy. Have you heard of CommuniCo?'

Sterling shook his head. Business was a foreign country.

'It's a specialised telecommunications company that the old man started after the war. It used to be Whitman Electronics Limited, but it got fancy. Now CommuniCo is heavily into mobile phones, smartphones, networks and the like, and is strong in Europe, particularly

Germany. When the old man retired, Jimmy took over as CEO. Those two are scary enough, but the grandson, Marcus – the bloke with the ferry bat on the quay when we were crossing the river...' Emma shuddered. 'I wasn't banking on meeting someone like him, and I certainly don't plan to bump into him again.'

'I still don't completely get it,' said Sterling. 'What were you planning to do when you got there?'

'Find out what had made Grandma so angry. And God, she was angry. I thought the old man would be able to tell me. What I didn't know then, and still don't know for sure, is that maybe he's part of the problem.'

'Poking around Bawdsey Manor and stirring things up. You've got bottle, I'll say that.'

Emma gave Sterling a look, of the kind he was coming to recognise. 'I suppose you could put it like that, but I didn't know what I was getting into. I phone up, mention my grandmother and 'Fang', ask what it's about, and before I know it I'm invited to visit. Alan Whitman-Wood says it's too complicated to discuss over the phone, and when I mention the wheelchair he says they've got all the facilities. Anyway, they make me welcome, find me a room and sort things out for me. All charm and smarm.'

'The trouble was that I soon found out that I couldn't come and go as I pleased. The bloke on the gate was on his break, or Alan Whitman-Wood was busy, or would it be OK if I waited till the evening. They didn't need to lock me up to keep me as a prisoner. That trip down the drive was the first time out of the house since I got there. And when I'd had all this time to think, I realised that what I needed to find out was at home amongst Grandma's papers, not in Suffolk. Maybe there was a letter in there somewhere. The more I looked at it, the clearer it was that Grandma had carried on with our project, but she had a little side project of her own. I reckon the phone calls she made were to old man Whitman-Wood. You know, she wasn't just angry. She was bitter. Vengeful, for someone of 94.'

Sterling rocked back on his chair. It helped him think – that's why he did it, he decided. The logic ground inexorably on. 'If you've got this right, it would explain a lot. What happened to her. Who did it. What's happening to us. And who's doing it.'

'Exactly. And there's another thing. CommuniCo currently seems to be in some kind of financial expansion. It was like a hornet's nest down at Bawdsey, getting ready for it. I reckon the Whitman-Woods are going to be making mega-bucks.'

'How does that fit in?'

'Haven't a clue. But it does fit in somewhere. And the answer is back in Kent, not here. Tick tock,' Emma said abruptly. 'That's filled you in. I'll tell you more later. Right now, we need to decide how we get out of here and back home.'

'So it's definitely home you want to go? Isn't that what they'll be expecting?'

'Correct, Einstein. But I've got to get home to find what Grandma found out. It's in her files somewhere, and the Whitman-Woods didn't find it. We'll worry about the details when we get there.'

'So, cards on the table, you reckon the Whitman-Woods are responsible for your grandmother's murder, Emma?'

'Exactly, directly or indirectly. That's the working hypothesis, anyway. You haven't met them. I tell you, Alan Whitman-Wood might be 90-odd, but he's capable of anything, and so is his grandson.' Abruptly, she changed the subject. 'Have you got a mobile? Let's have a look. Have you phoned my dad with this?'

Sterling nodded.

'Don't use it anymore.' said Emma. 'Don't even be tempted to use it. Don't even switch it on. The Whitman-Woods can access anything. I've seen the set-up at Bawdsey, and the staff they have to run it. If you use your phone, we're finished. Same with the Internet. I'm almost glad I had to leave my iPad in my cell. Now I won't be tempted to use it. From now on, everything we do has got to be under the radar.'

'Your cell. Under the radar. All the other stuff. It's a bit melodramatic, isn't it?'

'Listen, *Frank*.' Emma pierced him again with her eyes. 'This isn't some silly bloody game. They weren't going to just let me wheel myself out of Bawdsey Manor. OK, it wasn't a cell, but I told you, that was the first time I'd been out of the house since I arrived. They clearly couldn't decide what they were going to do with me. Marcus is a brute. He wasn't going to mess about. He isn't going to mess about. Take it seriously. Don't use your mobile. Don't go online and check your e-mails. Keep off Facebook. The only way we're going to get back is to do things the way I say. This isn't a comic book caper. This is real.'

'OK, OK. Noted. Facebook won't be a problem. I don't do that kind of thing,' said Sterling. He thought that might defuse the situation. 'Don't bite my head off if I suggest this. Why aren't we going to the police?'

'And say what? That a respectable telephone company chief executive and his 94-year-old father kept me prisoner in their mansion? That I didn't think I'd get out alive? That I might have information that could have changed the direction of World War II? You're a private investigator. I expect you were once in the police. Even if you weren't, think about it.'

'You might have a point,' said Sterling. He cast his mind back to front-of-desk duties: the default location of sceptical disbelief; the reluctant form filling; the horror and irritation of CID staff when they were invited to get involved. 'Well, maybe we'd better make a move. Derek said there was a station here. We can get a train to London and out again. Or hire a car. Or even get a taxi. Your dad would probably be pleased to cough up. It's quarter past one. We could be in Sandley by about seven at the latest.'

'Whoa. Not so fast. I still don't think you get it. The Whitman-Woods will already be scouring the stations at Felixstowe and Ipswich, and there will be people in place at Liverpool Street and Stratford in London. They'll be monitoring car hire and taxis for this whole area. All those things you suggested are exactly what they'll expect us to do, even if we've thrown them off the scent for the moment. No, we have to do this in a different way. We've got to slow down, not speed up. We've been lucky so far. We've got to build on that. And there's another thing. My regime.'

'Your… regime.' What now?

'I'm not like non-disabled people, Frank. The effort this morning has knackered me. My spasming has started and so has my usual range of mystery pains. I've got to get out of this wheelchair for a while and find a standing frame. Otherwise I'm going to start getting pressure sores. Then there are my exercises. I can't be gallivanting off to London straight away. All in all, it will be much better to lie low for a bit. Talking about camouflage, I wonder where these other chair-users are from.'

As Sterling bit into his fruitcake, Emma wheeled away into the heart of the wheelchair group. Its members looked older and frailer than her, and their chairs Morris Minors, but she was soon chatting and laughing with her new acquaintances.

Sterling was glad of the break. He congratulated himself for the progress he'd made with the case, but being with Emma Jameson was wearing. It wasn't just the way she was aggressive and uncompromising. He'd been pitched into an unfamiliar social world where nothing quite fitted his assumptions and in which he knew he had more adjustments to make. Her father had been prickly, but this was even more uncomfortable. And then there was the escape from Bawdsey. There was danger too. He looked around the café. A young boy with his mother looked wide-eyed at all the wheelchairs as a dollop of ice cream fell back from his spoon onto his plate. Through the window and beyond the jetty, he saw the little orange ferry bob and bustle across the estuary in the direction, he assumed, of Shotley Gate, since it was clearly not going back to Felixstowe. A pair of seagulls wheeled and squawked in the breeze.

He yawned and stretched. He knew there was still a long way to go.

Chapter 12

The Union Flag

'Pay dirt,' muttered Emma. 'We're on the move.'

There was a jolly air as the wheelchair group prepared to leave the café. The wagon train bumped over the small ramp at the café and moved generally single file to the pavement beyond the jetty. Sterling had his first chance to take in his surroundings. He seemed to have been accepted as a care-giver, so he would go with the flow. He and Emma fell into line in the posse of wheelchairs that stopped the traffic on the road splitting the staid, stone-built town hall and the gaily-painted Harbour Hotel from the jetty.

He liked the atmosphere of the old town – the jetty itself, the Trinity House lightship museum a little further down and the town's frontage overlooking the estuary. A little booth on the jetty welcomed visitors under the banner of the Harwich Society. In the mêlée of wheelchairs outside the town hall, he caught sight of a plaque commemorating Samuel Pepys's association with the town. The diarist and Navy Secretary had been friendly with a local MP. Then the troop, gathering some mysterious second wind, plunged into the maze of streets in the old town. It passed a pub, the Alma, and Georgian town houses and cottages of various sizes, right and left, interspersed with more modern constructions, until it came to an area filled completely with blocks of flats added in the 1960s.

Every so often, the wheelchairs and their riders would take sharp rights off-road down alleyways and through courtyards. The riders were skilful. They knew exactly where kerbs dropped and how obstacles could be avoided. In the alleyways, Sterling noticed that no space was narrower than the widest wheelchair. He was seeing things with new eyes. Down and right they all went in a crooked diagonal drift, and then they were in a main road at the other end of the small town.

Emma and Sterling, tucked in towards the end of the wheelchair train, followed the group through the electric glass doors of a bright and airy day centre.

Emma twisted her head around. 'Cool, eh?' Her eyes shone with quiet triumph.

Someone called out 'Andy, visitors', and a man with a black half-Rasputin beard appeared from a little office at the back. His jeans matched the beard but a short-sleeved, blue-checked cotton shirt and an open smile softened the sinister effect.

'Welcome to the West Street Centre,' said its manager. 'What brings you to Harwich, jewel of Tendring's crown?'

Sterling could not work out if there was any irony in the last bit. He left a response to Emma.

'It's rather complicated,' she said, waving her hand vaguely. 'We've got ourselves into a bit of a muddle, like, logistically. You know how it is with wheelchairs. I'm just wondering if we can rest up here for a little while. I need to do my exercises, and I could do with a standing frame if you've got one. We met everyone in the café, and they suggested coming back here.'

'Be our guests.' The man didn't push for further explanations, as if strange young wheelchair riders and their carers often popped in off the street in the company of regular clients. 'But we're closing in a couple of hours. In fact we wouldn't normally be open on a Saturday.' He waved at various piles of clothes and other remnants from the jumble sale that had taken place. 'Come on,' he said to Emma, 'I'll show you around so you know what's available.'

Sterling noticed another thing as he settled in to one of the armchairs in the centre, and it was not necessarily disadvantageous. He was becoming invisible. He closed his eyes for a catnap. Being with Emma Jameson hadn't stopped being wearing.

A few moments later there was an insistent tug at this sleeve. 'Frank. Frank.' He heard Emma say "Lazy bastard" under her breath. 'Wakey-wakey. This is no time to conk out. There's work to be done.'

He opened his eyes. There were two ways to play this. The first was tempting. 'You know what, I'm sick to the back teeth of your rudeness and filthy language. I'm not your skivvy. Just let me rest for a few more moments. And I'm not a lazy bastard. I'm the one who got you out of Bawdsey, remember?'

'OK, what now?' he said, opting for the second.

'Two things, Mr PI. First off, I'm going to need some clean clothes and toiletries. Come to think of it, as you haven't got your precious grip bag,' she said with a twinkle, 'I expect you'll need the same.' She produced a roll of notes from the pocket of her jeans. 'That should be enough, unless you've got the cash and want to claim it from Dad. I've been told there's a little department store in Dovercourt called Stanleys, about a mile down this road. I reckon you can get most things from there. For God's sake don't use a card or an ATM. I mean it. If you do that, I guarantee there'll be a black Range Rover, the Whitman-Woods' SUV of choice, cruising around here within the hour. Remember, we have to stay under the radar.'

'Right. And the second thing, my lady?' Sterling felt that he was getting dangerously used to taking orders. Hadn't he left the police to put an end to all that?

'You heard the man. This place closes at five. So the second thing is we need somewhere to stay. I can manage one night somewhere that might not be particularly accessible. Given the circs, we might have to share. While you're doing all that, I'll suss out transport for tomorrow.'

'I'm going to need a list of what you want.'

'I'm coming to that, dolt.'

You just can't admit to overlooking anything or being less than perfect, can you, girl? Sterling thought to himself.

'Got paper and pen?' said Emma.

Sterling fumbled for his notebook.

'Bra and panties, times two. Most things times two come to think of it, in case we get delayed tomorrow.'

'Sizes?' Sterling's face reddened. The day centre had become very quiet.

'You haven't done this before, have you, Mr PI? Have a look. What do you think?' she said mischievously, thrusting herself at him. She had raised her voice, and other people were interested.

'Stop messing about, Emma. We haven't got time, remember?'

'Knickers, small. Bras – well, say 34C. Let's hope they don't squeeze them up too much. Jeans, size 12 to be on the safe side. T-shirts, 12, same style as this one if you can find them, a top in case it's cold. Some kind of rain gear in case it's wet. Socks for trainers size 6. Pyjamas or nightie. I don't really mind which. Set of toiletries and some make-up from Boots. Perhaps you can use a bit of initiative. Don't make me dress frumpy, Frank. And maybe get a…grip bag to carry it all in, your stuff as well.'

The eyes of the day centre followed him into the street. He was glad to set off briskly westward in the direction of Dovercourt. Twenty minutes later he was outside the department store, and half an hour after that his new grip bag had the clothes and equipment he and Emma thought they needed. It wasn't too bad in the shop. The older shop assistant in Ladies' Fashion dealt professionally with his requests and purchases for Emma, and he'd quickly ignored the smirks and sly glances of the younger girls. Boots had been easier. There was a little holiday section that sold travel toiletry packs, and he'd supplemented one of those with a make-up kit. He'd sorted himself out quickly. On the way back to the old town, he noticed a supermarket set back from the road. Anything he'd forgotten they could probably get from there tomorrow. It was four o'clock. Now he had to find somewhere for the two of them to stay. It won't be too difficult, he thought – it's a port, after all.

He walked back to the day centre feeling buoyant. At Bawdsey Quay they had been in disarray. At Felixstowe Ferry, walking towards the town, it felt hopeless. Now they were getting organised. They were on track for the dash to Kent. As he approached West Street and the day centre just beyond the railway and bus station forecourt, he saw pub signs further down. The Union Flag caught his eye, so he passed the day centre and strolled down. He was in luck. A small sign in the window advertised 'Accommodation'. He noted the ramp at the door and the wide, furniture-free aisle up to the bar. I'm learning, he thought. What was it like at his local back in Sandley, The Cinque Ports Arms? He didn't know. He'd never had to think about it.

The pub was cosy. On the walls were nautical paraphernalia, sextants and barometers, and pictures of Harwich in a more majestic era. The bar was semicircular and backed onto what looked to be the kitchen behind it. To the right was an open door leading to some stairs. Behind the upturned bottles of spirits was a large mirror with a British bulldog prominent, wearing a Union Jack waistcoat. Pasted to the mirror were various notices. 'Free beer tomorrow', with date unspecified, caught Sterling's eye. At four in the afternoon, the pub was all but empty. A lone man with a pink, drinker's face and purpled nose sat on a stool at the bar by the open door, gazing sightlessly at his pint.

Sterling called out 'Anyone serving?' and from the kitchen shambled a large man with a gold chain around his neck, an open shirt and a gold ring in his left ear. He moved painfully, dragging a leg like a wounded bear and grimacing slightly, either from pain or simple effort.

'Yes, sir, what can I get you?' His accent carried the flat vowels of someone who'd never lived far from London or the ring of counties surrounding it.

'I'm wondering about your accommodation,' said Sterling.

'Yep, I've got one room available at the back. Twin beds. Small en suite bathroom. Just for you?'

'No, there are two of us, one with limited mobility.'

'Right, well, why don't you take the key and have a look?'

The price seemed reasonable. Anyway, needs must, thought Sterling. He looked around the pub. Although the publican sported a large belly and shuffled around his small domain, and although the pub did not look as though it had been decorated for two decades, it was clean and orderly. The British Bulldog mirror shone and sparkled, and the tables were highly polished. The room would be the same.

'Thanks,' said Sterling.

'Go through the door to the toilets over there,' said the publican, pointing to his right. There are some stairs straight in front of you. The room is at the top. I'll be here or in the kitchen when you come back down.'

One of the training courses Sterling did when he was on the job had been to do with witness protection, the bit about keeping people safe from intimidation, and worse, before trial. It was strange how he'd never needed it till now. On the other hand there had been no mention of wheelchair users. Perhaps the odds of them being witnesses were long. Whatever, thought Sterling, Emma would never be able to manage the narrow, steep flight he clumped up, and although the room itself was perfectly acceptable – spartan, but clean and airy – the bathroom next to the door was tiny. There was no bath, he noted, only a shower cubicle. He opened and looked out of the window at the back between the twin beds. There was a wrought iron contraption underneath it that must be a fire escape.

In his nostrils was the catering smell of chip fat and burgers, and he could see an extractor fan in the courtyard behind the pub's kitchen. The pub and its open space was hemmed in by the same kind of block of 1960s flats the wheelchair group had passed from the harbour to the day centre, but Sterling noted what seemed like an alleyway in between and a door in the wall. Some pubs only bother keeping up their façades, but standards were just as good at the back of The Union Flag as at the front. Sterling couldn't remember a back door painted so smartly. It was a fresh bright blue.

He closed the window and sat on one of the twin beds. On the opposite wall was a small print of two hares sitting upright in a country lane next to a field of wheat in the evening time, alert but carefree. Sterling looked at his watch. It was getting on towards half past four. The centre would be closing soon. He weighed things up. The pub and the room were close to the day centre, so Emma wouldn't have far to wheel. The location was perfect for the bus and railway station concourse, which they'd presumably be starting from on Sunday morning, just a three-minute journey around the corner.

The fact that it wasn't accessible (Sterling was beginning to get the language), unlike a mainstream hotel with a lift and other adaptations, kept them under the radar. The fire escape and the alleyway were reassuring. You never can tell when you might need a quick and discreet getaway, he thought. But those stairs. How was he going to get Emma into the room? He would need to carry her up and find somewhere to keep the wheelchair down below. But he'd done the carrying before at Bawdsey, so he could do it again. Emma wouldn't like the bathroom. He could hear her now. 'How the fuck do you expect me to use this poxy little hole?' Again, needs must, girl. Like it or lump it.

At the bottom of the stairs, Sterling peered through the crack in an external door that led into a kind of covered way which stretched from the street at the front of the pub to the alley running parallel to the street at the back, the alley he'd looked out at from the window. Back at the bar, Sterling clinched the deal for the room. Mention of a girl in a wheelchair brought little comment, and he was told that there was plenty of space for a wheelchair in the cleaning cupboard in the Ladies.

'Anyone can stay, as long as they pay,' said the publican genially. 'You're lucky really. The ferry is sailing for Denmark tomorrow, and I reckon accommodation in the town will be full tonight. Always is before a sailing. But my regulars cancelled.'

Sterling thought he'd be able to use that to head off Emma's complaints, because, he had to face it, she was bound to kick up a fuss. 'I'll be back in half an hour.'

'OK, see you then. We do food from about 7 and tonight's 70s night with a band – Early Doors. It should be a great evening.'

Sterling loved the music of his father's generation, and maybe the band would be a find. But he thought of Emma again. If anyone could put a dampener on things, it was her.

Chapter 13

Tendring's Finest

Up the road in the day centre, there was a winding down air after a busy day. Most of the wheelchair users had gone. The centre manager was tidying up and clearing cups and plates into the kitchen. Emma was watching television on the big screen with a couple of companions. Sterling sat down beside her.

'Nice grip bag,' she said, looking across. 'Are you going to claim it on expenses? You might have to negotiate if you use it beyond this case. Dad didn't get to where he's got to by being loose with money.'

Don't rise to the bait, thought Sterling. 'I've got what you asked for,' he said. He opened the bag like a pedlar and set out his wares. Emma switched from the television to the bag and worked through the contents.

'Not bad. Not bad at all.' She held a T-shirt against her chest. There was a complicated little glittery whirl of colour on the front more elegant than kitsch. Emma looked at the label. 'Thank God it's not 'Hand wash only'. What else?' She rifled through the rest of it. 'Neat little make-up kit. Toiletries….' She looked across at Sterling. 'The boy done good. I've been busy myself. Andy let me use his computer to plan our journey tomorrow.' She brandished some paper. 'If we go by bus it's nice and obscure – Harwich to Colchester, Colchester to Chelmsford, Chelmsford to Basildon, Basildon to Lakeside, Lakeside to Romford, and by that time no one will ever find us.'

'Yeah, they'll have died of boredom, and we'll have died of buses. It's more like the Long March than trying to get home,' complained Sterling. 'We'll be exhausted.'

'Stop your moaning. I've also done my exercises, had a shower and been on the standing frame. All in all, I'm feeling human again.'

'I'm glad one of us is. Well, I've got us a room. It's at one of the pubs down the road. It's not ideal, Emma, but it's pretty discreet, and not an obvious place for a wheelchair user. It's up some stairs, so I'll have to carry you, and the bathroom is really small, but it's only for one night.'

Sterling was waiting for a tart comment, but none came. Instead, Emma shrugged. 'Needs must when the devil drives.'

'Actually, my thinking exactly. I reckon we're getting in tune.'

'Frank, you've got a long way to go before you're going to be in tune with me and my situation.'

It couldn't last, thought Sterling, but nothing could dampen his current mood. 'Whatevs,' he said, mimicking one of her expressions. 'At least I'm having a go. Come on, this place is closing. Say your goodbyes and we'll go and have a drink.'

'Bye Emma.' 'Come and see us again, Emma.' There was a chorus of farewells. But there were none for Sterling. He'd stayed invisible.

The ramps over the door of the pub were smooth. The path up to the bar was uncluttered with furniture or obstacles. Sterling could tell Emma was pleased. She wheeled up and smiled at the publican. 'Mine's a Smirnoff Ice. Frank, what do you want?'

He looked at the labels on the pumps. 'London Pride, please. Pint.'

'Find a table,' said the publican. 'If you're going to see the band later on, get a table over there.' He pointed to the corner to his left and front. 'I'll bring your drinks and change over.' Emma smiled again. She liked this. Account was being taken of her requirements.

'God, that's so good,' she said, taking a sip. 'I haven't had a drink since I set off for Suffolk.' She did calculations in her head. 'Five damn days ago. I was almost teetotal. What's this about a band?'

'There's a 70s evening. We'll be able to blend in,' said Sterling. He wondered how he could tell her he thought 60s and 70s music was the best that ever was, is and would be, and her reaction wasn't promising.

'I hope there's a decent telly in our room.'

'Well, it's all right. It's one of those wall-mounted things.'

'So, a toss up between some boring old farts playing clapped-out music or *Casualty*. What a Saturday night I've got in store. I suppose if we're down here I can get a few drinks down me.'

'We'll need to eat as well, Emma. We can come down at about seven and get this table. The band starts at 8. Maybe we can see what it's like and you can go back up for *Casualty* if it's no good.'

'Sounds like a plan.' She tipped her drink back. 'Come on, let's have a look at the room.'

Sterling showed her where the wheelchair would be stowed at the end of the evening. Then he crouched on his haunches with his back to the wheelchair and she flipped forward onto him, draping her arms around his shoulders. Her damp hair brushed his neck and he caught the lemon scent of shampoo.

'Remember, bend your legs, not your back,' she ordered.

'Alright, alright,' he grunted. 'I've got the hang of it.'

Step by step they laboured up the stairs, and then they were in the room.

'Before you put me down,' said Emma, 'let's have a look at the bathroom.'

Sterling shuffled over.

'You're right, Frank. It's not Universal Design, that's for sure. Not much of the pub is for that matter, though I've seen worse. Not even room to swing a cat in here. Good job I could have a shower at the day centre. Still… it'll do. Prop me up on the bed, please.'

Sterling did as he was told. He slumped down on the opposite bed. 'I can't do much of that dragging up the stairs. I'll get the bag from downstairs and then I need to cool down. After that I guess we have to work out how we organise everything. What's Universal Design anyway – at risk yet again of showing how ignorant I allegedly am.'

'Allegedly – you *are* ignorant. Where have you been for the last ten years? Still, you'd better know. Universal Design is about making places accessible for disabled people, removing barriers and adding aids, but at the same time keeping places natural and attractive for everyone. It's building and other design that includes everyone – you could just call it "good design" – not even "accessible design". So if there was good design in this pub, you wouldn't have to haul me about. There'd be a fold-out stair-lift to get up here. There might be temporary handles that could be slotted into the walls in the bathroom, special light switches, strobe light alarms for deaf people...any number of possibilities. And in the end, non-disabled people would find it natural and even benefit.

'But we ain't got Universal Design here, that's for sure, so here's how it's got to work,' said Emma, when Sterling had collected the bag from downstairs. 'I can just about change all my clothes myself if you lay them out for me on the bed. I might ask you to make some adjustments when I've got them on. When I need the bathroom, you can take me over and get me in it, and I can probably do the rest. Don't leave me though, Frank. I could get stuck or something, and if I do I'll need you to help. At home someone comes in a couple of times a week to make things easier. Tomorrow morning, I'll need a shower, so you'll have to be involved in that.' She caught a look from him and stared back. 'I assure you, it's going to be just as difficult for me as it is for you. We've just got to get on with it. OK, let me select my clothes. Then we can get something to eat. Christ, I'm hungry.'

Sterling did as he was told, and then looked out of the window over the courtyard. A young man in chef's check trousers and white smock came out of the pub's kitchen. He emptied a bin into a larger one, leaned against the wall and lit up a cigarette, inhaling greedily and letting a plume of smoke float from his upturned nostrils – enjoying the lull before the evening rush. Sterling always felt faintly discouraged if he saw any of the staff involved in making his food, and this time was no exception. He hoped the chef would wash his hands after the smoke. He could hear little grunts of effort and oaths from behind him as Emma struggled to change her clothes.

'Right, can you lift me over to the bathroom? And I'll need you to get my make-up and stuff out.'

—⚹—

It was half-past six when Sterling and Emma were ready.

'I'll just pop downstairs and get your wheelchair out,' said Sterling. 'The timing's perfect. We'll get a table near the band and order some food before the rush.'

Emma reached out from the bed and put her hand on his arm. 'No chair, Frank. Please. Let's just get me into one of those comfy chairs in the pub. I don't want to be disabled tonight. I want a night off.'

Sterling nodded. 'I get it. This time I'll carry you in my arms. It will be easier going down the stairs. I know, I know. Legs not back. How much do you weigh, anyway?'

'Eight stone. I hardly eat anything. It's easier that way.'

They shuffled down the narrow stairs, Sterling's elbows brushing the walls either side to give them stability. Now she smelled of the Coco Mademoiselle perfume he'd seen in her make-up bag, and her breath warmed his neck. In the pub, the table they had before was still empty.

'Second drink of the day,' said Sterling when they were settled. 'Almost as good as the first. And happily for us, the kitchen is now open. Knowing Bryan, the food will be good too.'

'Bryan being the publican I suppose, Mr PI? You know how to get your feet under the table, I'll give you that. In fact, you haven't done too badly so far, all in all.'

Sterling toasted her with his pint.

After that, dinner had arrived and then their plates had been cleared away. Now the band was setting up in the corner in front of them.

'Stand by for the old farts', murmured Emma, but as the bustle and noise increased around them, she didn't seem as jaundiced about the evening as Sterling expected. He looked around the pub as it filled up. There were many men like his father – grey-haired blokes, some balding, some pot-bellied but most lean and well preserved. In the mid-70s they would have been in their mid-twenties. Their wives and girlfriends looked good too, in loon pants and miniskirts, and the occasional tie-dyed T-shirt. There were plenty of beads about. As it had been for Sterling and his father, the music of the 70s was a family thing. His own generation was well represented, and there were even a few teenaged grandchildren. It wasn't just the rock 'n roll of the 50s that left its echoes.

A man and a woman approached the table with some younger people trailing behind. 'Can we join you on this table?' said the man. 'Or maybe take the chairs and sit to the side.'

'No, join us,' said Emma. 'I don't want to move, but there's plenty of room around the table.'

'Thanks,' said the man as the group coalesced awkwardly around a stationary Emma. His brown curly hair was streaked with grey, and there were deep striations down his cheeks. His hands were callused and rough from a lifetime of labour.

His wife smiled and settled herself. Her fine auburn hair was cut elfin style, like Julie Driscoll from Trinity, or Twiggy, and her features were pale and delicate. Her deep-set dark eyes took in the odd couple, Emma and Sterling. 'I'm Mandy, she said. 'This is Kevin, and our daughters Tracey and Jodie. That's Grant,' indicating a man a little younger than Sterling with a fashionably shaven head, 'Jodie's boyfriend.'

Sterling half-rose from his chair. 'Nice to meet you. I'm Frank. This is Emma.'

'Haven't seen you here before,' said Kevin. 'Mind you, it's a first for Tracey, isn't it, love? She's down from London for the weekend, licking her wounds.'

'Dad,' protested the girl. She looked down at the table and tugged at her ear lobe.

The band had been setting up and tuning. The lead singer, a ludicrously tall and rangy figure in blue jeans, cowboy boots, stripy blue shirt and black waistcoat, with a pork pie hat perched on his small head, then abruptly approached the microphone. 'Hiya Harwich, Tendring's finest. Are you ready to rock in the 70s?'

'Yeah,' came the room's raucous reply, and so it began – with "Brown Sugar" belting out through the speakers.

'Blimey,' Sterling said to Kevin after the first few numbers. 'These blokes are good.'

'Best in Essex,' shouted Kevin over the hubbub.

'What's Tendring?' Sterling shouted back.

'It's the district we're in. Tendring District Council. It's an in-joke. Here in Harwich, we think we're better than Clacton and all the other places.'

As the music continued, the drink flowed. Emma seemed to be enjoying herself, even while her semi-permanent mocking little half-smile said how passé she thought it all was. Sterling found himself doing a commentary at the end of each song. He had the zeal of a missionary seeking a convert. '"Layla" is about Eric Clapton's love for Patti Boyd, George Harrison's wife. "Lola" is about a boy meeting a transvestite in a Soho bar.'

'Who the heck is Eric Clapton? And Ray Davies? Never heard of him,' Emma would reply, but gradually she just listened. By the time the band got to the final riff of the Grateful Dead's "Ship of Fools", Sterling was astonished to hear her say 'I liked that. That I did like.'

'Loads of bands have done "Ship of Fools",' said Sterling. 'In the 70s Bob Seger did a nice melodic little number. Lyrics not up to much. The one The Doors did was about a spacecraft leaving a dying Earth. But that was the best – the music and the lyrics. Anti-government, anti-capitalist. Just my dad's ticket. It's about not working for a pittance or a fortune, but for a way to sink the status quo. That's my interpretation anyway.'

'Yeah, well, good riff at the end,' said Emma. 'Mine's another Smirnoff Ice, Frank. Deaden the pain.'

Jostling at the bar, Sterling felt a slight form slip beside him in the crush of supplicants holding notes in outstretched arms as Bryan and his staff scuttled and rushed like ants to satisfy all the demands. Tracey from his table, the one from London licking her wounds, looked up at him. Her mother's eyes were dark, but hers were a clear grey-blue, more like her father's.

'So Frank, I've been trying to work it out – are you two an item?'

He brought down his arm and turned to her. Were they an item? Interesting question. 'Not really,' he said. 'Not in the way you mean. We've been kind of thrown together. It's complicated.'

'Well, if it uncomplicates itself, let me know.' The girl turned to the bar. She'd arrived a few moments after him, and well after the crowd of men trying desperately to be served next. A second later, a young barman was taking her order. 'I'll get yours too, if you hurry up and tell me what you're having.'

'Thanks,' he said.

She pressed into him fractionally as she turned away from the bar with her tray of drinks. No one else would ever know. That, the beer already sloshing around inside him and making his head buzz, and the band's rendition of a bluesy number he knew really well but couldn't quite identify, filled him with a strange mixture of feelings. Excitement was there, and a sense of the unexpected. There was a kind of sad nostalgia too. A little hopeless romanticism. There was that. He'd been in situations like this before, and they hadn't always ended well. At the table, he took a long pull of this pint and looked at the beer mat. 'Drink responsibly', it said. Maybe there was something in that. He needed to be right for the next stage of the journey.

'OK', said the lead singer of the band. 'A bit of cheating. This one's earlier than the 70s but I know you won't mind. Here we go – "Sukiyaki" – let's do it as a singalong!'

The room erupted. People stood up with their glasses raised.

Sterling looked across at Emma. 'The only Japanese song ever to get in the British charts – a young guy who's lost his girlfriend looks up at the sky as he walks so his tears don't fall on the ground.' He joined in with the rest of the room with the Japanese lyrics.

'Now I've heard everything,' said Emma. 'You want to be careful, Frank. You'll be an old fart before your time.' She yawned and looked at her watch. The band stopped for a break. 'I need to go up. All this excitement,' she looked around the room with a raised eyebrow, 'has knackered me again.'

'Sure,' said Sterling. 'See you in a bit.' He was still mouthing the words of "Sukiyaki". 'It's not really called

"Sukiyaki". They changed it for Western ears. In Japanese "Sukiyaki" is actually a kind of beef hot pot.'

'Frank, forget about that stupid song for a moment. I'm not going to just wave my magic fucking wand and get up to our room by myself, am I?'

'Oh damn. So sorry. Let's sort it out.' He turned to Kevin and Mandy, who were deep in their own conversation with the group around them. 'Kevin, Mandy, I'm going to need some room.'

The group looked on without understanding.

'Legs not back,' said Emma, and Frank got down on one knee in front of her.

Then something strange happened. From those nearest the table, still maudlin from "Sukiyaki", the veil of confusion lifted. 'Ah, look, sweet,' said a woman's voice. There were whoops and cheers in a ripple around the room, as if Emma and Sterling were the pebble thrown in a pond and the noise was the result. The drummer in the band, who had not left for the bar with the others, did some drum rolls and smashed the cymbals. As Sterling took Emma in his arms, there was a ragged chorus of a well-known rock anthem.

'Oh God, oh Christ,' muttered Emma, burying her face in Sterling's neck. Her apparent modesty egged the crowd on. Now there were hoots and whistles and clapping as Sterling stumbled and staggered across the room towards the door at the back, ears roaring, skin burning and stupid half-grin of denial on his face. There was a leering, knowing edge to the noise as they disappeared through the door. When he glanced back for a fraction of a second, he saw the girl Tracey staring, a complex look of surprise, disappointment and confusion.

Later on in the back room at the top of the stairs, Emma said, 'Plonk me on the toilet and close the door. Jesus, I'm desperate. My regime is shot to hell.' And later on still, when Sterling had helped her prepare for bed and slipped in between the sheets of his own bed opposite, and when the music and all the noises of the pub had long subsided into the stillness of the night, he heard the sound of weeping. Whether the tears were angry or sad, or a mixture, or something else entirely, he could not tell.

Chapter 14

Sally

The sun was leaking in through a gap in the blackout curtain. Sterling had woken abruptly. The dream had been unsettling. He wondered why he had been dressed in a fawn mini-skirt, intent on admiring his shapely though pale legs and inviting other people to admire them as well. Angela would have a theory. A homesick feeling attached itself to the sense of unease. But something else wasn't right, and this was more to do with his policeman's intuition.

He got up quietly and slipped on his trousers and shoes. Emma was on her back as he'd arranged her last night, snoring softly, her mouth open. He checked his watch. 7.30. Later than he'd thought. His head felt heavy as he eased himself down the stairs, which creaked and groaned in weary protest. Four pints of London Pride was one pint too many. I can't do this anymore, he thought. I'm getting old. He glanced around the door into the pub. The seventies were long gone. Only the little dais on which the band had perched gave any inkling that they had ever been there. Bryan and his staff had cleared the tables and given everything a good clean. What discipline that must have taken at midnight after such a busy evening, but you could never take away the lingering odour of stale beer and bodies the morning after the night before. Whatever was troubling Sterling wasn't in the pub.

The door to the side alley was locked, but the key, a clunky, old-fashioned thing, was in the lock. He felt the tumbler click and fall as he turned it. Then he was in the dark space between the pub and a laundrette next door. Edging up to the end of it, and taking care to keep himself in deep shadow, he stole a glance up and down West Street. Sunday morning in Harwich old town. Nothing stirred, not even a seagull. Opposite the pub, someone had forgotten to turn off the flashing 'Restaurant and Takeaway' sign of the Indian. In the sunshine the flicker of blue and red could hardly be seen. Then he caught a movement at the far end of the street towards the harbour – a glint of black and chrome. It was cool in the alleyway. Early morning in April. Spring temperatures. A nip in the air. A sharp breeze coming off the sea with a salty tang. But that was not what made him shiver.

Upstairs, he shook Emma with a gentle urgency. 'Emma, wake up. Wake up.'

Her eyes focused and she coughed. 'What the f....'

'Emma, come on, wake up. We've got to go.'

'Why, what's happened?'

'There's a black Range Rover cruising around the town. We can't let them find us here.'

'So much for keeping under the bloody radar last night. We might as well have hung a banner over the pub. *Emma Jameson is here.*'

'I don't think they've found us. I think it's speculative. They're cruising around Harwich because they can't find us anywhere else. We can get out of here. We've just got to get moving.'

'Well, I've got to have a shower. And I've certainly got to have a shit. I've got my regime to take care of.'

'No shower. No time. Just…you know…if you have to. What do you need me to do?'

'Take me over to the bathroom.' Emma was testy, but there was fear in her eyes, and she had stopped complaining. 'There are four of those Range Rovers,' she said. 'A whole stable. And sixteen blokes, including Marcus Whitman-Wood, looking for us – all probably dressed like the bloody Blues Brothers.'

'We'll get out of this. Tell me what you want to wear and I'll get it out and pack up the rest. I've got to settle up with Bryan. Remind me. What time is the bus?'

'Ten to nine. To Colchester via Manningtree.'

'Right. We need to get mobile and then time things.'

Fifteen minutes later, Emma was in her wheelchair in the alley at the back of the pub running parallel to West Street and Sterling was at the bar.

'What do I owe you, Bryan?' Sterling peeled off the cash but held on to the notes as the publican reached out. 'We haven't been here, right?'

Bryan shook his head, as if that might blow away the bleariness. 'Yes, you have. All evening. With Kev and his kinfolk. All night with that girl.'

'Bryan, you know what I mean. The girl's scared. I'm scared.'

'I know. I know, you daft sod. I hope it all works out. The alley leads up to a lane and you can turn right there back onto West Street. Go straight across down Golden Lion Lane. That will take you into George Street. Go left up there and there's the station. A nice, quiet, discreet route. That's what you want, isn't it? The band plays here every month. Maybe you'll come back. You livened things up a bit at the end.'

When Sterling reappeared, Emma started where she had finished the day before. 'This alleyway stinks. Come on. I need to get out of here before I start gagging.'

'There's a lane at the top. We turn right into it and cross the road down the lane the other side. Golden Lion Lane. The non-scenic and obscure route.'

At the junction of West Street, Sterling looked up and down. It was 8.20, half an hour till the bus, half an hour before the promise of escape.

'We'll cross quickly. We can't do anything else.'

In Golden Lion Lane, the wheelchair rattled on the cobbles, surely noisy enough, thought Sterling, to wake the whole of Harwich. He felt very exposed. The red hand rims would catch the eye of any even half-awake observer.

'Bloody hell,' said Emma, her lower body shaking and jerking as the wheelchair juddered along. 'Just what I bleeding well need after a night on the piss.'

'George Street,' muttered Sterling. 'Left here and the bus stop and rail station are just up here and around the corner. In front of them was a patch of wasteland dominated by the massed ranks of dandelions enclosed by a thin temporary galvanised steel palisade. 'World's End Property Development' proclaimed the sign. 'Too right,' said Emma. Beyond it they could see the abrupt end of the railway track.

The street itself was nondescript. Each side of and opposite the bleak wild patch was a higgledy-piggledy mass of housing, some almost brand new and some probably there since the street had first developed.

'We've been lucky so far,' said Sterling. 'But we're really in the open here. Let's get a bit closer to where the buses go and see if there's somewhere we can stay out of sight.'

As they laboured up George Street's rough pavement, they expected a black Range Rover to appear any moment at the top of the road. The game would be up. The heavies would emerge. Sterling would get beaten up against the wall, and worse, since the stakes were apparently so high. Emma would be tipped without delay from her wheelchair, bundled into the vehicle and borne away to an uncertain fate at Bawdsey Manor.

Emma twisted around in her chair, a half-smile on her lips. Sterling had seen it in the same instant. He took a tighter hold of the grip bag and pressed forward for a stronger push, his head parallel with his shoulders, his arms stretched out rigid. Salvation was just up ahead, or more specifically, the open door, in front of the station concourse, of Harwich's Salvation Army Citadel, complete atop with crenellations. And here was a bonus – not just an open door but a ramp.

It must be like coming into an Arctic research station cabin out of a howling minus thirty degrees storm, but escaping fear rather than cold, thought Sterling. He felt a wave of relief, even if it was temporary. And here was another bonus: from the window of the little reception area was a 180-degree view of the main road, the street they had just bundled themselves up and the station concourse in front of them. A military strategist couldn't have chosen a better vantage point. The Citadel commanded the terrain.

Someone was about – otherwise the door would not have been open – and today was the busiest day – but for the moment they could see no one. Emma still did not want to be overheard. Sterling had to lean down to hear what she was whispering. 'I'm not complaining about our luck, Frank, but I bloody well hope there's no faith-healing session fixed for this morning.'

They waited behind the door, Sterling surveying the panorama in front of him and glancing frequently at his watch.

An elderly woman appeared from the main part of the building, in full uniform except for bonnet, her grey hair tied in a bun. Her Mrs Merton glasses were speckled and needed a clean, and her buck teeth and slight stature gave her a mousey look.

'Can I help you?' she said. Sterling did the mental translation. 'What are you doing here?' This was a good occasion to let Emma take over. He looked down at her.

'We were hoping to attend the morning service.'

'Well, you're a bit early for that. No one else will be here till 10 o'clock. I'm just setting up.' Sterling translated, based on tone as well as content. 'You're in my way. Get out.'

'Perhaps my carer can help you – put out hymn books and so on.'

The woman looked at Emma, and then looked Sterling up and down, as if by doing that she could judge his competence. 'See that pile of hymn books over there? Put one on each chair.'

Sterling looked at his watch again and surreptitiously rolled his eyes at Emma. They couldn't afford to miss the only bus out of Harwich on a Sunday morning. Ten minutes. He set to work with gusto. 'Keep an eye out,' he said, looking at Emma. The damn girl was smirking.

The time edged up to quarter to nine.

'Frank,' she hissed.

As he joined her, a bus pulled into the concourse. It was unlikely that it was going anywhere but Colchester.

'OK, now or never,' said Frank. 'See the crook in the road. If we can edge around that we'll be out of sight from the main road. Then we'll be able to get on the bus.'

'What's all this whispering?' said the woman. Sterling's quick-fire job with the hymn books hadn't mollified her.

Sterling and Emma, intent on the view through the window and in a cocoon of intimacy and concentration, ignored her. Sterling was muttering under his breath, while Emma nodded.

'Ten seconds to the crook in the road. Twenty seconds to the bus stop. How long to get on the bus?'

'It looks pretty new. The driver will lower the platform. Twenty seconds.' Emma fumbled in her bag. 'Here's my bus pass. It's a free ride for me. Pass it over the machine and it will issue a ticket. Got cash for yours? Right. No point in hanging about. It's now or never. Let's go.'

The woman stepped in front of the wheelchair. 'Excuse me,' she said primly, 'but I thought you were staying for the service.'

'What the f….? Change of plan, for Christ's sake. Get out of the way,' shouted Emma, as she grabbed at the hand rims and Sterling propelled her from behind. The woman jumped out of the way and the wheelchair rattled over the ramp and sped across the road into the concourse area.

'Eight seconds,' gasped Frank as they reached the crook in the road, and 'twenty three-seconds' as they reached the bus stop.

There was a hiss of air pressure as the driver let down the platform and Sterling wheeled Emma aboard.

'There was no need to rush. I'm not going for a couple of minutes.'

In the middle of the bus, in the area for pushchairs and wheelchair users, Sterling and Emma looked at each other. Sterling felt himself start to giggle.

'Bloody hell,' said Emma, joining in. 'No need to rush. God. I was trying to work out the odds of being spotted.'

'Too many variables,' said Sterling. He was looking at the Citadel as the bus swept past in a wide right hand arc into the main road. The Salvation Army woman was standing at the door staring out, arms akimbo. Her stance needed no translation. But it wasn't that that stopped his giggling. Through the back window of the bus, he saw a black Range Rover emerge slowly from a junction in West Street a hundred metres behind. Had he and Emma been spotted getting on the bus? He willed the woman to go back into the Citadel. If the men in the Range Rover started talking to her, the game was up. He sank further down into his seat and Emma seemed to shrink down in sympathy.

Chapter 15

Elf and Safety

'I think we're OK,' said Sterling. 'We've been going about twenty minutes and it wouldn't have been hard for them to catch up if they found out we're on the bus. It's not as though there's a choice of destinations.'

Emma nodded. They were both looking anxiously through the back window. The bus had left Harwich and the adjoining town of Dovercourt and urban sprawl had given way to verdant north Essex countryside. Gradually, the fugitives began to relax into the motions of the journey.

'You were right then,' said Emma. 'It was speculative. They haven't a clue where we are, and I reckon we're definitely doing the right thing going home this way.'

'Yeah?'

'Yeah. I spent enough time with these people to know what they're like. The Whitman-Wood operation is hi-tech. Very hot on technology actually. Computers. Smart phones. Electronic surveillance. All the gizmos. They'll have sussed you out already, Frank, and not just from the CCTV at Bawdsey Quay. The cars are top of the range. No expense is spared. They even have their groceries delivered. You saw that. The thing is, that's how they think everyone lives, in fancy houses, on the Internet all the time, not connecting with daily life. None of those blokes has been on a bus or a train for years. They've got all this money and all this technology but less imagination than my little finger.'

'I bet they went to Felixstowe station to check on trains. They might have thought about buses too, but it's the car-hire places and taxi stands they would have been to first. They may be watching Liverpool Street and Stratford International, but they honestly haven't the nous to work out how we might be getting about.'

Sterling shifted in his seat. It wasn't that comfortable. He wondered what the river was to the right of the bus. As they passed through the undulating countryside, it would come sparkling into view and disappear again. The bus had a distinct if intermittent rattle coming from somewhere. He began to listen for it, trying to work out a pattern, or even a trigger. Did it start when they took a right hand bend, or at a certain speed? He wondered how accurate Emma's theorising was. It made a kind of sense. How far was it from Bawdsey Quay to where they were now – just coming into a small hamlet in north-east Essex – only about 14 miles as the crow flies, and it had taken 24 hours one way and the other. That's (he tried to work it out) about 0.6 miles per hour. Yes, worked out like that, it was plausible.

'Another thing. They're arrogant, surly bastards. Marcus Whitman-Wood, the grandson, is a scary bloke, but that's to our advantage. Because he's got the charm of a pit bull, no one's going to want to tell him anything. Remember the ferryman at Bawdsey? He won't be the only one old Marcus will have rubbed up the wrong way.'

'Let's hope you're right.' Something else had occurred to Sterling. How much was Emma trying to reassure herself? Cussedness might prompt people not to be helpful, but fear was surely much more persuasive in making people tell the truth. For the moment, he kept those thoughts to himself.

When the bus dropped down to the riverside they stopped talking and looked out across the water. Flocks of birds rooted and fossicked amongst the mudflats. A swan sat by a bus stop, wings spread out like a Victorian matron in a long skirt at a picnic.

'So free,' murmured Emma. She fidgeted with the hand rims on the wheelchair.

Sterling saw the signs for Mistley and Manningtree, and then the bus left the river and moved uphill and inland, west and slightly south towards Colchester, through a flat terrain of orderly fields and well-tended nurseries. Almost exactly an hour and a half after the drama at the Citadel, Emma and Sterling found themselves pulling into Colchester bus station.

'Remind me,' said Sterling. 'Where are we going next?'

'Chelmsford,' said Emma, looking at her watch, 'in about 20 minutes. Bus number 71. Time for a bite to eat and a cup of tea. I reckon I can manage without the toilet till we get there. I'll wait here and look after the grip bag. We don't want any hitches with our new grip, do we?'

'A return to form after last night, Emma,' said Sterling.

She looked at him, a hard, hostile look. 'That was better in than out, Mr PI.'

Sterling moved off, trying to keep a smirk off his face. He was about to say 'Keep you on your toes'. Careful, he thought. Don't make it worse. 'Any special dietary requirements, madam?'

'Something with a bit of bacon, and one sugar in my tea. And hurry up. We haven't got long.'

There was a kiosk at the edge of the bus station. A girl in a striped red and white visor and dark ponytail served two bacon rolls and tea, supplied by the cook behind her, whose hairy arms and five o'clock shadow, coming through even in the mid-morning, gave the operation a sinister air. She put the food and paper cups in a self-assembly cardboard tray whilst Sterling added the sugar from a dispenser on a shelf that protruded from the side of the shack. A lump of sugar, discoloured light brown by tea or coffee, had hardened onto the lip of steel tubing sticking out of the glass pot where someone had dipped it into a hot drink. An old man stood to the side, dragging at a roll-up and staring into the distance, steam from his tea curling sinuously into the morning air. I could be at any bus station in England, thought Sterling, and it would be the same.

In front of the bays, Emma was moving her wheelchair back and forth. 'The bus goes from stand five. Thanks,' she said, taking a roll and her tea. 'You can put the tray in my lap. I guess there are marginal benefits in all this crap I put up with.'

Sterling wheeled her to the right bay, joining a ragbag of fellow Sunday travellers. He finished his roll and tea and found a bin as the double-decker pulled in. Emma was fiddling with the hand-rims again, plucking restlessly. It came to Sterling that this was what must happen at every stage of her journeys. It was about contrasts and comparisons. The ferryman on the river Deben on the Saturday and the genial, elderly bus driver at Harwich station today; the ferrymen at Landguard Fort before the crossing to Harwich. What was it going to be now? The signs were inauspicious as they queued up. The driver had a brusque, impatient air. He spoke loudly and without clear enunciation to the older passengers. He tossed change carelessly into the receptacle for coins. His pasty face had an unhealthy sheen to it, and a truculent, bitter look, as if life had dealt him a bad hand driving a bus on a Sunday in the heart of Essex. He sighed as Emma came into view. Even the air pressure sounded reluctant as the bus platform lowered.

'No eating and drinking on the bus. And no exceptions,' said the driver to Sterling.

Emma stared, eating and drinking noisily. 'Hey,' she said sharply. 'Talk to me, not him. I'm not bloody invisible.' She passed her paper cup to Sterling. 'Can you bin that? Hope I don't get indigestion,' she said flashing her bus pass.

'I didn't see it properly. Hand it over.' The man, now focusing with insolent exaggeration on Emma and the wheelchair, peered closely at the photo and then into her face. A *douanier* couldn't have been more officious. 'Where to?'

'Does it matter?' said Emma. 'I travel free wherever I go.'

'Where to?'

Emma sighed. 'Chelmsford.'

'And him? £3.50 for him if he wants a single.'

Inside the bus, Emma was shaking. 'Frank, I want to go upstairs.'

'Upstairs? How?' said Frank.

'Leave the wheelchair there and help me up. Put me on your back. You know the drill. You're getting enough practice.'

God, thought Sterling. But he was wise enough now not to say anything. He crouched in front of the wheelchair with his back to Emma, slipping automatically into the way of it.

The bus driver on the other hand knew nothing about inhibitions. 'Oi,' he said, 'leaning out of his cab and looking down the bus. 'Oi. What's going on?'

'What does it look like?' said Emma. 'I'm going upstairs.'

'You can't do that. Wheelchairs, and their contents, go in the disabled space with all the others. 'Elf and safety.'

'I can sit anywhere I damn well please,' said Emma.

'No you bloody can't.' The driver opened the door of his cab, pushing back a young girl trying to get on, and took a couple of paces down the bus. He loomed over Emma's wheelchair.

Sterling stood up out of his crouch and inserted himself between the two. 'Yes, she can.' He could smell the tobacco on the man's breath and see the flabbiness of the spare tyre around his middle. He looked him in the eye. 'She can go anywhere on this bus, like any other passenger.' He was getting the hang of it. Her paralysed legs weren't holding her back. The driver's hostility was. That and the dauntingly narrow, steep and twisting stairs to the upper deck.

'You want to be very careful when you talk about health and safety,' said Emma. 'You'll get the bus company in big trouble if you start using that as an excuse to stop me doing what I want. It's called direct discrimination on the grounds of disability. And it's illegal.'

On the lower deck, passengers watched the standoff, joined by a gaggle of bystanders looking through the window. They couldn't understand what was being said, but it was livening up a dull East Anglian Sunday morning, and if they had been children, they would have been shouting 'fight, fight.'. The word 'illegal' seemed to undermine the driver's confidence. He looked at his watch, turned around and made his way back to the cab.

'If you go upstairs, you do it at your own risk,' he called over his shoulder.' He was so fluent it was likely that he had had practice. 'Bloody cripples,' he mouthed.

'What did you say?' said Sterling. But it was like when he and his mates were baiting teachers at school, tapping radiators, looking for an exasperated reaction and then claiming innocence ('what, miss? Not me, miss'). He'd made the challenge, but he got no reaction and had no proof of what had been said.

He turned back to Emma, slipped into the time-honoured position and felt her lean forward and slip her arms around his neck. 'Legs not back,' he murmured. 'Legs not back' she echoed into his ear as they staggered up to the top deck.

'Let's sit right at the front, Frank. Look at the countryside.'

'Thank God for that,' said Sterling. 'Less haulage.'

Colchester was slipping away before Emma's muttering and swearing began to recede, and Sterling began to cool down from the exertion of getting them on to the top deck with the grip bag. The ride too was getting smoother as if the driver's rage was subsiding.

'I didn't know you knew about health and safety,' said Sterling.

'I know a bit. I make some of it up. Why not?' said Emma. ''Elf and bloody safety is the stick they use to beat cripples like me. I got so pissed off I mugged up a bit on it. It's all pretty straightforward, whether or not you're disabled. If that driver hadn't been such an arsehole it would have been better for everyone. It boils down to three

things in almost every situation. Hazard identification –
finding out what the dangers are. Risk assessment –
judging how dangerous the hazards are. And then risk
control – either getting rid of the risks or controlling them.'

'I remember that vaguely from the police,' said
Sterling. 'I never listened that much. Boring.'

'No wonder you're a PI, then, you know-nothing,'
said Emma. 'Take me riding on a double decker. What's
the biggest hazard? I reckon it's you dropping me down
the stairs and doing your back in in the process, as well as
bashing my head in. But you've carried me before. We've
got a way of doing it. I'm only eight stone and you're
quite a big bloke. The stairs aren't very long. And the bus
was stationary. So there are hazards, but if you assess the
risks you can get over them. You can manage them. You
bend your legs, not your back. I hold on tight. The driver
keeps the bus stationary. Look at that notice. The bus
company recognises that for all passengers, disabled or
non-disabled. Nobody is meant to move out of a seat
until the bus stops. So you ring the bell. The bus stops and
only then do you get up. And not all drivers are idiots.
I once saw a driver get out of his cab and help bring a
wheelchair on. Our driver could have come up behind to
catch me if I slipped off you. Anyway, we controlled the
risk and here we both are. Not difficult. Not dangerous.
Me not being able to use my legs is only one bit of the risk
assessment. Impairment is irrelevant. It's just so stressful
because of that shit-for-brains we trust to drive us safely.
God, the irony, actually. And can you give me one good
reason why I can't sit anywhere I like on this bus?'

'Well,' said Sterling, 'playing devil's advocate, so
don't bite my head off, supposing you don't have a carer,
or someone to carry me about like I'm doing.'

'Fair point. But I don't suppose it's beyond the ingenuity of the company that made this bus to design one that has a lift for pushchairs and wheelchairs and so on.'

'Blimey, Emma, think about how much that would cost. You don't even have to pay a fare.'

'Ah yes. Expense. Often used as an excuse not to make changes. But a big company like this one can't use expense as an excuse not to help disabled people. It might be different for a small business – I don't really know. All I know is that struggling to get equal treatment is bloody tiring.' Emma rested her head on the seat and closed her eyes.

Not just for you, thought Sterling. Dragging her about and being a foot soldier in her battles brought on an exhaustion of its very own.

Chapter 16

Sterling Opens Up

'What about you, Frank?' said Emma abruptly. She'd opened her eyes again.

'What about me?'

'Well, you know about me and my family. You know a lot about my business. It seems only fair that I should know something about you.'

'Fair,' said Sterling.

'You know what I mean. Don't be a dickhead.'

'I'm just doing my job. You don't need to know any more than that.'

He looked down from the top of the bus as they went through the dribbling remains of Colchester. Outside a row of shops he could see a girl of about fourteen waiting at the crossing on her bike. She had a small head, shoulder-length blonde hair and a plump body. It looked as though surplus bulk was pushing up from her trunk, thickening her soft neck and giving her the beginnings of a double chin. Her eyes had a bulgy look. 'GORGEOUS' was emblazoned on her black T-shirt in silver sequins – or at least, that's what Sterling assumed. A kind of pink long-sleeved half-cardigan hid the 'G' at the left and 'S' on the right as he looked.

He had been harsh. Loosen up, he thought. Work more at establishing a rapport. It might help. 'I've been a private investigator for about a year. I've got an office in Sandley above the library. You were right yesterday about me being in the police. I was in the Kent force for fifteen years or so from the age of 18. I was in the CID when I left. Couldn't take orders anymore' – he smiled a small smile – 'which is an irony considering how you're currently bossing me about. I got into plenty of scrapes as a kid and all that sort of followed me into the police.

'Dad and I lived in a few of the east Kent towns – Deal, Ramsgate, Dover - when I was growing up...He got restless. I've been divorced these last five years. No kids. I'm single now but not entirely neglected, you might say. My mother walked out when I was a baby. I never knew why, but Dad never bad-mouthed her. He's dead now, so I guess I'm an orphan.' He sighed. 'On to my special subjects...I'm fond of beer, as you now know, and the music of the seventies, thanks to my dad – a lot of things thanks to him, actually. Politics: I'm what you might call 'unaligned', much to Dad's disapproval, since he was a trade unionist and a socialist. But who can trust politicians? That's my take on it. Religion: agnostic – just in case there is something.'

Some things he chose not to mention: the small flecks of grey appearing in his dark hair in what passed for side-burns; the slowly but apparently inexorably thickening waistline; and especially, the way women drifted away from him in what Andy Nolan sadly but not unsympathe-tically dubbed the 'procession of abandonment'.

Then he thought of something else. 'Disabilities, sorry, impairments: none, unless you count my alleged hot-headedness. Is that enough for you?' Part of him was surprised at his openness. Another part knew how skilful Emma was in getting people to share confidences.

'Interesting,' said Emma. 'So I'm in non-disabled, competent and colourful hands. Thanks for telling me all that. It could be worse, I suppose. Of course, we're all only ever temporarily-abled, technically speaking.'

'Temporarily-abled? Here we go again,' said Sterling. 'Jargon. Gobbledegook.'

'I mean it, Frank. Think about it. Sooner or later, everyone's going to get something – emphysema, cancer, a dodgy pair of knees, cataracts, multiple sclerosis. It's just a matter of time. Being one hundred per cent OK is only ever temporary. And sometimes you can get a temporary impairment. What about this: in those 15 years as a cop, were there never times when you were off with stress or anything like that?'

Sterling looked out of the window again. He didn't want to think back to the time he was off for four weeks after retrieving that bloated, decayed young body with no eyes swirling around Deal pier, a young woman abused, battered, murdered and then tossed away by her wastrel husband, or even when his own wife said she was leaving. 'Hang on a sec. Does a nervous breakdown count as an impairment? Does cancer?'

'They can do. Being disabled is not just about stuff like being blind, or being a cripple in a wheelchair. It includes depression, HIV. And let's not forget deafness and my own tedious father. So we're all temporarily-abled because sooner or later, something is going to get us. And we can all get impairments that don't last.'

'There's a whole little world here, isn't there, a mumbo-jumbo minefield,' said Sterling. 'Some people are in the know, and some aren't.'

'It's not mumbo-jumbo. You really hack me off, Frank. If you get the language right, it changes the way you think about things. And if you think differently, you start to act differently. You start to act properly.'

'Well, being one of the ignorant, I certainly managed to wind your dad up.'

'Not difficult. He's my dad, but he can be a stupid prat.' She looked across at Sterling – one of the sly glances he'd come to recognise. 'Did he do the music thing with you – how he hasn't heard any music for x number of years and what a tragedy it is?'

Sterling remembered "A Boy named Sue" and smiled slowly.

Emma laughed. 'I knew it. What about the mondegreens gig?

'Mondegreens?'

'Grandma told me. Dad used to drive her wild too. It's from the first verse of a poem:

> Ye Highlands and ye Lowlands,
> Oh, where hae ye been?
> They hae slain the Earl O' Moray,
> *And Lady Mondegreen.*

Except that the last line should be '"And laid him on the green." So it's repeating what you think has been said, only you use the wrong words and sounds.'

Sterling nodded again. 'I get it.'

'Self-pitying bastard,' she said. 'Always out for the sympathy vote. It sounds clever to begin with, but it soon gets on your nerves. Especially growing up with him around. What about the cinema riff?'

D a v i d   R   E w e n s

'No, not that one,' said Sterling. For him, Nicholas Jameson's testy self-confidence and air of authority, which might have been intimidating, was rapidly being undermined by his daughter's forensic mockery.

'You'll love this. He takes his scabby girlfriend to the local indie cinema. They could only see foreign films because they're subtitled. He wanted to know why subtitles weren't available for English-language films. Of course, he got fobbed off. The cinema manager implied Dad already had enough choice, and even if they had the right subtitling equipment, some non-deaf people might be put off. Fair enough, you might say, until the cinema put on singalong, subtitled versions of *Mama Mia* and *Grease*. Dad went ballistic. If they could do that, why couldn't all English-language films be subtitled? Even though they've now got the equipment so he can see more films, he complains if the meal deals in the café are only available on non-subtitled nights. Actually, he's got a point, I guess,' she reflected, almost wistful. 'It's just that he can be such a pain making it.'

The temptation to say 'Like his daughter' was almost overwhelming. Better keep quiet, thought Sterling.

'Your dad sounds interesting,' said Emma.

Sterling turned to her. 'He was. He was a good bloke. He was from the Fens originally – somewhere near Cambridge. Customs man in Dover. Didn't complain when I didn't want to go to university. Didn't complain when I joined the police. I learned loads of things from him. He was quirky.'

'That explains a lot,' said Emma. 'Tell me some more later. I've got to close my eyes for a bit.'

—w—

As the girl slept, Sterling looked out again from the top of the bus. This leg was different from the one to Colchester. The bus went from suburb to village to small town across flatter countryside, and was never far from East Anglia's main artery, which Sterling recognised as the A12 to London. A pattern emerged. Leaving a settlement, Mark's Tey or Kelvedon or Witham, the bus would slip onto the dual carriageway, and just as it appeared to be gaining momentum, would slip off into the next village or town, each one as orderly and quietly elegant as the last, with pretty half-timbered Tudor cottages and Georgian town houses in the East Anglian style next to more modern and recently constructed town and village centres.

Gardeners were cutting the grass in their back gardens and shoppers loading their cars. In the Chelmsford hinterland, a man in a trilby manoeuvred a large bookshelf unit onto to his back, hitching it up in stages and tottering arthritically off, bent almost double, hands behind back clasping the shelving. It looked as if the faintest puff of wind would blow him over. Amidst all the suburban and village scenes viewed from on high by Sterling, it seemed outlandish that he and Emma were on a desperate journey – the laboured, meandering mode of transport in direct contrast to their plight.

'Where are we now?' said Emma as she opened her eyes.

'A large walled chunk of suburbia not far from Chelmsford,' said Sterling. 'I think.' He looked out at rows and clusters of newly built houses enclosed by a never-ending ribbon of red brick punctured by the odd road. 'I think I saw a sign that said 'Chelmer Village'.'

'Not far then,' said Emma. 'Thank goodness. Yet again, I'm dying for a piss.'

As they were getting off the bus, Emma locked eyes with the bus driver. The loathing looked as if it was mutual. 'There,' she said. 'That wasn't so bad, was it?'

The driver looked away, ducking down to get his cash box. But Sterling rubbed his back. No matter how conscientiously he bent his legs, eight stone was eight stone. He hoped their lunch venue would have ramps. Emma would have the usual barrage of complaints otherwise, and he could do with a rest.

Chapter 17

Simone's Ragtag Army

'That bloody girl,' said Emma, as she and Sterling struggled out of the pub. 'She was more interested in checking her text messages than serving us.'

'Yeah,' said Sterling. The obstacles – no ramps as well as surly service – were getting him down as well, but so was Emma's default position in the face of any slights against her and her impairment, real or imagined. He thought for a moment. Could he bear another tongue-lashing? 'I'm just asking here, but wouldn't it be easier sometimes to be a little less... in yer face? Maybe not take such a hard line with people who don't get it about being disabled.'

Emma took her hands from the rims of the wheelchair, which gradually slowed to a halt. 'What, you mean start bloody simpering and lisping, and fluttering my bleeding eyelashes. Stick out my tits. Or maybe go all helpless and pathetic.'

'I don't mean any of that. On the job, there were courses on dealing with the public. What was it we did? Assertiveness. Eye contact. Being polite and firm at the same time.'

'Bugger that,' said Emma. She started wheeling again furiously, while Sterling struggled to keep up. 'None

147

of that crap would have worked with that ferry at Felixstowe, or on that last bus, would it? Naked aggression is the only language most non-disabled bastards understand. And remember for that matter. It actually helps me to take no crap – it's what the boffins call psychologically supportive.'

'Just raising the point,' said Sterling.

On the corner there was a convenience store. 'What about something for the journey – sweets, snacks, something to drink,' said Emma.

Sterling looked at the ramp and the automatic electronic sliding door. 'Fine. Yeah. I'll wait here.' He held up the grip bag. 'Don't worry about the grip.'

'Alright, alright. Lazy bugger.'

'Well, society's not disabling you here, is it?'

'Smart arse,' said Emma, spinning away to the entrance.

'If you're getting crisps, cheese and onion are my favourite. Any kind of sandwich will be fine.'

Sterling and Emma had left the bus station some way behind as they were searching for somewhere to eat and rest Their next destination, as they went from transport hub to transport hub towards London by bus, was Basildon, but Sterling couldn't remember the number of the bus or what time it was leaving. Now he looked up at the bus stop sign on the pavement outside the shop. 'Towards Basildon', it said. Nothing could be more convenient, he thought, except perhaps the invitation to text a Traveline number with the code for the bus stop to find out when the next bus was coming.

You do so many things in life on a kind of autopilot. Sterling switched on his phone. There was a beep as he sent the text, and within twenty seconds the reply from

Traveline had arrived, with good news. The 100 bus would be arriving in eight minutes, comfortably after when Emma would have left the shop.

Then he realised. He looked at his phone as if it was a hand grenade with the pin removed. With suddenly trembling fingers he switched it off. A moment later, Emma emerged through the sliding door, a Spar bag in her lap.

'Enough for a feast,' she said. Then she saw his face. 'What?'

Bluster. Prevarication. Airy dismissal. These were possibilities, but in Sterling's bitter experience it was always best to face the music early. 'I've cocked up.'

'How?'

'I forgot we were on radio silence. I turned my phone on and sent a text.' Sterling nodded towards the bus stop sign.

Emma sighed. Disabled issues made her furious and foul-mouthed. Other things, potentially far more dangerous, made her stoical.

'Easily done. If I'd had my iPad I'd probably have succumbed myself. No use crying about it. When's the bus?'

'Look. Just coming now. Maybe we'll get away with it.'

'Maybe. We'll have to see. But knowing the Whitman-Woods and the technology, I rather doubt it.'

—✺—

The bus journeys to Chelmsford had been anonymous. The number 100 bus to Basildon was different. Sterling and Emma joined a community. It reminded Sterling of the Sandwich buses he'd been on only a few days ago, although those communities had been a pale imitation of this. It was a single decker. Thank goodness, he thought. There'd be no going upstairs.

'Yo,' said the beaming driver in a deep voice. His pate glistened in the afternoon light. His symmetrically arranged teeth gleamed. A dark-skinned Gulliver filled the Lilliputian driver's cab. 'Where can I take you today?'

'We're going to Basildon,' said Emma, showing her pass. 'A single for him, please.'

'Ah Basildon. Town of dreams. The new Elysium. The urban Arcadia.'

There was hubbub from the back of the bus. 'Drive, Cedric. We've got a service to get to.'

As Sterling and Emma settled themselves in the space allocated for wheelchairs and pushchairs, smiles and greetings met them. A little girl stared at Emma with large brown eyes, as dark as her skin, and carried on even as Emma stared back.

'Louise,' said her mother, a plump young woman with an open face wearing an extravagantly multi-coloured outfit in the kaba fashion of West Africa – red and blue and green hoops with white edging on the sleeves, neckline and hem. 'Don't be rude. She doesn't mean anything,' she said to Emma. 'She's just curious.'

'I don't mind,' said Emma. 'Hi Louise. Is that your brother?'

'Yes,' said the girl. 'Sam.'

Sterling watched Emma in action. She was formidable when she thought it was necessary, and formidably prickly and challenging. But now he saw her other side again, as he had among the wheelchair users in Harwich – a young woman at ease in diverse company, chatty and charming. She soon knew that the mother's name was Simone, and the bus knew she was Emma. Somewhere between Chelmsford and Basildon, the little boy was sitting on her lap, listening raptly as she explained why her legs didn't work – how she'd fallen off a horse as a teenager, the critical loss of feeling and movement and the long journey of adjustment – told wittily and without self-pity.

'So all in all, they're fu… they're not much good. But I can pop wheelies.' The little boy giggled and held tight as she did little spins.

Most of the passengers seemed to know each other, pilgrims on a mission to a favoured church in Basildon. 'He's an excellent preacher,' said Simone of the minister. 'Michael', she said, indicating her husband, immaculate in a dark suit and white shirt, 'loves the sermons, and so do I. It reminds us of home.'

'So where are you from?' said Emma.

'The Gambia, though Louise and Sam were both born here,' said Simone. She pointed to the hooped colours on her outfit. 'The red is the sun shining on the Gambia River. The blue is the river, which runs through the middle of the country, and the green is for the land, the forests and our agriculture. The narrow white hoops stand for unity and peace.'

'Cool,' said Emma.

'We're all exiles on this bus,' piped up an Irish voice. 'Sunday is when we go home.'

Sterling looked around. He couldn't remember ever having seen such a motley crew. All human life was here, and in the middle of Essex, the only English accents seemed to be his and Emma's.

'Why are you going to Basildon?' said the Irish voice again. It came from a young woman with wide-apart green eyes and pale freckled skin, who sat towards the back with her own partner and three young children. She introduced herself as Moira.

'Actually, we're on the run,' said Emma, 'and Basildon is only the next stage of the journey. We're kind of heading to London.'

'What have you done?' said Simone. The little community had fallen silent. There was only Cedric's baritone humming and the rattle of the bus.

'I thought we were meant to be going under the radar,' whispered Sterling, his head bent across to Emma's.

'I very much doubt that these folk would co-operate with Marcus Whitman-Wood. Anyway, I trust them,' Emma whispered back. 'Nothing,' she said more loudly to the group. 'But we might find something out. Something dangerous. There are some people who don't want that.'

'Why are you going by bus?' said Michael. 'Surely there are quicker ways to get to London. Especially on a Sunday. Especially from here.'

'Yeah, but more conspicuous. The people who are interested in us don't know much about public transport.'

'Yeah, how poor it is,' said an elderly woman with alert eyes, white hair and a mischievous smile.

'Hey, hey, Lily,' rumbled Cedric from the driver's cab.

'Present employee excepted,' said the woman. 'It's just like *The Fugitive*. Not that any of you would remember it.'

'I do,' said the Irish woman. 'Harrison Ford and Tommy Lee Jones. It was a film.'

'No way,' said Lily. 'It was on our first telly around 1965. David Janssen was the star.'

Sterling switched his attention to the view from the window. He'd heard a few Essex girl jokes, and casually considered Essex to be just an extension of London. Very inaccurate, he thought. In the distance, he could see a line of low hills. In the latest village the bus was trundling through, there was a clapboard church steeple painted brilliant white, and an old flint stone school with 'Girls' Entrance' and 'Boys' Entrance' sculpted above modern replacement doorways. The Victorians must have thought things would stay the same forever.

Not long afterwards Cedric was speaking again. 'Gather up your belongings, pilgrims. The Promised Land.'

Picturesque Essex was gone. In the middle of Basildon, Sterling saw 1960s brutalism – long swathes of square glass and steel office blocks and concrete car parks. This *was* Essex as an extension of London. As the bus approached the long line of bus stands, Emma and Sterling scanned the area.

Emma stiffened. 'Uh oh. Trouble.'

Parked opposite the stands was a black Range Rover hard against the kerb, like an impossibly large and malevolent bluebottle. It was clear from the bustle and straightened backs in the vehicle that the bus was expected.

'They're going to get us as we switch buses,' said Emma.

'Hang on. Hang on. We need to think,' said Sterling. 'Do they know for certain we're on this one?'

'This is the one they'll have tracked from your text message. They'll have got the time of the text and assumed that we got on the first bus that came along.'

'OK, but do they know where we're going next? The text I got only said buses to Basildon. Actually, I can't remember where we're going next. You've been organising the itinerary.'

'Grays. Lakeside. The direction that gets us to London.

Cedric had been listening. 'If it's Lakeside, stay aboard the magic bus,' he rumbled. 'That's where I'm going next.'

Sterling thought about it. 'Doesn't it just postpone the showdown? They'll just follow the bus to Lakeside and get us there. Or the next place. Now that they know where we are and what we're doing.'

The bus community, aware of the Range Rover from Emma and Sterling's animated discussion and anxious glances, began a debate of its own, apparently based on last week's sermon at the church.

'Gandhi,' Sterling heard the strong-minded Simone say.

'Occupy,' said Moira.

'UK Uncut. Flash mobs,' said someone else.

Sterling was confused and irritated. He and Emma were in a spot, there seemed to be no way out and their new friends were prattling irrelevantly. But Emma's eyes sparkled. She'd made the connection that Sterling had missed. The three women – English, Gambian and Irish – were having quiet, intense further discussion. There was that female solidarity again, excluding and sidelining him.

'Cedric,' said Simone, 'when are you leaving for Lakeside? You haven't got a break here, have you?'

'Soon as you all get off the bus, lady. You're gonna be late for church.'

'Yes, we are. But it's in a good cause. What's the point of church if we don't help our neighbours and put our Christian duty into action?'

'Be careful,' said Emma to Simone and Moira. 'Especially with the children.'

Sterling watched about thirty men, women and children get off the bus. He still didn't get it. He tasted bile at the back of his mouth and swallowed. Surely whatever was about to happen couldn't have a good ending. Yet being seated on the bus had disguised both Simone's size and her leadership qualities. She filled her dress as she sashayed across the Sunday afternoon road towards the Range Rover. Whereas Simone's figure was generous and full, Moira's two-piece fuchsia suit hung from her slight frame. Her thin legs, sticking out from her skirt, took almost two paces to Simone's one. Behind these leaders, their menfolk, their children and the rest of the bus community shuffled along behind – Simone's little rag-tag army.

'Can we get going, Cedric?' said Emma.

'Sure thing, girl.' Like Sterling he was puzzled.

They all watched as Simone and Moira, and the whole bus crowd, surrounded the Range Rover, linking arms and pressing hard. They kept the children at the sides and on the edges. Now Sterling understood. He concentrated on Marcus Whitman-Wood, who was getting more and more agitated in the driver's seat. He tried to force open the door. He gesticulated angrily through the open window. He squirmed in his seat and looked all around for a means of escape. Even through the thick window and above the rattle of the bus's engine Sterling could hear the loud gunning of the Range Rover, juddering like a Formula 1 car on the grid before the start flag. In gestures and noise the intimidation intensified, but the crowd was unyielding.

Just before Cedric steered the bus around the corner and out of sight, Sterling caught a last glimpse of the ambush. 'It's like on a nature programme' – he deepened his voice to mimic the breathless, solemn tones of a narrator – '"ants overpower a larger predator through sheer numbers".'

'Idiot,' said Emma, but her heart wasn't in it. Her eyes had stopped shining and she was gloomy again. 'You're right. This will probably just give us some breathing space. The trouble is, now they know how we're getting about and roughly where we are. What's going to happen at Grays or Lakeside?'

Chapter 18

Sojourn at Socketts Heath

'Why go all the way to Grays?' said Lily. 'Why go all the way to London for that matter, if London is only a stepping stone to Kent?'

Neither Emma nor Sterling had noticed that the old woman was the only one not to have got off the bus with the church crowd.

She came down the aisle of the bus and sat heavily in the seat that Simone had previously occupied. She patted her heart. 'Goodness, I haven't had this much excitement for years. Who would have thought it, just coming back from seeing my sister in Clacton?'

Emma smiled at the old woman, as if she was pleased to be the source of the excitement.

Then she said, 'Surely, if we're going to Kent, we have to go through London. There's the Dartford crossing, but we're going by bus. Anyway, that's an obvious crossing point.'

'There are plenty of ways to get across the Thames,' said the old woman, 'and the more you get into London the easier it is. The Blackwall tunnel. The foot tunnel from the Isle of Dogs to Greenwich. Stratford International station. In fact, any number of road and railway bridges, any number of tunnels. You could go by bus, train, tube, Docklands Light Railway, riverboat from the Isle of Dogs. But from what you say those men will be keeping an eye on all the obvious places, and now they know roughly where you are your options are more limited. Trains go to Fenchurch Street and Liverpool Street. Buses go from Lakeside to the next hub. And of course, no offence intended, you're conspicuous. So don't bother with London at all.'

Facetious ideas slipped into Sterling's head. Yeah, swim over the Thames. Put buoyancy tanks on the wheelchair. He kept quiet.

'So....' said Emma.

'So, go down to Tilbury Docks and take the passenger ferry to Gravesend. From there, just go up to the railway station and get a train. No one would think of watching Tilbury or Gravesend.' Lily's air of quiet triumph fell just short of smugness.

'Sounds like a plan,' said Emma. 'How do you know all about transport in this neck of the woods, Lily?'

'I grew up in Romford. When I was doing my teacher training at Avery Hill back in the late 40s, I had a teaching practice placement in Gravesend. My father and I looked at it, and we worked out that if I went back home to Romford for those six weeks, I could get a train to Tilbury Docks and the ferry across the river. The school was a 15-minute walk the other side. That was a wonderful time. And my husband worked at the Department for Transport, so I knew everything from him. He's long gone. I'm 85 myself.'

'85,' said Emma. 'No spring chicken then.' She had the knack of making cheeky into charming.

'I live at Socketts Heath, just short of Grays. You can get a bus the other way from there. Cedric knows where I get off. The only snag is, by the time you get to Tilbury Docks, the ferry will have packed up.' She took a long look at Emma and Sterling and made a decision. 'I've got a flat on the main road. The stairs are quite steep, but you can stay there with me if you want. It's Monday tomorrow, and things will be back to normal then. It depends how much hurry you're in.'

Emma looked at Sterling. 'I'm knackered, Frank. I need to stretch. I'll be spasming soon, and the pain's already started.'

Sterling turned to Lily, seeing her clearly for the first time, and not as a vague voice from the back of the bus. Women of her age favoured bright red lipstick and she followed that fashion. Her skin was pale and unlined, and although her brown eyes had a sunken look in her face, they were bright and firm. She had talked sense and looked trustworthy. 'Lead on Macduff,' he said.

'We're all getting out at Socketts Heath, Cedric. Usual place,' Lily called out, and the driver waved a huge hand.

Now that the deal had been struck, the trio fell silent. They immersed themselves in the motion of the bus as people boarded and disembarked and as they edged on westwards to Grays over endless Thames-side conurbation. Sterling felt relieved. Perhaps his mistake at Chelmsford wouldn't be too costly. Perhaps they would have been traced anyway, but he couldn't really be convinced of that. At quarter past three that spring Sunday afternoon, Emma and Sterling checked the traffic and got off the bus in the No Man's Land called Socketts Heath.

'Goodbye, Cedric. Thanks for looking after us,' said Emma.

'You take care now. Let Lily look after you. Safe onward journey.'

The bus edged off into a gap in the dual carriageway traffic as Sterling, Emma and Lily gathered themselves at the bus stop. Even on a Sunday, the traffic hummed and roared, the air was dusty and there was the usual waft of fumes in the air.

Lily pointed over a pedestrian crossing to the bus stop on the other side. 'When the time comes, you'll need to catch the 73 bus to the centre of Tilbury, and then the 99 to the ferry terminal. Come on. We'd better get you indoors in case that Range Rover cruises by.'

Sterling noticed how brightly the wheelchair stood out in the Sunday sunshine. He upped his pace to catch Lily up. After she had taken one or two more steps, she stopped and grimaced.

'My back,' she said, rubbing and stretching. 'It was all that sitting down on the bus.

Emma twisted and looked up at Sterling. 'Temporarily abled,' she murmured, with an expression that said 'I told you so.'

The old woman missed nothing. 'What?' she said.

'We were having a discussion on the Chelmsford bus,' said Emma. 'How some ailment will always get you in the end.'

Lily blew out her cheeks. 'Too right,' she said. 'I'm a tough old bird, but there are my eye drops for glaucoma and paracetamol for the arthritis. It gets so bad at times I can't wait to conk out. 85. It's long enough.'

'Don't conk out yet,' said Emma with her cheeky smile. 'Not till we've gone, anyway.'

Lily laughed. How does the girl get away with it? thought Sterling. They drew up at a door between a print shop and a florist's in the middle of what planners would call a parade, with mock-Tudor panelling and gables for the flats above.

'Here we are.' Lily opened the door and Sterling could see a flight of thinly carpeted, worn stairs stretching steeply upwards into darkness. He tried not to sigh. Another mini-mountain.

'If you could open up upstairs, Lily, I'll carry Emma up and then come back down for the chair. We need to get that out of sight inside as soon as possible.'

'LNB,' murmured Emma In the dark hallway.

'I know. I know. If you carry the grip, I'll carry you.'

'The grip. I'd forgotten that.'

Sterling was sweating again when he finally closed the door of the flat. He joined Emma in the front room by the window, where he'd put her back in her chair. The flat had a musty smell of stale biscuits, heavy velour curtains and unopened windows. As he stood next to her they looked out of the window. Even as time crept on into Sunday evening, the traffic showed little sign of abating. Beyond the window and the bus stop below on the right was the huge roundabout that Cedric had negotiated, and beyond the carriageway to the north, a large new secondary school was just visible through some trees. The view was panoramic, which explained the easy chair Lily had in the window alcove, but to the left and right flat vistas stretched out along the road that joined London to south Essex suburbia. A tune he struggled to recognise popped into his head and he began humming. Then it came to him – "Nowhere Man" by the Beatles. That's what he was, and nowhere land was where.

'I can spend hours in that chair,' said Lily. 'I never expected that I'd end up here. I never even knew there was a place called Socketts Heath. I loved my husband, but he was a gambler, and when he died and I discovered all his debts, this was all I could afford. Still, it's bigger than you'd imagine, and there's always something going on outside. Now, what about a cup of tea? Then we can get ourselves organised.' She moved stiffly off towards the back of the flat. Emma and Sterling heard the clink of china and the sound of a kettle being filled up.

'So what do you think?' said Emma.

'We've been lucky again. We should be safe enough here. It's obscure enough. If Marcus Whitman-Wood comes by in the Range Rover on the way to Lakeside, which is pretty likely, he'll never know we're so close. Funny really. And the Tilbury-Gravesend ferry is a good idea. I never even knew it existed.'

'Me neither. Anyway, I couldn't have gone much further today.'

'The regime,' said Sterling.

Emma looked at his deadpan face. 'Are you taking the mickey?'

'Certainly not,' said Sterling. 'If I haven't got the hang of it by now, I never will.'

'Thanks, Frank,' said Emma in a softer voice. 'I appreciate it.'

'Of course, I'm pretty knackered myself. All bussed out, you might say.' Sterling found a polite and considerate Emma, and one using his first name, unsettling. 'Ooh, Battenberg,' he said as Lily came in with a tray of tea and cake. 'I haven't had this since I was a kid.' He could tell she was pleased. Some people are givers, and some are takers. It was clear which camp Lily was in, and maybe she didn't have much in the way of opportunity.

'My nephew Billy – well, really my great-nephew – loves it. He'll probably pop in later. Now, dear,' she said to Emma when the tea and cake was gone, 'tell me what you need and we'll get you sorted out.'

'I need to stand somehow,' said Emma. 'Get the blood circulating better around my legs and give my bum a rest. If I don't do some standing I'll get pressure sores.'

'What about my Zimmer frame?' said Lily. 'I hate the thing, but they left it ages ago when I broke my hip. It's around somewhere if I can find it.'

'That might work. I might need your help with that, Frank. Can I have a shower or a bath? We didn't have time this morning. And a massage. My legs need a massage to keep them in tone. Frank, could you do that?'

'Sure,' he said. It felt odd. She'd stopped giving orders and started making suggestions and requests. Lily must be a good influence.

'After all that,' Emma smiled, 'I reckon I'll be ready for a bit of telly.'

Lily beamed. She had company. It was clear that she loved making herself useful.

Emma propped herself up in front of the window with the Zimmer frame, while Sterling stood next to her with his arm around her waist for extra support. Her arms were rigid and Sterling noted her whitened knuckles on the frame. This was hard work.

'Just another few minutes, and then I'll be ready for that massage.'

'OK,' said Sterling. 'Where do we do that?'

'Where am I sleeping, Lily?' said Emma. 'If it's a bed in the spare room I can lie out on that.'

'Follow me,' said the old woman. With Emma back in her chair, they went back along the hall towards the stairs but then turned sharply into a bedroom. 'I've put you in here, Emma. Frank, the sofa in the sitting room at the front folds out into a bed. I'll leave you to it, shall I?'

Sterling laid the girl out on the bed.

'Are you OK with this, Frank? Lily won't have the strength. I haven't had any toning for days. My legs really need it.'

'It's OK. I can do it. I'll just need some guidance.'

'Prop my head on the pillows so I can see down. Put the towel over my pelvis. When I've undone my jeans, slip them off.'

Sterling did as he was told. Emma's legs had the same light golden colour as her arms and face, and, for all he knew, the rest of her. They were well-proportioned but lacked definition. He lowered his eyes, but not before he caught a glimpse under the towel of the underwear he'd bought in Dovercourt.

'It's only a massage, Frank,' said Emma, seeing his discomfort. 'You'll get into it. What you need to do is kind of rub and knead, rub and knead, from the top of my thigh and down. Then the other leg. Then turn me over and do the backs. Kneel on the bed with your back to me and you'll be more comfortable.'

'Nice tan,' said Frank as he set to work. 'I've noticed it before.'

'Nice solarium,' said Emma. 'Just because I'm a cripple doesn't mean I can't have a bit of luxury here and there. This is good, Frank. You've got the knack.'

He worked his way down one leg and then started on the other, with little grunts of effort. 'Right, I'm going to turn you over. Grab the towel.'

Emma squealed and laughed. 'Careful, Frank, you prat. You'll tip me on the floor.'

'Sorry, Madam. Only just finished my training.' Sterling started the same process on the backs of Emma's legs.

'Idiot,' she said, but Sterling could tell she was smiling into the pillow.

'Right, Madam, that's you done and dusted. How would you like to be arranged now?'

'Shut up, Frank. Just tip me on my back again and prop my head up. I wish I could say that felt wonderful, but of course I can't feel a damned thing down there. At least it helps keep me in some sort of nick. I haven't had a massage since I went to Bawdsey.'

'Who does it when you're at home?'

'Someone comes in. Ellie. A physiotherapist. Dad sometimes.'

'He seems to do a lot for you, one way or the other.'

'Yeah, well. I s'pose.'

Sterling flexed his shoulders and rolled his neck. 'Actually, do you mind if I join you?' he said. 'What with being hunted by a pack of thugs, all the buses, the rumble at Basildon, the lifting and carrying, the shouting and swearing, I'm pretty bushed myself.'

'Not forgetting looking after the grip,' said Emma.

'Not forgetting that.'

'Yeah, you can join me. Hop on.'

Sterling eased himself onto the bed. There was just room for the two of them. An old-fashioned eiderdown covered sheets and blankets. He lay back, head propped on a pillow next to Emma, and looked up at the ceiling. There was a dried out, ochreish watermark towards the corner, cylindrical but with a bulge at the bottom, like the cooling tower of a power station. The ceiling itself could have done with a lick of paint, like the rest of the jaded flat. But it was clean and neat, and in the circumstances he was far from complaining.

'It's full-time, managing this impairment,' he said.

'You're a fast learner, Frank. Using all the right words. Yes, it's all a pain, every bloody bit of it. There's a constituency in the disabled community that's all for making society change to accommodate us – lifts on buses, zero tolerance for people who abuse us like that crappy bus driver – but at the same time recognising that our impairments play a part in limiting us, and give us pain, discomfort, sadness, inconvenience.'

'Is that what you think?' said Sterling. 'It seems, dare I say it, reasonable enough. Like a two-pronged approach.'

Emma looked at the ceiling. 'Doesn't that look like one of those towers you see at power stations? It's what Dad would call a siren song. Luckily, he'd say, I can't hear siren songs. But his point is that having that attitude would give disabled and non-disabled people an excuse to focus back on impairments and not on what can be done to get over them. He's a pain, Dad, but I'm with him on that. We both think society's got to change, and other people must too. We've done enough adapting of our own. Leave us to deal with our pain and sadness, but get us the changes we need. It's the social model that will do that, not your so-called two-pronged approach.'

'Yeah,' said Sterling.

'Yeah what?'

'Yeah, it is a cooling tower.'

'Thought so.'

'The social model. I haven't heard that before. Where did you get all this from? You and your dad are really in the know.'

'Dad's campaigned, mainly for deaf people, for years. He met someone at a conference, a blind bloke, Scottish, who radicalised him even more. Paul Mackay. He talks with this really clipped Dundee accent. "Och, Emma, this" and "Whisht, Emma that". He certainly packed away the whisky when he stayed with us. Dad and I both learnt loads from him. He connects disabled politics with the mainstream.

'All the ideas you're hearing about have got names, Frank. There are even people who regard their impairments as gifts. The "I-wouldn't-be-the-person-I-am…" school. "I've-found-out-stuff-about-myself-I-never-knew-was-there…"'

'Let me guess what you think about that.'

'Go on then.'

'I think you'd say that's crap.'

'Too bloody right. Of course being a cripple is a big influence on me. Of course I'm….'

'….Bitter. Twisted,' said Sterling. 'Sorry, couldn't resist it.'

'Sod off, Frank. Yes, of course it's affected me, but it's not a bloody gift. And it's certainly no cause for celebration. Yes,' she nodded, 'there's even a celebratory wing of the disabled movement. Wankers.'

'But isn't that positive? You know, helps people cope better.'

'God knows what goes on in some people's heads.'

Emma and Sterling stared up at the ceiling again. The room was quiet apart from the faint hum of traffic.

'Am I glad I fell off that sodding horse? Of course I'm bloody not. Would I like a normal life? Of course I would. In the meantime, I guess the next thing is to have the wash I didn't get this morning. Ready?'

Sterling rolled off the bed and crouched next to Emma. 'LNB,' they said simultaneously.

'OK, usual method. Put your arms around my neck while I put one of mine around your shoulder and the other under your knees. Good job this bed is quite high. On three. One, two, three.'

He remembered that Emma's body was heavier than her legs, and compensated for that. He noticed again her well-muscled arms, her wide shoulders and her generous chest. Her right breast pressed against him as she held him tightly. He pushed his legs up, swung her around and tottered off towards the bathroom.

'Hell's bells,' said Emma. 'This is tiny. I'm not going to manage this by myself. Put me down in the bath and then we can have a think.'

Sterling grunted as he bent his knees and lowered the girl. She barely fitted into the narrow space. He sat on the lavatory seat next to the bath.

'What we'd better do is for you to get the grip bag. I'll get the stuff I need. You'll have to help me strip off. Then fill the bath and I'll do the next bit. Then rinse me off with the shower attachment and help me get dressed. Actually, I might as well get into my pyjamas. We aren't going anywhere else today.'

'Shouldn't I ask Lily to do this? You know, another woman.'

'Frank, Lily is 85. She can't haul me about. What's the problem all of a sudden? I can tell you, ten years of crippledom means that whether it's a young bloke or an old woman who bathes me makes no difference except how competently they can do it.'

'Alright. I was just suggesting.'

'Let's get on with it. Lift me up a bit under my arms so I can take off my knickers. Now put me down.' She unbuttoned her cardigan and tossed it aside and then pulled her T-shirt over her head. 'Start running the water.' Then she unhooked her bra and tossed that aside.

Sterling concentrated on the taps and getting the temperature right. But he couldn't help noting again the lopsided nature of his client's daughter's body – muscled and broad-shouldered at the top but slim and shapely, with firm, generous breasts, tapering down to her diminished legs. He noted something else too – unexpected and unwelcome, since he was working a case – the inconvenient stirrings of an erection. He knelt on the floor and felt the water with his hand. A small spider scuttled over the side of the bath.

'See if you can find some bubble bath, Frank. A soak will do wonders. Why don't you leave me for fifteen minutes while I wash my hair and that,' said Emma after he'd added the liquid and stirred it in. 'Then maybe you can rinse my hair and the rest of me, and help me get in my pyjamas.'

If she'd noticed his discomfort, she'd uncharacteristically chosen to ignore it. 'Fine,' he said. 'I'll leave you to it, then.' And the truth was, he was glad and relieved to escape for a short while.

Chapter 19

'I Gave them Nothing.'

Emma and Sterling were sitting side by side on the sofa in the front room. Emma was propped up on cushions in her pyjamas and a dressing gown Lily had found, and they were eating chicken pies, potatoes and two vegetables from trays in their laps.

'Nineteen fifties food,' Emma whispered. 'These veg have been boiled to within an inch of their lives.'

'Shut up. Ungrateful girl,' said Sterling.

'Just saying. I'm not complaining. I know we've been lucky.'

Their hostess creaked back into the room from the kitchen at the back of the flat. She wasn't a fusser or a bustler – just quietly efficient, like many women of her generation. Sterling was thinking other things too. He assumed that older people got set in their cantankerous and disapproving ways, but on current evidence, this woman – born in, what, 1928 – had a cheerful and flexible attitude. Since she'd offered her hospitality, there had only been acceptance and generosity. There had been no frowns of disapproval about Emma's squeals and giggles in the bedroom, or her disappearance into the bathroom with Sterling. He sighed. As well as the danger, it had been a confusing few days. When it was all over – if they got out of it in one piece – he'd have to take stock.

'Everything OK?' said Lily.

'Fine, thanks, Lily,' said Emma. 'Brilliant dinner. Winter greens. My favourite,' she said slyly.

'I'll make another pot of tea. Or I think I've got a drop of cider.'

Emma's eyes shone. 'Cider for me, please.'

As the old woman turned, the doorbell buzzed loudly in the quiet room.

'Jesus,' said Emma. 'That gave me a fright.'

Sterling edged to the window and glanced cautiously down, flicking the heavy curtain back, half-expecting to see large men in dark suits clustered around the downstairs door.

'It's not them,' he said. They all knew who he was referring to. 'But goodness knows who it is under that rapper's cap.'

The young man below fidgeted restlessly, combining that with a slight sway to the music apparently going into his ears through small white ear buds. His jeans were baggy, barely covering his backside, and his unlaced trainers a garish yellow and royal blue. Sterling could see a large white '99' crudely stitched on the back of his red sweatshirt.

Lily joined Sterling at the window. 'Ah, Billy,' she said. 'Wonderful. My nephew, or more accurately, my great-nephew. I wonder, dear. I wouldn't usually ask, but it's been so busy. Would you be kind enough to pop downstairs and let him in? Just say you're visiting and tell him Lily sent you down to save her legs. He'll understand.'

'Sure,' said Frank. He put his tray aside and went downstairs.

'Hi Billy,' he said to the skinny young man in the doorway. 'Lily sent me down to save her legs. I'm visiting with another friend. I'm Frank Sterling.'

Billy looked into Sterling's face, confused. But there was something else. Sterling had been a policeman long enough to recognise the signs. Lily's great-nephew was stoned.

Sterling followed him up the stairs. Billy weaved, even though the passageway was narrow.

'Billy,' exclaimed Lily in the flat.

'Hiya, Auntie,' said Billy, with less obvious enthusiasm.

'This is Emma.'

'Hi,' said Emma.

'Yo,' said Billy. He struggled for eye contact, gave up and looked away. If he noticed Emma's legs, he didn't say anything. His manner was offhand. He seemed unwilling to share his great aunt's attention with anyone else. 'I didn't know you were having visitors, Auntie, apart from me.'

Sterling caught something in his voice, a slight whine. The boy was resentful.

'Something to eat, Billy?' said his aunt.

'Nah. I had something earlier.'

'Billy comes every Sunday. He really looks after his old aunt,' said Lily.

Yeah? How? thought Sterling. By helping her spend her pension? He's cocky. Used to being pampered. The young man in question gazed vacantly at the wall, his foot beating a frantic tattoo on the floor. Emma glanced at Sterling and they both carried on eating. An uneasy silence settled over the room like an invisible mist.

Lily was sensitive to the atmosphere and tried to jolly things along. 'Billy's between things at the moment.

He still hasn't quite worked out what direction he's going in. He's been a bit unlucky. How's the rapping coming on, Billy?'

'Good. Just got to do a demo tape and get that out. Get a contract. Then I'll be laughing.' He adjusted his cap so that the visor pointed up and left, as if the act would confirm the contract.

Sterling looked at the fidget staring at the wall. He could recognise a hopeless case when he saw one, but why couldn't Lily see it? Then he thought of his own blind spots. He shouldn't be so quick to judge.

Lily removed the dinner plates and turned on the television. Maybe that would do the trick. Emma took a deep pull of her cider from a half-pint glass inscribed with three scimitars on a red background and *Essex Beer Festival 2003*. Eight eyes focused on the television. The Sunday news was on – the usual dross, Sterling thought – crisis, scandal, war and misery, with a feel-good story to cheer things up at the end. A 60-year-old Essex man from Billericay had found his long-lost twin sister in Billericay, Massachusetts. Then there was a switch to the local news. And that's when their troubles, Emma's and Sterling's, started all over again.

The dark young presenter with rich red lipstick put on her serious face. 'News is coming in of a vicious assault at Lakeside bus station. The victim is understood to be a bus driver just finishing his shift. We go over to Michael French, our reporter at the scene.'

'Thank you, Kerry. Yes, the driver, Cedric Longhurst, had just left his bus when he was apparently set on by four men and badly beaten up. A witness said that there had been an altercation and then the attack was launched. Reports from the hospital indicate that

Mr Longhurst has been left with three broken ribs, a cracked cheekbone and various other injuries, not thought to be life-threatening. He's recovering now at Thurrock hospital. Police tell me that they are pursuing various lines of inquiry, including one that involved an incident near the bus Mr Longhurst was driving at Basildon earlier in the day. They are also not ruling out a racial motive. Now back to you in the studio, Kerry.'

'Thank you, Michael. We have just received this footage direct from the hospital, where a news crew spoke briefly with Mr Longhurst. Some viewers may find some pictures distressing.'

Emma and Lily gasped as they saw Cedric's battered face. His left eye was closed and his dark skin overlaid with dark red weals and bruises of dirty yellow. He looked directly at the camera. Watching Essex saw a resolute and perhaps morale-boosting message defying street muggers and robbers.

'I gave them nothing,' said Cedric in a hoarse baritone. 'You hear me. Nothing.'

Emma and Sterling knew exactly who the message was for and what it meant.

The narcissist Billy, his self-absorption receding a little as the drugs wore off, picked up the atmosphere. 'Mate of yours?' He answered his own question knowingly. 'Yes, he's a mate. What's it all about?'

'Emma and Frank are on the run, Billy,' blurted Lily. 'It's just like *The Fugitive*.'

'Lily, that's a big exaggeration,' said Emma.

'No, surely not.' Lily's excitement was running her mouth. 'Not from what you said on the bus. To thirty people,' she slipped in, as if one more, and her relative to boot, would make no difference.

Now Billy's pupils dilated for reasons other than illegally ingested substances.

'Go on, Auntie. What's going on?'

'Lily, the fewer people that know what's happening the better,' said Sterling. He meant to speak softly but there was steel in his voice. 'And remember, looking at what's happened to Cedric, it might be safer for Billy to keep out of it.'

Common sense and courtesy to her guests wrestled in Lily's face with wanting to please her nephew. Sterling could see Emma's anxious eyes. He realised she was holding her breath.

'Frank's right, Billy. It's not our business. I'm sure Emma will tell me all about it afterwards, and then I'll tell you.'

Billy subsided into the armchair. His chin sank into his chest. The foot-tattoo began again, a light thumping on the floor. If Lily knew that he was sulking, she chose to turn a blind eye.

'I gotta go,' said Billy just before nine o'clock.

'Already?' said Lily.

'Busy week coming up, Auntie. I'll call in Wednesday.'

'Do you want me to go down, Lily?' said Sterling.

'Would you, dear?'

'Sure.'

Billy went first down the narrow stairs. The dull light bulb in the hall cast a gloomy pallor over the threadbare carpet. Billy opened the door onto a wall of noise. He turned around to Sterling in the doorway and looked up. Sterling realised how short he was – just over five feet by the looks of it, framed in the orange glow of a street lamp so his face was hard to make out.

'The girl never moved from the sofa,' said Billy.

Sterling realised that with the wheelchair in the bedroom, Billy hadn't known that Emma was disabled. 'No,' he said. It might be better for Billy to stay in the dark.

'Suppose you want to protect your asset.'

'Protect my asset?'

'Saw it in a film. Spy film. I expect there's a bob or two in it for you, getting a result from what's going on. Whatever *is* going on. She's pretty too,' leered Billy.

'On your way' was a favourite expression in the Kent police, back in the day – for lippy juveniles hanging around on street corners, drunks outside pubs, assorted loiterers. Don't say it, thought Sterling. Don't rise to it. 'Yes, she is, Billy. Nice to meet you.'

But Billy wasn't ready to go just yet. 'I'm thinking, you could probably do with some help. From someone who knows what's what around here. And who's who. Someone who can keep you out of hospital. You don't want to end up like that black bloke.'

'Well, mate, that's something to bear in mind. I'll have a think about that, discuss it with Emma, and maybe get back to you. We can get you through your auntie, can we?'

'Yeah, Lily's got my number. It would be a sensible thing to do.'

Like open-heart surgery without anaesthetic on a sewage farm, thought Sterling. 'See you then, Billy.' He half-expected some complicated fist bumping and hand clasping, but Billy moved off in a pimp roll without looking back. Sterling watched him swagger out of sight around the corner. He leaned on the door jamb and looked out into Socketts Heath. The sun had long gone but the streetlamps and car headlights bathed the area in a patchy flickering light of their own. The air was cool and the sky was clear. A faint breeze rustled around the doorway, lapping at the junk mail and the litter on the pavement. A leaflet for Grays Unitarian Church promised a warm Sunday welcome for all the family, and a regular Wednesday coffee morning with free cakes. A corner flapped up in the air and then fell back again, as if the effort was just a little too much. An old man with rheumy eyes shuffled past with a mongrel dog. The dog limped sadly on and looked at Sterling without interest. Sterling and the old man exchanged nods. Then Sterling withdrew back into the passageway, the roar becoming a hum as he closed the door.

Back upstairs, Lily was once more claiming to Emma that black was white. 'He's a very good lad, Billy. He visits me regularly, and I see more of him than I do his mother. He's been unlucky. The school didn't really understand him, and then he sort of got in with the wrong crowd.'

Sterling said nothing. He thought of his own blind spots again.

'I'm sure you're right,' said Emma. Her eyes glazed over and she looked exhausted. 'You know what, Lily? I'm ready for bed. Can you do the honours, Frank?'

After the bathroom regime, Frank laid her down in bed.

'So what does Billy know?' she said. They didn't need a preliminary conversation about his degree of trustworthiness.

'Not much. He's offered to help. We can contact him through Lily.'

'Good to know,' she said ironically. 'He's streetwise, that's the trouble. He can find things out, do some sniffing around.'

'My thoughts exactly. Still, if we're lucky we'll be on our way in the morning and Billy will no longer be in the picture.'

'Here's hoping. Goodnight, Frank.'

Chapter 20

All the Saints and Angels

'Where's my handbag?' said Lily.

Sterling was sitting with a bowl of cornflakes in the small kitchen at the back of the flat. He'd left Emma in the bathroom, 'finishing off', as she put it. He'd slept poorly on the sofa bed in the front room. The dull hum of the traffic in the main road outside, the restless shadows it made on the lounge walls, and a nagging, ever-present anxiety about their situation all combined to keep him wakeful. Getting Emma up and ready added to his exhaustion.

'On your shoulder, Lily,' said Sterling. He felt embattled – a surly, prickly young paraplegic, and now a forgetful old woman. It wasn't just that either. The whole situation was outlandish. He could barely believe he was fleeing from a bunch of thugs by bus and ferry, at an average of six miles per hour, camouflaged by wheelchair users, protected by Christians, and sheltered overnight by an octogenarian. If he and Emma got out of this, who would believe their story? And what exactly was the story? There was so much he didn't know.

Lily sat down and put the handbag on the small table. 'I do things like that all the time. I tell you, sometimes I've had enough. How's Emma this morning?'

'Alright,' said Sterling. He'd become familiar with Lily's refrain about having had enough. 'A bit grumpy. The usual.'

'Well, I suppose she's got quite a bit to be grumpy about. But from what you've said and what I've seen, she does get a lot of help from people.'

'Yes,' said Sterling. He thought hard about his discussions with Emma, and his experiences in her company. 'She's gloomy about why they do it though. Guilt, relief and pity are why people step in, according to her. Guilt and relief because they aren't crippled, and pity because she is – and what she calls the "There-but-for-the-grace-of-God syndrome". It's almost superstitious, she reckons, as if helping her will keep them lucky.

'Of course, not everyone is onside. We've had more than a few rucks on our way here, Lily. Some people have just seen her and her wheelchair as an inconvenience, and haven't seen her as a person. Not surprisingly, that incenses her. There's impatience with disabled people out there, and even hatred.' He thought of the ferrymen at Landguard Fort, and the bus driver at Colchester. 'And ignorance.' He remembered his own casual attitude before he'd ever met the Jamesons. 'And maybe some people are scared because she's different. Of course, she can rub people up the wrong way.'

'What about you, Frank?'

'Ah well, Lily, I'm a man on a mission. I'm getting paid to get her safely home, and perfectly willing to accept whatever help we get along the way, and for whatever motives.' He stirred his cornflakes. 'At least, that's how it started off. Actually, I'm not as cynical as Emma. There's something about her. She's rewarding to help and she makes people feel good about it. It's easy to help her. There's no danger involved – not from her in her wheelchair anyway. She makes you feel as if it's you and her against the world. She's the underdog in all this stuff that's going on, and people love sticking up for the underdog.' Sterling stirred his cornflakes. 'All these opinions from Emma and me…What about you, Lily? Why did you get involved?'

Lily clasped her hands around the straps of her handbag. 'Well, you *were* easy to help on the bus, and she's hardly dangerous. All those other things you said make some sort of sense – even her gloomy reasons.'

Sterling waited.

'I get lonely,' said Lily. 'Life's too quiet up here. I rattle around by myself too much. So it's good to help. Get involved. Have a bit of an adventure.'

'Frank!' called a voice from the bathroom. 'Where are you? I could do with a hand here.'

'I get it, Lily,' said Sterling, ignoring the summons for a few moments. 'You've been especially kind. Really dug us out of a hole.'

'You'd better go and see to Emma.'

'Yeah. Her ladyship. Coming,' he shouted more loudly.

Finally, breakfast was over. Finally, the grip bag was packed and everything assembled. Finally, the wheelchair and Emma, from separate journeys, were united at the bottom of the stairs. Finally, not greatly refreshed, she and Sterling were ready to go. Groundhog day was starting again.

'The bus is in five minutes from across the road,' said Lily. She gave a little grin. 'Do you want me to do a recce?'

'Go on then,' said Emma, entering into the spirit of it. They all knew that if a black Range Rover cruised by they were sitting ducks, and that no recce by a creaky old woman would save them.

Sterling remembered his spell in the elite rapid response squad in the Kent police – armed, super-fit, highly trained young men and women. Things have changed for me. Things have changed a lot, he thought.

Lily had walked stiffly back to the front door. 'All clear,' she said. 'Thank you for staying with me. Good luck getting across the river. Good luck with everything.' The words came out in a torrent. Shortly, she was going to be alone again.

'Thank *you*, Lily,' said Emma. 'I've got your address and phone number. We'll be in touch.'

Then she wheeled briskly to the pedestrian crossing. She wasn't the kind to look back.

Sterling squeezed Lily's hand. 'Take care. Thank you from me.'

'The light's green, Frank,' called Emma. She was tense as he caught up. She jerked back and forth in small darting movements, her fingers tight on the hand-rims. 'I never bloody know how it's going to be each day. Whether the platform of the bus will lower. What the driver will be like. What unexpected hassles will turn up. I get so tired it does my head in.'

'Not forgetting the small matter of CommuniCo and Marcus Whitman-Wood,' said Sterling.

'Yeah, all that. Goes without saying. Thanks for reminding me. I was actually leaving all that to you.'

The bus arrived shortly afterwards. It was a modern one with a platform that lowered to the perfect height for the wheelchair and a retractable ramp that moved smoothly out for it. The driver was a slight woman with a wide, easy smile. Her hands seemed dwarfed by the size of the steering wheel. Whereas Cedric was Gulliver in his cab, she was a Lilliputian in hers.

Emma edged meekly into the space for wheelchairs and pushchairs. 'After yesterday, I need to pace myself.'

Sterling looked back as the bus moved smoothly into the traffic and approached the big roundabout. Lily was in the doorway at the bottom of the flat. He saw her put her hand up in a gesture between a salute and a wave, turn, put a hand to the bottom of her back, and disappear into the hallway.

—⁓—

Even here Sterling felt the presence of the Thames.

The terrain was flat and mundane but canted gently southwards as the bus moved east. A couple of student stragglers went into the sixth form college by the road, a red brick, post-war structure of square solidity. Sterling and Emma stared quietly from the window as they entered Chadwell St Mary, according to its sign, its stone church and cottages overrun by a 1950s housing estate. It was the time of day of young mothers with pushchairs, and pensioners with shopping trolleys.

Then they were in the Essex countryside, seemingly empty of life but for a few sheep. Most towns and settlements stretch out their tentacles before they take dense and consistent shape – a petrol station here, a row of cottages there, a timber yard. Tilbury began abruptly. One moment there was countryside and the next a huge, sprawling ex-council estate, row on row of predominantly grey pebbledash terraces along grey suburban roads, with the occasional green space and hedging – a town built to house dockers and stevedores for the post-war boom and London overspill.

'Poets and novelists. And Canada,' said Emma.

'What?'

'This bit's all novelists and poets. These old council estates were often given those names, presumably to imbue the working class with a bit of culture. Or they got Australian and Canadian names, to remind people what they were missing.'

'Maybe,' said Sterling. If you built a new town, just finding a supply of names might be a challenge, never mind the cultural aspects.

The driver had stopped the bus in the heart of the town. She stuck her head around from her cab, her frizzed hair dramatic in the sunlight coming in from the front window, and looked into the bus. 'Tilbury Civic Square,' she said. 'Change here for a bus to the ferry terminal.' She looked at her watch. 'The next one's in about three quarters of an hour. You just missed one because I was running a bit late. Sorry about that. There's not actually very much around here. You could pop into the library.'

'Best get out of sight,' said Emma when they were on the pavement. 'And they might have a computer so we can do a bit of research while we're waiting – if we're careful.'

She nodded approvingly as the heavy old library door swung automatically open as she approached. The building was ugly and squat, the library sharing the premises with an outpost of the local district council, but inside the atmosphere was bright and cheerful, and it was warm. Tilbury might have been built for a predominantly white working class, but now the clientèle was over-whelmingly diverse and dark-skinned – a new kind of migrant, from further away than London up the Thames.

Emma wheeled up to the counter, which was at her height. 'I wonder if you have computers with access to the Internet,' she said to the librarian.

'Are you residents?' said the librarian, whose silver glasses reminded Sterling of his grandmother.

'No…tourists,' said Emma.

'Right,' said the librarian. Sterling followed her eyes as they looked out of the window. The war memorial, which he and Emma had skirted on the way in, a white rectangular monolith with clocks on each face at the top and lists of the fallen inscribed in dark lists down each side, was solemn and starkly eye-catching enough, flanked by the maple leaf of the Canadian flag and the Union Jack. But beyond that was a brief interlude of patchy greenery on either side of a grey road that stretched out into a vista of flat nothing.

In the far distance Sterling made out what he thought might be low tenements and a block of shops. The woman gazed on, as if evaluating the likelihood of Emma and Sterling's tourist status, or whether as a tourist destination Tilbury might be up there with the Taj Mahal, the Niagara Falls, the Great Barrier Reef…A teenaged boy came into view on a tiny bicycle with wide handlebars and began the long pull down the endless road. It looked laborious, standing up on the pedals. His legs were too long for him to be able to sit on the saddle.

The librarian's reverie continued for a few seconds and then she turned back to Emma. 'Well, Monday morning. It's hardly busy. The computers are through that door at the back and to the right. I'll come and log you on.'

'Thanks,' said Emma. 'We appreciate it.'

Sterling and the librarian shifted a chair so that Emma could get close enough to the keyboard. From his machine, Sterling could see into an adjacent children's area, where a little girl with hair tied up in little topknots read haltingly to her mother. Every so often she looked his way and smiled.

'Right, Frank. You do a bit of rooting around on CommuniCo, and I'm going back to 'Fang' and Grandma's radar work in World War Two. For God's sake don't go direct to the CommuniCo website. They'll be monitoring traffic. Start with Google.'

Sterling felt the usual rising of hackles. 'Yes, Ma'am,' he muttered.

'Stop your bloody chuntering. We haven't got much time.'

Sterling couldn't resist it. 'Welcome back.'

'Meaning?' said Emma.

'I'd got used to the polite Emma at Lily's. The one that asked rather then ordered. The one that wasn't foul-mouthed and bad-tempered. The almost human one.'

'Get over it, Frank. And get searching.'

'I've made my point,' he said primly.

Through Google, there were plenty of hits on CommuniCo. He started with Wikipedia, which recapped what Emma had told him in the Harbour Café at Harwich. CommuniCo had begun life after the Second World War as Whitman Electronics Limited (WEL), owned and run by Alan Whitman-Wood, a former scientist at Bawdsey Manor Radar Station and one of the leading developers of radar. WEL was a niche company, servicing and working in partnership with larger firms, especially in Britain and Germany, but also globally. Radio communication and latterly mobile telephone technology were particular specialisms. The wiki contributor was unequivocal. Alan Whitman-Wood had been a young genius, adept at innovation and invention at the very edge of technological and communications development, with a record number of patents in the field. As his own flair and creativity had declined, he had become an expert in assembling and managing teams of inventors and innovators, and evaluating and assessing their work. Sterling's eyes glazed over as he grappled with the technical details – bandwidth, the decline of analogue and the rise of digital signalling, 2G and 3G technology and an array of other advances.

But where WEL differed from other companies was getting its innovations and products to market. Whereas Alan Whitman-Wood was a scientific leader and visionary, his son was an entrepreneur skilled in business. From the 1980s he was responsible for harnessing his father's evaluation skills, and along the way, old-fashioned WEL had become CommuniCo, its headquarters now at Bawdsey and the old radar station.

Interesting, thought Sterling, but hardly enlightening for the situation currently facing him and Emma. Why had she been kept prisoner, and why was she being hunted? Still, the background was useful, even if the wiki entry was uncontroversial. What else might there be? He went back to the Google list of hits. Most links were to the CommuniCo website. He heeded Emma's warning. Then something towards the bottom of the screen caught his eye: 'CommuniCo float going according to schedule', and a link to the business page of a national newspaper.

'Wednesday 11 April is D-Day of a different kind for 94-year-old Alan Whitman-Wood, a leading WWII radar scientist. This is the day when his brainchild, the leading-edge electronic, communications and computer technology company CommuniCo, is floated on the London Stock Exchange, led by Whitman-Wood's son James, the company CEO.

'CommuniCo, formerly Whitman Electronics Limited (WEL), has planned meticulously for the initial public offering and expects to achieve its £30 per share target with ease. Underwriters Schredemann believe that CommuniCo's research and development division, based in Bawdsey on the Suffolk coast and strongly linked to Cambridge University, is the strongest in a tight and competitive field.

'"We have always been a successful private company here in the UK and Germany, with excellent partnerships with the big players in telecommunications, and a global reach,' commented James (Jimmy) Whitman-Wood. "Becoming a publicly owned company will secure our future, get us access to the extra finance for the next, major stage in our expansion, and of course contribute to UK plc's global future. We are a successful British company with roots stretching back to the 1940s, thanks to my father."'

Sterling turned to Emma. 'How long do you reckon they were going to keep you at Bawdsey Manor?'

Emma's eyes stayed fixed to her own computer screen. 'What?' she said, preoccupied.

'The Whitman-Woods. How long were they going to keep you?'

'Dunno. A few days. Forever. I never got the chance to find out. Why?'

'I might have found something.' He slanted his screen towards her and she scanned down the article. Sterling watched the flicker of her eyes as she read quickly. There was a small pucker in her forehead and she mouthed words silently.

'What does it all mean? It makes no sense to me.'

'Nor to me. We'll need to look into it a bit more, and I don't reckon we've got enough time now. But it looks as though CommuniCo is currently a private company, which probably limits the amount of money it's got. If it goes public, and issues shares, then that will mean more cash – if the launch is successful. Being a hi-tech operation, it needs upfront money for research and development. Maybe the Whitman-Woods were hanging on to you in Bawdsey because of something to do with all this and your grandmother. Maybe that's the "Fang" connection.'

'Sounds plausible. You have your uses, Mr PI. So whichever way we look at it, and even if we don't understand the ins and outs, this coming Wednesday is a big day for the Whitman-Woods.'

'Looks like it. Let's try and think this through in more detail. Your grandmother finds out about something from way back in the war to do with Alan Whitman-Wood, maybe to do with this "Fang" thing. She contacts him. She's murdered soon after, presumably to silence her – so the Whitman-Woods are obviously candidates. Not knowing any of that, you contact Alan Whitman-Wood and ask about "Fang". He realises, from the conversation, that you don't know what she knew. He invites you down, supposedly to explain, but really to hang on to you and keep you out of circulation. When the right time comes, we're assuming this Wednesday, they can let you go. They just didn't factor in the efforts and speedy work of a brilliant private detective, and your bold bid for freedom.'

Emma ignored Sterling's levity. She was focused elsewhere. 'I should have stayed at home and found the answer to Grandma's murder there.'

'If we're right, after Wednesday, whatever you do or find out won't matter to them. I can almost see the PR line they'd take. 'We offered her hospitality and every courtesy and this accusation of abduction is how she pays us back.' They'd probably say you were insane. Anyway, they're after us to stop you doing something that will really hurt them, something they stopped your grandmother doing.'

'The thing is, we still don't know what that is,' said Emma.

Sterling nodded at her screen. 'What have you been doing?'

'I went back to the Cauville Raid, the one that did for my grandfather, on a German radar installation on the Normandy coast.'

'And did you find anything?'

'Nothing new. But then, we don't have much time and I don't have access to specialist sources. The story is pretty well known. RAF aerial reconnaissance planes spotted what British intelligence agencies believed was a German radar transmitter. It was remote, near an old country house on a cliff, and didn't look that well defended. A commando raid by sea wasn't considered feasible, so the plan was for a parachute assault – to steal as much German equipment as possible for analysis.

'At the time, the raid was generally considered successful. After a couple of fire fights, the attack group was picked up at a nearby beach with the equipment on specially built trolleys. But there were controversies. The main one was how my grandfather came to be captured and killed. There was talk that he was wearing the wrong uniform, which made him stand out. That was one bad thing. Another was that the captured equipment apparently didn't tell the British much more than they already knew. After the war, all kinds of rumours swirled around. Maybe the Germans had expected the attack, and even encouraged it. Those kinds of double bluffs were common.'

'Well, you're the expert, pretty much,' said Sterling. 'All interesting enough, but pretty vague. When did all this happen? 1943? How could that be important 70 years later?'

'Dunno. But something got Grandma going, and the Whitman-Woods are involved up to their necks.' Emma shivered as a gust of cool air found its way to the computer room. She put her hand on Sterling's in a warning gesture. The small sliver of light at the bottom of the door turned to a darker shade. Sterling looked through the partition at the little girl reading to her mother. She had stopped, and looked with a troubled, anxious face towards something at the front desk, beyond Sterling's line of vision. He and Emma went very still.

A harsh, penetrating and surprisingly reedy high voice addressed the librarian – one used to command. 'I'm looking for a girl in a wheelchair, and her carer. Did they come in here?'

'Shit,' whispered Emma. 'Talk of the devil. Or one of them, anyway. Marcus Whitman-Wood.'

Sterling looked around the room, trying to keep calm. Next to the partition with the children's reading area was a rack of shelves with local history books. As quietly as he could, he wheeled Emma behind it. This is pathetic, he thought – the worst, most ineffective, stupid hiding place. An irrelevant thought popped into his head – it had to be some kind of defence mechanism and always happened in times of stress – this time his father's favourite picture,

And when did you last see your father? They'd been up to that gallery in Liverpool to see it.

Whitman-Wood's demanding tone had the desired effect – from Sterling and Emma's point of view. Unerringly, he raised people's hackles, and in double quick time. Sterling heard the bureaucratic shutters come rattling down. 'My role, sir, is not to give information about who is or is not currently in the library. It is to offer information, advice and guidance about our stock, to maintain an appropriate atmosphere and to supervise, and in some cases assist in, the process of borrowing and returning books and other items. Are you a local resident? Do you have a library card? If you do not, then your right to use these premises is very restricted.'

Angela couldn't have done it better, thought Sterling.

'Where are you going? What do you think you're doing?' Now there was alarm in the librarian's voice.

Emma took Sterling's hand as he crouched beside her. Marcus Whitman-Wood came through the door. You do look like a Blues Brother, thought Sterling, but without the pork-pie hat, and much, much more menacing. The little girl in next door stared, the whites of her eyes in dramatic contrast with her dark face. Sterling looked at her mother, desperate.

'Come on, sweetie, don't stop reading,' said the woman. 'Look. What's going to happen next?' The little girl realised what she had to do.

Emma pointed with a timid finger between *A History of Tilbury Fort* and *Thames Coastal Defences During the Dutch Wars* at the computer screens they had just deserted – a page on the Cauville Raid on one, and the wiki CommuniCo page on the other. The evidence of their presence was screaming silently. Whitman-Wood only had to take two more steps into the room and they were finished. He moved forward and Emma closed her eyes.

Five seconds later, their adversary had left the room. Sterling peered around the shelves. Just in time, he calculated, the screensavers must have started to sing the praises of Thurrock District Council, which they were doing in garish colours.

It wasn't over yet. There was that high reedy voice again. 'I wonder, am I, as a *non-resident*, allowed to ask how you get out of Tilbury if you haven't got a car. Does answering that fall within the remit of your job description?'

He's got a sense of humour, thought Sterling, or at least a sense of irony. He heard the librarian's stiff reply, about catching a bus to Grays from the stop outside or a train to Fenchurch Street from the railway station up the road. Gratifyingly, she made no mention of the passenger ferry to Gravesend from Tilbury Dock. When the automatic doors finally swished shut and the draught was once again revived and then just as abruptly extinguished, the little girl giggled.

'Jesus Christ and all the saints and angels,' said Emma. 'I hope this library's got a disabled toilet. Otherwise I'm going to wet myself.'

'Accessible toilet,' said Sterling. 'Get it right, girl.'

'Bloody hell, Frank. What a time to go PC.'

Chapter 21

A Taste of the Thames

'There are an awful lot of tourists about in Tilbury today,' said the librarian as she came into the computer and local history room.

'Like buses,' said Emma. 'You wait for ages and then they all come at once. Thanks for not spilling the beans.'

'A deeply unpleasant and dubious man, and clearly up to no good. With the social skills of a rodent.' She considered for a moment. 'No, rodents are much more sociable. But if he knows you're somewhere around here, I'm afraid it's very open, and as I said to him, there are only the buses and the station half a mile up the road. Can I ask where you're going?'

'Down to the ferry and across to Gravesend,' said Sterling. 'We were going to catch the next bus, but right now that doesn't seem like a very good idea.' He looked at Emma. 'How did he know we were around here?'

'Billy,' they said together.

The librarian was thinking about something else. 'I can get you down to the ferry without you having to go outside to catch a bus. The mobile library is due here in about five minutes. I'll get Malcolm to run you down.

194

And the beauty of it is that he parks around the back and backs the van in. You'll be out of sight.'

'Brilliant.' said Emma. 'Thank you very much. Have I got time to use the loo before we go?'

Amazing, thought Sterling. With this girl, something always turns up. And Marcus Whitman-Wood's lack of grace was a bonus. If he had not been going around East Anglia putting people's backs up, he and Emma would never have got this far.

Malcolm, a slim, wiry man with a restless, energetic manner, acted as if he smuggled wheelchair users and private detectives every other day of his working life. He was gallant, taking Emma's hand as the lift transported her up into the mobile library and fussing around so that she was settled. 'It's only a five-minute journey,' he said, 'but you've got to be comfortable.'

Leaving the back of the library, Sterling was reminded of private security vans taking prisoners to and from courthouses. Only the press photographers were lacking. From the window of the children's area of the library, the little girl next to her mother and the librarian waved a farewell. Sterling did a little thumbs-up through the door panel. How did they do it, the two of them? He'd had more help from ordinary strangers, in Emma's company, than in all the rest of his life. OK, some of that was in the police, and you don't get much support in the police, but it seemed exceptional. He couldn't recall reading anywhere that East Anglia was an especially friendly locality. Remembering his breakfast conversation with Lily an hour ago (could it have been so recent?), he saw few signs of guilt or pity and plenty of instinctive and spontaneous sticking up for the underdog.

—m—

To get to the ferry's wooden-planked landing stage, the mobile library had to go through a narrow metal-girdered bridge and down a steep ramp. Malcolm left them looking out towards Gravesend to the south across the grey, turbid Thames. He had a schedule to meet out towards Stanford-Le-Hope and Corringham, just this side of the border with Canvey Island, he said, and he was late.

'Another day, another ferry,' said Emma. She and Sterling had edged between the river and a scattering of parked cars. Behind them the girders loomed up to the dock road. Sterling sat on one of the bollards. A few metres away a young grey seagull pestered its mother. 'Feed me. Feed me,' it squawked. In a large four-by-four with a marque Sterling didn't recognise, a woman in a white blouse was pouring a drink from a Thermos flask as the man in the driver's seat scanned the river in a restless sweep with his binoculars. The checks on his lumberjack shirt were large and loud. It looked safe and cosy, and emphasised how horribly exposed Sterling felt with Marcus Whitman-Wood and his black Range Rover close by.

'There it is,' said Emma, and halfway across the river Sterling spotted the bulk of the ferry, the superstructure at the front giving it a kind of eager look as it ploughed towards the Essex shore.

'It'll be good to be back in Kent,' said Sterling. 'Home.'

Emma looked at him. 'Bloody hell. The man really means it. You can't be homesick, Frank.' He watched her doing calculations in her head. 'Not after three days. Not for Kent. And surely not for the backwater we live in.'

The throaty roar of an exhaust pipe caught Sterling's attention. He recognised the sound from his police days.

A Subaru Impreza saloon in metallic purple was at the top of the ramp, complete with hood scoop, vents and rear spoiler.

Emma was looking too. 'That is one naff, vulgar-looking car,' she said.

'And always driven by a boy racer,' said Sterling. 'When I was on the job, we were always flagging them down on the M20.' He peered hard at the figure in the rapper's cap. This is not good, Emma. It's Billy, on his mobile telephone. The monkey's here. The organ grinder must be close by.'

The ferry was bearing down towards the landing stage. Billy was gesticulating as he spoke agitatedly into the telephone. Emma tensed, and Sterling had come to understand that it was as much to do with potential conflict at boarding as their pursuit. 'It'll be tight,' he said. 'I'd better stay here with you. There's no point in going up the ramp to Billy, and you'll need help getting aboard.'

'OK,' said Emma. She was too unsettled to think of swearing.

Now the ferry veered around so that it was parallel to the landing dock. There'll be a nautical term for that, thought Sterling. The skipper spun the wheel and the engine thrust into reverse. All the forces combined to slow the boat and make it drift gently to shore, the water bubbling and frothy at the stern. A deckhand in a dirty hi-vis jacket fussed around with ropes and then leapt off the vessel and made it secure. He swung out a retractable boarding ramp, larger than the ones at the Deben and at the confluence of the Stour and Orwell, but with little metal ridges. People whom Sterling had not noticed before materialised from various obscure corners of the landing stage. They were almost without exception frayed in some way, not just physically, and looked down at heel.

The man in the jacket glanced at Emma by the bollard, and then at Sterling, thoughtful. 'The gangplank's wide enough for the both of us and the wheelchair. Can you lock the wheels?' he said to Emma.

'Yep. Done.'

'Lift on three,' he said to Sterling, and then Emma and Sterling were on the ramp.

'Same performance at the other end,' said the man, and then Emma was on the ferry and in the 'passenger lounge', a space of scratched wooden lockers that served as benches and smelt of diesel oil.

'Thanks,' said Emma. 'You've no idea how good that was,' but the man had already gone, supervising everyone else's boarding.

Sterling looked through the wide salt-scoured window up to the top of the girdered ramp. It was like watching in a mist. Billy was still in the car. Perhaps he doesn't fancy his chances by himself, thought Sterling with a surge of anger. He'd be right, too.

Then he saw it, next to the bollard. Forlorn-looking. Deserted. Unclaimed. Something suspicious in a public place - the kind of scenario that could clear a railway station or a tube train. The grip bag.

'Bloody hell,' said Sterling. He'd been consciously avoiding oaths. Emma's mouth was foul enough for both of them.

'What?' said Emma, as she watched him spring up.

'I thought you were in charge of the grip,' said Sterling. 'Right now it's still on the landing stage.' Losing one grip bag was unlucky, and forgivable in those earlier circumstances. Losing the replacement was simply derelict. Sterling couldn't bear the idea of it.

The deckhand was about to draw in the boarding ramp and untie the ropes from the bollards.

Sterling pointed at the bag. 'That's ours.'

'Well, you can get it, but we've got to go. We're late already. Back in forty minutes.'

'Leave the sodding thing, Frank,' called Emma. That clinched it. Mr Hothead. He leapt onto the landing stage. He'd have words with Billy whilst he was about it. Bag in hand, he watched the ferry drift from the landing stage and the engine note rise to a sudden crescendo. Then it sprang off in the same eager way that it had seemed to approach. He saw Emma's clenched fists shaking in rage and frustration. Even worse, at the top of the ramp he heard a screech of brakes and a squeal of rubber, and then felt a weary inevitability descend on him like a particularly pervasive spell of morale-sapping drizzle as a black Range Rover lurched to a halt in front of Billy's purple car.

Billy got out of his car from the front passenger door and jogged lightly down the ramp, looking back with a kind of anxious curiosity. Odd. Why didn't he go to meet his new mates?

'Frank,' he panted as he approached. 'It's me. Billy.'

'I know who it is, you bastard. And I know who you've brought with you.'

'Half a moment, mate. You've got that well wrong. I didn't bring them. They found you all by themselves.'

'Like hell they did.' Sterling looked over the river. The ferry was receding into a speck. Gravesend, its waterfront a jagged jumble of far-off wharfs and buildings, seemed much further than a mile away. He looked back up the ramp. He could see Marcus Whitman-Wood and three of his men. The big man was directing them towards Billy's car.

'I locked it,' said Billy, 'and blocked the entrance so that you'd be sure of getting away.'

The men started bouncing the car violently.

'Hey,' shouted Billy, but they were oblivious.

Sterling could see what they were doing. He remembered the technique from traffic management, when a car was locked and mis-parked, or had broken down. The purple car was bounced away from the ramp way and soon the Range Rover was parked at the far end of the landing stage. The man with the binoculars in the other four-by-four had stopped scanning the shore. The woman next to him had her coffee mug halfway between her lap and her mouth. Close by had become much more interesting than the horizon for the moment.

He turned to Billy. What he was saying, and doing, seemed plausible. And it was hard to imagine Marcus Whitman-Wood being in cahoots with anyone. 'We'll sort it out later.' He had a feeling of déjà vu. He'd had enough of ferries. Enough of river crossings. But this one was worse. This time he was stuck on a landing stage. The ferry was gone and his pursuers were looming. As usual, an irrelevant thought popped from nowhere into his head, this time about his father's favourite poem, about brave Horatius on the bridge, facing down Lars Porsena of Closium and his Etruscan hordes. Sterling himself was a poor captain of the gate, Billy an even less credible Spurius Lartius, and Herminius was nowhere to be seen.

Close up, Marcus Whitman-Wood was as menacing as on the shoreline at Bawdsey, or trapped by Simone and her rag-tag army in Basildon, or in the Tilbury library. He was shorter than Sterling, but stocky in his dark suit. His bullet head sat below a haircut Sterling once thought was just cut spiky but which might better have been described as 'high and tight' – shaved short at the sides with a crew cut on top. His associates had the same style, like a uniform. His face was a curiously pink colour, and his hands white and lardy, like a butcher's. His blue eyes looked harsh and mean. Sterling felt a lurch in the pit of his stomach, as when he was a kid at the top of the rollercoaster at Dreamland in Margate and then plunging down. His sphincter relaxed involuntarily. It was a good job there was nothing in his bladder.

'Missed the ferry, Mr Sterling?' Whitman-Wood had done his homework on the identity of Emma's assistant.

Sterling had been with her virtually non-stop for three days. What would she say in the circumstances, even if she was terrified? 'Fuck off,' he said.

Whitman-Wood looked over to Gravesend and back to Sterling and Billy. He seemed to be weighing things up. What could they tell him? Nothing. Nothing he didn't already know – that Emma was on the ferry to Gravesend and could be picked up the other side. He cocked his head to the burly men standing in pecking order behind him and indicated the river. Clearly, they were used to his ways. The men converged on the two of them, who retreated to the edge of the landing stage. It was quick and brutal. First Sterling was taken by the arms and hurled into the river, and then Billy.

The cold hit Sterling. There was a roaring in his ears. Water went up his nose and filled his mouth, water thick and murky with mud and ooze. He thrashed around with his arms and kicked his legs, feeling his clothes grow instantly heavier with water and weigh him down.

His chest tightened. Then his head broke the surface of the river and he started coughing. He struggled to stay above water and realised he was still holding the grip bag.

Billy came up a few metres away. Already they were drifting down river from the landing stage, which loomed black and impossibly steeply above them. Billy could swim. He moved towards Sterling with easy overarm strokes.

'Bloody hell, bro. I didn't expect that.' Considering what had happened to his car and then to himself, he actually seemed cheerful.

Sterling hated the water and was beginning to flail. He could feel panic rising. It would be so easy to let the grip float away, but then, what would have been the point of leaping off the ferry?

'Give me the bag. We can paddle to the shore beyond the jetty.'

Grey water eddied and swirled around mud flats, which seemed to Sterling to be well beyond his limited range. In the distance beyond the shore he could see some kind of industrial plant, all disembowelled pipes and squat square buildings, belching steam and smoke. He could taste the sulphur in the air. Then he heard the putter and knock of an engine in the river behind him, sounding sickly. Every so often it would stutter and die out. With a concerted effort, he paddled around to see what was happening.

'Oi. Oi,' shouted Billy. 'Over here. What word do they use?' he said to Frank. It came to him without prompting. 'Oi. Mayday. Mayday. SOS.' Now Billy was splashing frantically, as if he was fighting off a shark attack.

The boat changed direction, alternately puttering and knocking and then silently drifting to the two men struggling in the old river. A pole was offered to Sterling first, and he felt himself pulled and bundled determinedly but not roughly into the bottom of a large tender. He lay dripping and panting on the floor of the boat, relief and even jubilation flooding through him. He stared up at the sky and savoured the moment. He could hear Billy join him, chattering excitedly, fearing nothing. A pair of dark eyes in a deadpan face looked down on him.

'Thanks,' said Sterling.

The face nodded. 'Law of the sea,' he said.

Beyond him to the front, two more men were fiddling about with the engine, its casing lying on one side. One spoke to the skipper, who had gone from Sterling back to the wheel, in a language Sterling didn't recognise. There was a 'cough, cough' as the skipper pressed the starter motor. The sound echoed over the water as the tender drifted downstream. 'Again,' the man seemed to say. And then the engine burst once more into life, and the vessel was transformed from drifting hulk to purposeful, useful service boat, even if the knocking continued.

'We will take you back to the shore,' said the skipper.

Sterling looked at the jetty two hundred yards upstream. He saw that Marcus Whitman-Wood and his men had turned back from the ramp and were watching the tender as it worked its way back.

'I'd rather you didn't,' said Sterling. 'We were going to Gravesend on the ferry before we fell in the water. Why don't you give your boat a little run out over there? I'd be happy to make sure you aren't out of pocket.'

The skipper looked across the river, judging distances. He looked back at the Tilbury shore, registering the men in black on the landing stage. Beyond it Sterling noticed a small cruise ship at the terminal. This was where the tender was from. This explained the language he didn't recognise.

'Keep your money,' said the skipper. 'You're right. The engine needs a good run out. We'll take you over.' He issued instructions to the engineers and the tender swung south to Kent.

Sterling and Billy stood at the back of the boat, wrapped in makeshift blankets. Provocation and defiance are always risky. Sterling's V-sign from outstretched arm to Marcus Whitman-Wood contained plenty of both. The hothead in him just couldn't resist it. The trouble is that they invite retribution. The alarm on his face when the engine faltered and threatened to die away, and Marcus Whitman-Wood, stopping in mid-stride, looked on with renewed interest, made Billy laugh.

Chapter 22

Rats in a Trap

The sailors on the tender were from the Ukrainian coast of the Black Sea, and Sterling had been right to assume that they were employed on the cruise ship. They dropped him and Billy at the ferry jetty at Gravesend. The skipper was pleased. The engine was running smoothly after the run across the river and the knocking noise had gone. 'Law of the sea,' he'd said laconically again when Sterling renewed his thanks. If he'd seen any of the shenanigans on the Tilbury side, he showed little interest. Perhaps, coming from the Ukraine, he was used to minding his own business. 'We must get back to the ship,' was all he'd said in farewell. Sterling and Billy watched the tender go. River water dripped on the jetty. Sterling considered kneeling and kissing Kent ground, even if it was actually a jetty jutting out from Gravesend. It was good to be home, or in the general vicinity. Seeing Emma beyond the gangplank and near the gated entrance to the ferry terminal brought him to his senses. 'You prat,' she'd say, and garnish her scorn with swearing.

Whereas the ferry landing on the Essex side was apart from any built up area and the rest of the docks, the landing in Gravesend was clearly within the town, and the connecting bridge was for pedestrians. Emma would have struggled to get to the gate onto the roadway. As Sterling and Billy approached her, Sterling held up the grip bag. It still dripped river water.

Billy stared at the wheelchair. 'Hey, bro,' he said softly, 'I didn't know she was a cripple.'

Emma took in the scene, deadpan. She nodded at the bag. 'What, did you have to dive for it?'

'Kind of,' said Sterling.

Then she switched her glance to Billy. 'What's this double-crossing little bastard doing here?'

'Whoa,' said Billy. He looked pained, but the geniality on the Essex side hadn't left him.

'We got that wrong, Emma,' said Sterling.

'Yeah?'

'Yeah,' said Billy. 'I was looking out for you. If it wasn't for me, you'd be in a black Range Rover with the bad guys.'

'Listen. Enough bickering,' said Sterling. 'Billy can tell his story when the time comes. I can tell you about our little swim. But right now, we've got to get out of here. We've been rumbled. Whitman-Wood knows exactly where we are. I reckon it's about twenty miles by road from Tilbury, up to the Dartford crossing and back down here on the Kent side. The ferry was probably going back to Tilbury a few minutes ago, so all in all we've got an hour at the outside. We've got to get our arses into gear. And it's got to be route one. We can't be doing with buses and suchlike anymore. And thank God no more ferries. The whole point was to keep under the radar. Well, we're certainly not doing that anymore. I need to change, clean up and get dry. Then let's get back home as quickly as we can.' He stared at Emma. He needed her to agree.

'Alright,' she said, with just a hint of the sulky. 'Makes sense. I s'pose. What about him?' She still couldn't bring herself to speak directly to Billy.

'OK, guys. I know Gravesend. Auntie Lily brought me over on day trips. The best and quickest way out of here without a car is by train from the station, and we can change on the way.'

'Let's go,' said Sterling.

The two sodden tramps, the wheelie and the grip bag crossed the busy road near the ferry terminal and went up the slope towards the centre of the town. A church surrounded by a well-kept railed garden appeared in front of them.

'Through here,' said Billy. 'And then into the shopping centre.'

Emma wheeled up to a statue in front of the church and paused, the tramps squelching after her. Sterling looked up at the woman on the large plinth, dressed in what looked like the clothing of a native North American.

'Pocahontas,' said Billy. His voice took on the mechanical cadences of a recital, as if he was a kind of tour guide, but there was tenderness too. 'The Red Indian wife of John Rolfe, merchant and adventurer, originally of Brentford, Middlesex. She protected Captain John Smith, colonist, of Jamestown, Virginia from her own tribe in a land dispute. Died on board ship back to America off Gravesend of TB. Or maybe plague. The truth is, no one really knows. But it's Aunty Lily's favourite statue. And mine.'

Sterling glanced across at the young man in his rapper's cap and baggy jeans, the jeans now weighed down by water and dragging on the paving stones. This was unexpected.

'Never mind about Pocahontas for God's sake,' said Emma. 'You're both soaked, but I'm in a mess too. The regime expects. The regime demands. I need a loo.'

Billy dragged his eyes away from Pocahontas. 'Just up here.'

Sterling heard it first, the insistent, growing thrum and throb assaulting his ears. Then the wind got up, a sudden gale where there had been relative stillness. The sky, already a dull grey, darkened even more. When he looked up, his face matching those of his companions, it was at a small black helicopter, a Range Rover in the sky.

'Shit,' said Emma.

They could see the pilot and a passenger looking down, the pilot pointing. Now the passenger was speaking with intense concentration into a microphone. The helicopter did what helicopters do, and hovered. To Sterling, Emma's wheelchair looked astonishingly red and bright in the grey air. There was no hint of a mistake. They were the subjects of the surveillance.

'I still need a loo,' said Emma.

'Follow me,' said Billy.

As they went into the shopping centre adjacent to the church grounds and out of sight, the chopper wheeled away. There are only two good things about this, thought Sterling. For now we can't be seen from the air, and there's no way a Range Rover can get in here. But then there's the bad thing: we're trapped.

'Can you manage,' he said at the door of the accessible toilet. 'or do you want me to....?'

Emma took in the facilities with an expert eye. 'I'll be OK.' She was quiet, chastened.

'I'll wait outside. Then we can decide what to do.'

Billy leaned on the wall. Even he seemed more subdued. His foot tapped restlessly. Surprisingly, he still had his rapper's cap, but he looked a sorry specimen. I probably look worse, thought Sterling. We can't go on like this. He could hear the faint noise of the helicopter. It would be hovering over the shopping centre, keeping up a regular communication with Marcus Whitman-Wood. Three days of flight, running across eastern England, and now run to earth in a shopping centre at the wrong end of Kent. He was cold and wet, and what was worse, hopeless. He felt the stares of passers-by in the passageway by the stairwell. He hunched himself up, as if that might make him a little less conspicuous. Come on, Emma. This waiting around is making things worse.

Sterling didn't at first notice the door of the lift opening next to the stairs, or the sturdily-built young man with thick golden-blonde highlighted hair with dark roots emerge with a trolley of cleaning materials, a mop sticking up like the aerial of a bumper car. But he soon saw Billy straighten up and dart forward.

'Yo, Jon-Jo, what are you doing here, man? Hardly seen you since school.'

He and the boy Jon-Jo did a kind of complicated greeting involving hand-clasps and fist-bumps.

'Got this job, cleaning, innit? What happened to you, bro?'

For Sterling the rapper talk and accompanying performances were beginning to grate, and they hadn't got time for exchanging pleasantries with acquaintances. As Emma emerged from the accessible facilities, Billy was explaining to Jon-Jo how he'd come to be soaking wet in St George's Shopping Centre, Gravesend.

'Billy, mate,' said Sterling. 'We haven't got time for this. We've got to get to the train station.'

'Hold on, bro. How are we going to get to the station without being spotted by that chopper?'

'We'll cross that bridge when we come to it. Come on.'

Jon-Jo looked down at Emma. 'That is one bright wheelchair, girl. They're gonna spot you wherever you come out of here.'

'Doh,' said Emma. Something about Billy and Jon-Jo irked her as well. The sneer on her features went far beyond the merely scornful that Sterling had become accustomed to. But Jon-Jo was like Billy. He seemed impervious to insult. Sterling watched him chew gum in a mouth overcrowded with teeth.

'No other bugger has turned up to work today. I reckon I might be able to help.'

He cocked his head towards a door next to the public lavatories. 'Staff only' said the notice.

'Are we allowed in here?' said Emma. It was a kind of locker room with lavatories and shower cubicles, and a large store cupboard for cleaning materials. An old, battered sports shoe with no laces sat in the middle of the floor. On a large laminated Health and Safety notice pinned on a bulletin board, all red bordering and small print, someone had scrawled FFS in large black letters. The area looked as though it might be the one place in the shopping centre that was never cleaned. The air was still, warm and damp and a fusty smell of old clothes was everywhere.

Sterling had spent long enough with Emma to recognise her sarcasm, but sarcasm didn't seem to be in Jon-Jo's range. 'Nobody's gonna know. Like I said, there's nobody home but me. You guys better have a quick shower. If you want to keep those clothes, we're not short of rubbish bags, and I've got just the gear you need. Got some new wheels for you, girl.' Jon-Jo was getting enthusiastic, as far as Sterling could tell. He had an odd thought about Horatius on the bridge of the Tiber again. Perhaps this was Herminius, only he'd turned up late and on the other side of the river. It was enough to make him superstitious.

When Emma heard the plan, she baulked. 'No way. No bloody way, Frank.'

'It'll only be for ten minutes. Then we're home free. We don't have any alternative. Come on, Emma. You've been up for anything so far.'

After Sterling and Billy had swiftly showered and changed, Billy and Jon-Jo were gathering materials to construct the other element to fulfil Jon-Jo's vision. They spoke in their strange Essex youth dialect as they argued excitedly. There was a profusion of 'bros' and 'mans'. It's English, thought Sterling, but weirdly distorted.

'Decision time, Emma. Whitman-Wood is going to be here in about 25 minutes. That helicopter will still be around somewhere.'

'You'll push it, Frank, and talk to me all the time, won't you?' Her eyes flicked over to the young men. 'Clowns,' she mouthed.

'Of course.' Sterling nodded to Billy and Jon-Jo. Jon-Jo went out of the staff room and returned with a large grey four-wheeled waste bin, Gravesham Borough Council stencilled in large letters on the side.

Jon-Jo flipped the lid, lined the inside with some old tarpaulin and turned the bin on its side. 'This one's not for food waste, just cardboard and plastic and stuff, so it shouldn't smell bad.'

'Ready?' said Frank.

'Bend your legs, not your back, Jon-Jo, you dolt,' said Emma. 'Haven't you done the lifting and manual handling training?'

Jon-Jo rolled his eyes at Sterling behind Emma's back. Perhaps he wasn't so impervious after all. They lifted her in and placed her on her side, using cardboard, plastic and Styrofoam for padding.

'OK, we're going to tip the bin upright, Emma. Hold tight.'

'Bloody be careful. Ow.'

When Sterling looked into the bin, scared, pleading eyes looked up at him. He'd seen the look before, on the first river crossing, from Bawdsey Quay to Felixstowe Ferry.

'Frank, you're not going to leave me, are you?'

'I told you. No. Remember, I haven't had my fee yet. Here, take the grip. I'm going to flip the lid over now. It's time to go.'

While he and Jon-Jo had turned Emma into refuse, Billy had converted her wheelchair into a cleaning trolley. Now a large grey piece of plastic sheeting had been draped and pinned over the seat and wheels, obscuring the bright red seat and wheels. Buckets and other cleaning paraphernalia had been added. A mop stuck up at the back to re-create the dodgem car effect.

'Cool, bro, innit,' said Billy. 'What's it look like?'

'A wheelchair draped with sheeting and festooned with cleaning stuff,' said Sterling gloomily. 'But it's all we've got, and it might look different at a distance and from the air.'

Billy didn't look crestfallen. In fact Sterling took heart from his irrepressibility. Billy stood on the bench attached to the wall and loomed over his handiwork. 'Looks exactly like a cleaning trolley to me.'

The three Gravesham Borough Council employees emerged from their morning break pushing a large commercial bin and a cleaning trolley of innovative design. All were in the royal blue livery of the council, with its title emblazoned in white on the backs of their sweatshirts. All wore baseball caps in the same royal blue with GBC lettering. Naturally, there were three of them for the two contraptions, in case one tripped and sprained an ankle, got lost, was called away or otherwise fell by the wayside. It was probably in the council and trade union negotiated conditions of service agreement too. Sterling and the rubbish bin were in the middle of the convoy. He looked forward and behind. This is plausible. This might work.

Jon-Jo led them to the service lift and they piled in. 'We go up to the first floor and then through. We cross the High Street, which is in the open, and then go into the other covered area on the other side. Come out of there, cross at the crossing and down the slope to the station. So the danger points are crossing the High Street and the bit going down to the trains.' He spoke with authority, as if he was a vital cog in a Kentish Underground Railroad.

On the first floor they rattled out of the lift. Sterling eased up the lid of the bin.

'Alright, you worthless piece of trash?' he said softly.

'Ha bloody ha,' said a small voice from the depths. 'Don't run over any bumps.'

'Let's rock and roll,' said Sterling to the convoy.

Chapter 23

Billy Joins the Gang

St. George's Shopping Centre was no Westfield. No fancy shops adorned its halls and corridors. This was Poundland country, with a clientèle to match. But it was cheerful, and Jon-Jo was lord of all he surveyed.

'Yo, Jon-Jo,' hailed a young woman pushing a buggy. 'How are you doing? Who are your mates?'

'They're new. I'm training them up.'

Sterling pulled his cap down as he pushed. Next to him, the work trousers Billy had changed into were not much less baggy than his jeans, and still too long. The convoy wended through the mall, taking its place in the usual weekday flow and contra-flow of mobility scooters, young parents with small children, pensioners and an assorted medley of non-working poor people. As Jon-Jo approached a multinational coffee shop he let Sterling catch up and come alongside.

'This is where we're out in the open. We go up the street a bit and then across into the mall on the other side.'

'OK,' said Sterling. 'If the helicopter appears, best not look up.'

He followed Jon-Jo and Emma's disguised wheelchair into the brick-paved pedestrianised thoroughfare.

He could hear the faint stuttering of the helicopter blades high in the air. Surely it couldn't come too close to a built-up area. There had to be regulations. There always were. Usually he railed against them. That's why he'd left the job. But sometimes they were handy. He kept his eyes focused on Jon-Jo's back as he pushed Emma and the bin along. Was that a dragon's tongue lapping up above Jon-Jo's shirt just to the left of the nape of his neck? The tattoo made him feel old. That, and the feeling of being horribly exposed, added to his unease. Then Jon-Jo was turning right and they were back in the canopied glass and steel shelter of another shopping mall – or perhaps it was just an extension. Smooth marble replaced the brick. No doubt Sterling would hear from Emma about the quality of the ride as they'd rattled and vibrated over the brickwork.

'It worked,' said Billy. 'Bro, it bloody worked.' His eyes were shining and he was doing a little jig next to the bin.

'Don't count your chickens,' said Sterling. 'Isn't there another open bit to the station?'

'Yeah, across the road and down the slope. Like I said. But if it worked once, I reckon it will work again,' said Jon-Jo. 'OK, here's the crossing.' He pressed the 'Wait' button. Sterling looked down at the pattern of studs for blind people and thought of Emma again. Even with the dropped kerb she was going to get a jolt.

'Ow,' said the voice.

On the way down the slope to the station, with the red railway sign looking so welcoming and the helicopter nowhere in the sky to be seen, Sterling felt an endorphin-rush of relief even as he prepared for Emma's next verbal assault.

In the small station, the ticket collector, a short dark man with a drooping black moustache and the look of a Mexican bandit, looked on by the ticket barriers as the Gravesham Borough Council employees tipped their bin gently to the side and opened the lid on the concourse. He seemed incurious, as if it happened every day. Sterling and Billy reached in to lift Emma out as Jon-Jo converted the cleaning trolley back into the gleaming red and chrome Ferrari of wheelchairs.

'Bloody hell,' said Emma. 'What a bleeding kerfuffle. Why did you go over so many bumps? I was shaking to bits in there.' She ran her fingers vigorously through her hair and dusted herself down. 'Get off. Stop pawing at me,' she said to Sterling and Billy, who were offering ineffectual assistance.

'Where to?' said Sterling at the ticket machine.

'Not Sandley,' said Emma. 'Too obvious. Minster?' Have you got anyone who could discreetly pick us up? An assistant. An associate in your busy operation. An apprentice.'

'Funny girl,' said Sterling, but he thought of Mike and Becky Strange, who ran his local and had helped him out of a number of fixes during one of his first cases. Either of them would be ideal – efficient, savvy, unobtrusive and, he knew for certain, good in an emergency – unsurprisingly since they were ex-members of an always unspecified branch of the security services. It really was time for reinforcements. 'I know just the people. Minster sounds good.' A village just above the marshes on the Isle of Thanet about five miles from Sandley was perfect. Quiet. Obscure.

'Where's my ticket, bro?' piped up Billy. 'I can still help. Look what I've done so far.'

What, exactly, thought Sterling. He met Emma's eyes. She shrugged and turned away.

Billy was already thanking Jon-Jo. Sterling caught the glint of a small silver-foil wrap. Jon-Jo was backing off, arms outstretched in a kind of supplication.

'No, mate, that's not why I did it.'

Emma wheeled up to him. 'Why then? Why did you do it?' she sneered.

He looked down at her and back through the concourse towards the town. A young man, in some way deranged, agitatedly examined something on a windowsill, scrabbling at it with his fingers. He'd go away, and then come back, obsessive intensity redoubled, muttering all the time. A crisp packet whirled and fluttered in an eddy of air above a drain. An elderly woman limped past the door two-handedly pushing a tattered tartan shopping trolley, cigarette hanging from her lip, her eyes slits as the smoke swirled up into her face.

'You're not the only one who's oppressed, girl.'

Emma stopped fidgeting with the hand rims. A boy cleaner with blond highlights and a crowded mouth of teeth was unexpectedly speaking a language she understood. Not an airhead. Not stupid.

He flipped the lid back over the bin and pulled it upright. 'This job's shit. The money's shit. I've got A levels but I can't afford to go to college. Politicians are shit. The rich screw us and laugh. I'd tear this whole society down with my bare hands. So it's about me sticking it to the Man. I try and do that every day. Stops me going mad with the injustice of it. Just one little gesture, every day. I reckon that's what I've been doing this last half hour. Thanks for the opportunity. I better get back. My supervisor will be sniffing around soon,

I reckon, wondering why I'm wheeling an empty bin from one end of the mall to the other.'

Emma put out her hand. The sneer was gone. Billy's face said, 'You've changed since you were at school.' 'Thank you,' she said. 'You really have helped. And you really are sticking it to the Man.'

The bandit let Emma, Sterling and Billy through the barrier just as a train down to the coast pulled in. Sterling and Billy lifted Emma and her wheelchair into the nearest carriage.

'Hey,' said another railway employee from the platform. 'You're meant to wait for a ramp.'

'You should have been quicker,' said Sterling. 'We're on now.' He settled Emma into a space reserved for wheelchairs. The carriage door glided shut. Through the windows into the station concourse and beyond he saw no black Range Rover screech to a halt. No large men in Blues Brothers suits and shades leapt over the barriers and on to the train in an attempt to bundle Emma off. No Marcus Whitman-Wood stood on the platform and watched the train ease eastwards, arms akimbo. There was no longer even a faint sound of helicopter rotors in the spring air.

Sterling thought back to the ferry crossing at the Deben He could see the mean face of the Salvation Army woman at the Citadel near Harwich bus station, and feel the panic as he and Emma waited for the bus to set off. He could hear the gunning of Whitman-Wood's engine at Basildon, his SUV immobilised by Simone and her rag-tag army. He could see the wide eyes of the little reader at Tilbury library as he willed her to stay silent when the hunter came calling. He could taste the filthy Thames water below the jetty at Tilbury dock.

But now, as the train gathered speed across to the Medway towns, there was no drama at all. He settled back in his seat and closed his eyes. This was much, much better.

—⟶⟵—

There was a cluster of pay-phone boxes outside Chatham station and twenty minutes until the Ramsgate train. Sterling knew the Stranges' phone number off by heart. For him, no number was more important.

'Becky?' he said when someone picked up.

'No. It's Mike, Frank.'

Sterling no longer wondered how Mike Strange knew it was him phoning, or questioned his taciturnity. 'Mike, I'm in a bit of a spot. You know how it is. Is there a chance you or Becky can pick me up at Minster station in about an hour? Me and a couple of companions. One of them in a wheelchair.'

'No problem. It'll be me, not Becky. I'll bring the van. Anything else I need to know?'

'Someone's after us, and they mean business. It's mostly been by car. A black Range Rover. Actually, more than one. But then there was a helicopter at Gravesend. We managed to lose that. Now we're at Chatham station.'

'OK. Is there anyone on your trail now?'

'I don't think so. We got to Gravesend station and I bought tickets from the machine rather than the ticket clerk. We put them through the barriers. The people after us know we're heading home, but not how. This route is better than going up to Ebbsfleet and down to Ashford and beyond. I thought Minster because it's pretty obscure.'

'Why are you using a payphone?'

'My mobile calls would be monitored. Anyway, my mobile got wet.' Sterling had not bothered to check the state of his phone after his ducking in the Thames but for the moment it hardly mattered.

'I need to summarise,' said Mike, 'to help me plan. You've been a bit garbled. You're at Chatham station. Someone's after you but you think you've thrown them off track for the moment. There are three of you, one in a wheelchair. If I'm looking out for anything, it should be for a black Range Rover, or more than one. And maybe a helicopter. You want me to pick you up at Minster station in about an hour.'

Even in Mike's flat, neutral tone, it sounded preposterous.

'Weird, eh, Mike?' said Sterling.

'See you in an hour. From what you've said, you've got a good chance of getting to Minster before your trail gets picked up again. The train will be pretty safe. You've got my mobile number.' The line went dead.

Sterling looked at the receiver. Typical Mike Strange. He didn't waste a word. He found out what he needed to know to do what he needed to do – no more and no less. Still, he was ultra-reliable. If it hadn't been for Mike, Sterling would probably have been rotting in some shallow grave in West Flanders.

Sterling went back into the station. He'd always liked this one when he used to travel up to and down from London on trips with his father. It was sculpted into the landscape just beyond the tunnel that separated Chatham town from Rochester. In the approach, row on row of terraced houses flowing up and down the steep streets were more redolent of gritty northern towns, or the Welsh valleys, than a scruffy corner of the Garden of

England. The Victorian brick arches behind the platforms provided perfect cover, and it was within one of them that Emma was complaining vigorously about her sandwich. Things are getting back to normal, thought Sterling.

'That's the worst bloody sandwich I've ever tasted. Where's the bin?' She threw the sandwich and missed. A tired, tiny sliver of tomato dropped from the bread onto the platform. 'Well, pick it all up, Billy, for God's sake. Make yourself useful, why don't you?'

The genial Billy did as he was told, grimacing at Sterling.

'All good for Minster, Frank?' said Emma.

'Yep. I'll tell you on the train.'

'So Billy boy,' said Emma, when he was back. 'What's the story? Why should we trust you?'

Billy leaned against an arch. 'Auntie Lily told me to keep an eye on things.' He shifted uneasily, as if admitting it was a kind of betrayal. 'And the best way to do that was to go and see my mate at the hospital. He's a porter on the night shift, and I told him to let me know if the bus driver had any visitors. I got a text this morning to say that these blokes had turned up – the ones who chucked us in the river. They didn't get to see the bus driver but my mate hung about to see what was happening.

'He heard what they were saying. They knew you hadn't got to Grays or Lakeside, so they were watching the railway stations and the bus routes They'd lost you completely, so A and E was like them clutching at straws. You were unlucky and lucky. Unlucky because one of the blokes saw the poster for the ferry from Tilbury to Gravesend. They knew you'd been on one river ferry. It was a fair bet that you'd go on another. They must have checked the buses too – one bus to get you into

Tilbury and another to get you down to the jetty. My mate phoned me when they went off. They want you badly, don't they?'

'Yeah, they do,' said Emma. 'A bloody ferry poster in the hospital. What are the chances? OK, I get the unlucky bit, Billy-boy. Now tell me how we've been lucky.'

'Easy. I checked with Lily that you were taking the ferry and got down to the terminal. If I hadn't blocked the entrance they'd have taken you back to wherever they had you in the first place. And I kept Frank afloat. He can hardly swim.'

'I was trying to hold on to the grip,' said Sterling. He was sensitive about his poor swimming.

Emma wasn't listening. 'So, Billy, our guardian angel, by appointment of Saint Lily of Socketts Heath, aka your great aunt.'

'Right,' said Billy. If there was any irony, he didn't notice it. His face broke into a wide smile. He liked the idea.

'Maybe you'd better stick around,' said Emma, as the train going down the coast to Ramsgate pulled in.

Chapter 24

Council of War

'So this bloke is kosher,' said Emma. Her recovery was complete. She'd refused to sit in the space allocated for bicycle, pushchairs and wheelchairs. 'I'm not being tethered next to that chemical toilet,' she had said. 'The smell's horrible. Why did the train designers think it's acceptable to put us with the bogs, bikes and pushchairs? I'm a citizen, not an inconvenience to be shoved to one side.'

'Tethered. That's a bit of an exaggeration,' said Sterling. He thought it was possible to be a citizen and an inconvenience, but knew better than to say so. He and Billy had manoeuvred her into one of the table seats. The wheelchair stood behind them by the doors.

'You get what I mean. You should do anyway, after all this time.'

'Mike Strange, and also his wife Becky,' said Sterling. 'Both very kosher. Ex-security services, but don't ask me what branch. I think Mike was invalided out, but I don't know that either. They run my local and do an excellent job. They also helped me out in another case. I trust them absolutely. You'll see what I mean when Mike meets us at Minster. We can go back to the pub, regroup and have a powwow. Decide what to do next.'

'Sounds like a plan. Obviously I've got to get home, but we need time and space to work out how. You know, Frank, crossing your path hasn't been a complete disaster.'

'Blimey,' said Sterling. 'Steady on.'

Emma leaned back and closed her eyes. Sterling slumped back in his own seat and looked at the East Kent landscape. Should they not have been thrilled? Triumphant about having escaped? At least excited. But after Tilbury and Gravesend, and the dramas of the day before, all he felt was a kind of exhausted apathy. It's because it's not over, thought Sterling. It's just the end of the beginning. Only Billy's fidgeting carried on as before – his foot tapping restlessly, his eyes flicking to points in the landscape beyond the train as he too stared from the window.

Yes, thought Sterling. She's right. They needed time and space. They'd have Mike take them to the pub. That was safest for the moment. Whitman-Wood could not know of Sterling's connections in Sandley, and nowhere could be more secure than an establishment run by ex-spooks. He needed to rest. They'd do some more thinking down the line.

The Medway towns had given way to the fruit trees, row on manicured row, between Rainham and Faversham. At Sittingbourne station, the old timber shed next to the line looked more decrepit than ever, with gaps in the roof where corrugated iron sheets had dropped away. Further on, Sterling looked over a huge white stain of mobile homes at Seasalter across the Swale to the Isle of Sheppey. Behind the brightly painted beach huts on the shore, an elderly man was wrestling a red Calor Gas canister into position.

Further on still, Sterling gazed out at the twin towers of the ruined church at Reculver, remembering his father's bright eyes and restless hands as he talked about the Roman conquest and the later defences of the Saxon Shore. A young mother and her two children, a boy and a girl, were trying to fly a kite. It jerked and fluttered, and then dived back into the grass. Then the train was sweeping and rattling down across the marshy channels and dykes of the Wantsum stream, into the Isle of Thanet. He and his father had done this journey many times during a spell in Ramsgate. When the first bungalows replaced the water meadows, and country gave way to town, he knew he was close to home.

Half an hour later, after an edgy wait on the draughty Ramsgate platform, the fugitives got off their third train at the next stop, Minster.

Mike Strange stood on the other platform, neat in his work boots, plain dark shirt and anorak, a nondescript Kent everyman – just the innocuous look he intended. Emma saw the pedestrian bridge, complete with steep stairs and no obvious concessions for wheelchair users.

'How the f….' she began.

Mike pointed to the other end of the platform and a general crossing over the tracks. He'd been planning ahead. By the van, Sterling did the introductions.

Mike looked directly at Emma. 'I've checked the area. It's clear. There's no one after you. So we can be flexible. Do you want to go in the front or the back?'

Emma looked at Sterling. This is good, said her face. 'How long will we be in the van, Mike?'

'About 20 minutes.'

'OK, I don't mind going in the back.'

'I'll tether you up,' said Sterling, recoiling in mock horror at the V-sign and scowl Emma directed at him.

The three of them, Sterling, Emma and Billy had gone like contraband from the yard behind the high walls of the pub through the back door and into the snug. Becky had lit a fire.

'You can have a drink, freshen up and decide what to do next,' said Mike.

Sterling was eavesdropping on Emma's softly spoken side conversation with Becky. 'It's not about gender roles,' said Becky. 'We share everything right down the middle. He collected you and is sitting with you because that's just how the chips fell. I was out when Frank called. It could just have easily been me collecting you in the van. Anyway, I lay and light a far superior fire.'

Sterling warmed his hands. There was that feminine solidarity again. It made him feel a little uneasy and excluded. It's not a bad thing, he thought. It's just something I'm not part of. He tried to focus on what to do next. The feeling that they were not finished yet swelled up more powerfully than ever. The whole business was far from over. Mike sat to one side, still and silent, his arms folded. The pub was in the lull between the lunch crowd and early evening drinkers. Becky kept things ticking over. Mike will bring me up to speed later, she'd said. Billy's foot tapped. The boy needs action, thought Sterling. He just can't sit still.

'We need to get cracking,' said Emma. 'The fire, the beer, the sandwiches – there'll be a tipping point and we'll get so comfortable we'll lose our momentum for the rest of the day.'

'Hold on,' said Sterling. 'Technically, my work is done here. All I've got to do is reunite you with your father.

That was my brief. You're in Sandley. He's probably in Hamworth. He can come and get you. I can go home and put my feet up.'

'Don't be an arsehole, Frank. Not after all we've been through together.'

Billy's eyes glinted and the corners of his mouth turned up a fraction. 'Yeah, bro, don't be an arsehole.' There was more to Billy than first met the eye.

Mike Strange just sat. Sterling guessed that he was intrigued, but there'd never be any sign. Then he stirred. 'If you explain it all to me and Becky, we can ask you questions and between us that might fill in the gaps. Then it will be glaringly obvious what you have to do next, and then we can work out the hows, whys, whens and wherefores.'

'Right,' said Becky half an hour later. 'These are the bare bones.' She didn't beat about the bush. 'Your grandmother was murdered a few months ago. Her study was trashed but there was no sign of an actual break in, which suggests she let her killer in. You were doing a project together based on her war experiences. But she was also doing a side project, as a result of something that happened. Something that really upset her and made her angry. You found the word 'Fang' amongst her papers. She had a friend in the war called Alan Whitman-Wood. You thought he might know something. The police weren't really paying you much attention, so at his invitation you went down last Tuesday to Bawdsey Manor in Suffolk, where he's based, to ask him. At that stage you'd no idea that he'd be anything but accommodating, but after a while you realised that he and his son and grandson were kind of keeping you locked away.'

'Kind of...! They *did* keep me locked away! I was lucky to get down the drive and out, and lucky that Frank was mooching around on the quay.'

'I don't mooch,' said Sterling.

'Snoop then.'

'I don't do that either.'

'If you can let Becky finish,' said Mike, 'you'll be closer to deciding what to do next.'

Becky was smiling. 'So then you started this journey out of Suffolk, through Essex and back down here. Ferries, buses, trains.'

'Hitchhiking, library van, rubbish bin,' said Emma.

'Well, I'm summarising here,' said Becky. She was a deft, efficient, economical woman. Sterling had never seen her impatient. But maybe there was just a hint here. 'You had time for a bit of research in Tilbury library – before the library van took you to the ferry....' She's taking the mickey out of Emma, thought Sterling. He smirked to himself. 'The Cauville Raid in 1943, during which your grandfather died, and CommuniCo's public flotation in 2013 – this Wednesday you say, Frank.'

He started. 'Yep. 1.30 GMT. We think all this is something to do with the flotation.'

Mike leaned forward, his hands clasped over his knees. He'd said nothing for half an hour. 'I'm sure you're right. This is all about the flotation. That's the deadline. And it has all the hallmarks of desperation. Keeping Emma at Bawdsey. Searching for her when she escaped. Not searching. Hunting. The Range Rovers. The team of men. The helicopter. Especially the helicopter. And it's all telling us where the answer is.'

Becky blinked. Sterling knew why. What Mike had said constituted, for him, a speech.

'Someone tell me what a flotation is,' said Emma, 'and why it's important.'

'CommuniCo is a private company,' said Mike. 'Probably wholly owned by the Whitman-Woods. Without a stock market flotation, when investors can buy publicly traded shares, it could never make the next leap. If a flotation goes well and reaches bid price, it makes the owners a fortune, and they can still retain control if they keep 51 per cent of the stock. If it goes badly, it doesn't raise enough capital for expansion, the share price stays low and the owners lose control.'

'OK,' said Emma. 'Now tell me what could make things go wrong for CommuniCo on Wednesday.'

'Bad news, girl,' said Sterling. 'A hole in the accounts. Financial fiddling.'

'Yes, that. Or a company hopelessly overvalued,' said Mike. 'Would you buy a jumper from a shop if you could get it cheaper down the street? A company not making profits, or making fewer profits than can go to share-holders in dividends. A company with poor products.'

'But none of that is CommuniCo,' said Emma. 'Is it?'

'I don't think so,' said Mike. 'But there are other things. Bad news can be about reputation. To be honest, reputation by itself isn't necessarily a problem. If a company makes profits for investors, they're not always that fussy about dodgy dealings or bad news. But reputation can give a company a bad name, so investors go elsewhere, or suppliers and contractors don't want to do business. And it costs money, lots of it, to fight reputational slurs. Even rumours can be damaging.'

'I get it. I think. How do you know all this, Mike?' said Emma.

'He knows everything,' said Sterling.

'Moving on,' said Mike. When he got going nothing would deflect him. 'You got the part about CommuniCo and the flotation right. I think you're right about the other bit of it. It's plausible that your grandmother found out something and that, although they silenced her, the killers didn't find what it was that triggered everything off. It's still there in the house. The Whitman-Wood strategy is to keep you quiet, and keep you from finding the trigger before Wednesday. After that, it hardly matters. If you hadn't gone to Bawdsey, this chain of events wouldn't have happened.'

Emma rubbed her hands together. 'That was really helpful. Thank you very much, Mike and Becky. Obviously, there's only one thing for it.'

Sterling sighed. Here we go again. They'd done the whys and whats and wherefores. Now it was about how. Specifically, how they were going to get into Hamworth Place and do a search, because it went without saying that Marcus Whitman-Wood and his team, having failed to stop Emma en route, would be staking out the final destination. The other problem loomed for Sterling as he stared into the flames of Becky's fire. Even if they got into the house, Emma had already searched through her grandmother's papers. The police had also been in, including the forensics people, and nothing to do with Alan Whitman-Wood or his company had been found. Why would it be different this time round?

Chapter 25

The Expeditionary Force

Billy shifted in his chair. He homed in on exactly what was troubling Sterling. 'When your gran was done in, her study was turned over, yeah?'

'Very tactfully put, Billy,' said Emma. 'Thanks for that.'

'And nothing was missing.' When Billy has the bit between his teeth, thought Sterling, he gets like that. It was helpful. 'And then the police came. And they found nothing.'

'Correct.'

'But because of everything that's happened, you still reckon there's something there.'

Emma sighed. 'Billy, you prat, where is this going? Because I don't think we've got time for your cogitations.'

'Did she have an escritoire, your granny?'

'A what?'

'An escritoire. A secretaire.' Billy put his palms out in a beckoning gesture. 'Come on, girl. You know, a writing desk.'

'She had the big desk in her study. That was wrecked.'

'I'm thinking of something smaller – maybe somewhere else in the house.'

Emma's frown disappeared. Her eyes lost their glazed look. 'There was a little writing desk in her bedroom. Hardly a desk. Just a kind of small ancient ornamental contraption with a matching chair. The kind of thing you write 'thank you' notes at.'

'It's there,' said Billy. 'What we're looking for. There'll be a secret compartment. They all have them. The bad guys and the fuzz have eliminated all the other places. They've done our job for us.'

'How come you know all these fancy words, Billy? And all about secret compartments and the like?'

The tattoo of Billy's foot became louder and more rapid, like a rabbit thumping in the face of danger. He stared out of the window of the snug into the street. 'I took some wrong turns. Got in with some people who did stuff to order for a dodgy antiques dealer. The desks were the first thing we went for. I spent some time in Chelmsford nick. Auntie Lily stopped it.' He tailed off.

'Bloody hell,' said Emma. She shook her head. 'Still. Handy. And all in all you've done OK so far, Billy.' Praise from Emma was as rare as rain in the Gobi. In Billy, it looked as though she might have made a friend for life.

'So,' said Sterling. 'There's one promising place to look. But aren't we getting ahead of ourselves? How are we going to get into your house in the first place if Marcus Whitman-Wood and his blokes are watching it?'

'We wait till dark, and we go around the back. It's Monday. There'll be no one in. Dad and his scabby girlfriend will be at the Bridge Club. There's a gate in the wall with keypad entry and an alarm. We get in through there, up the back garden and in through the back door. The password on the kitchen key pad disables the house alarm and the security lights. Easy.'

'And who's going on this little expedition?'

'Me,' said Emma. 'Obviously. This is my gig and my house. Billy. Obviously. Mike, you look handy in a ruck. Fancy it?'

'Of course,' said Mike. 'Or Becky, who is equally competent, if I lose the toss and have to mind the pub.'

'I reckon three will be enough. Looks like you've got the night off, Frank.'

Sterling felt his stomach lurch, just as it had on Tilbury Dock. This was a brutal way to be made redundant. Being left out is the worst feeling, his father used to say. If you're left out; if a girlfriend walks out; if you're not picked for the team – pretend you don't care. Better yet, don't care. 'OK,' he said. 'You've got it covered. I'll bring your dad up to speed. Prepare and present my bill. Get a proper meal down me in here. And most important, have another pint.'

'Don't be a prat, Frank. You're not getting off the hook that easily. Who's going to help me out of the van? Who's going to push me up the garden path?'

'Damn,' said Sterling.

'And no contact with Dad until we're back here, Frank. Marcus Whitman-Wood will be keeping tabs on him, and we need things to be uncomplicated while we do the search. Dad's waited three days. He can wait a bit longer.'

Having done the organising, she winced. 'Spasming. It's all the excitement.' She turned to Mike. I need some kind of frame – somewhere I can stand up for a while. And the loo. This cider's gone right through me.'

Becky had come over. 'There's the weights room upstairs. We've got some bars. We could improvise something. And there's a loo next door. It's all better than being in the public area, but there's the stairs.'

Sterling and Emma looked at each other. 'LNB,' they chorused.

'I should charge your dad extra for the care-giving,' said Sterling.

'Cheeky, grasping bastard.'

'I mean it.'

'You're like a married couple,' said Becky. 'All this bickering.'

In the weights room, after Sterling had carried Emma up the stairs and helped her in the lavatory in the Stranges' private quarters on the first floor, Mike assembled a bar that Emma hooked her arms over and Sterling sat on a rowing machine to wait.

'This is so much better, Frank. It's not just the practicalities. It's all the planning and thinking, and never knowing how things are going to pan out.'

'Yeah, I get it. And when people are hostile, it's even more tiring. You'd better have your massage after this. Who knows what's going to be happening later. And maybe a lie-down to recharge your batteries. I'll ask Becky if she's got a spare room.'

Half an hour later Sterling rejoined Billy in the snug. Billy was drinking a bright coloured drink that Sterling didn't recognise. Becky brought over another pint.

'This is definitely going on my expenses,' said Sterling.

At quarter to six, Angela came in. 'Over here, Angie,' called Sterling. 'The usual for the librarian, Becky. It can go on my tab.'

'Return of the wanderer, Frank. No word for three days. No help with the crossword. I feel neglect. And in the meantime you seem to have become an employee of Gravesham Borough Council.'

Sterling looked down at his sweatshirt, rueful. 'Sorry, Angie. You have no idea how mad it's been. And this is just a bit of a break. We're hiding up here before the next bit. I've found the girl. She's upstairs, having a rest.'

'I saw the wheelchair by the bar. Who's this?' Billy was sipping his drink and struggled with eye contact. Angela could project a regal air. 'This is Billy. He helped fish me out of the Thames and got us on a train down here. He and his aunt have made themselves very helpful.'

Billy squirmed. He might not have been used to praise. He and Angela did the same complicated fist and hand bumps that he'd done with Jon-Jo. She might be a librarian in a country town, thought Sterling, but there was something metropolitan about her still. She'd promised him her story once – the real story with all the details – when this was over….

'The next bit,' said Angela. 'Intriguing. You've found the girl. You've brought her back. Surely your work is done.'

'I thought that. But it's turned out to be a little more complicated.' Sterling sipped his drink and looked at his watch.

A voice called down from the first floor. 'Frank, I need a lift here. Frank, get your arse from that chair in front of the fire and get up here.'

Angie looked at Sterling. She took a sip of her own drink. 'Well, she's certainly got you dancing to her tune,' she said softly.

'Don't be so sure.'

He fetched Emma from the top of the stairs, to where she'd pulled herself from the spare room, and put her in the wheelchair.

'Christ, I'm bloody parched,' she said as she wheeled around the corner into the snug. She pulled to an abrupt halt. 'Oh. Company. Who are you?'

'Well, I come in here most weekday nights to have a drink with Frank and we do the *Times* crossword together,' said Angela. 'I'm thinking that it's me who should be asking that question.'

Sterling thought back to the Landguard Fort on the edge of Felixstowe, and how Emma had been with Esther that lifetime ago, and earlier on in the afternoon with Becky, and all the other instances. That effortless female solidarity. There was none of that here. 'Angela,' he said, giving her precedence as the older woman and longer-standing friend, 'this is Emma. Emma, Angela.' The women nodded, wary.

'That drink…' said Emma.

'The bar's that way,' said Sterling.

'I'll get it,' said Billy. Even Billy got an inkling of the way the wind was blowing.

Angela got out the crossword and hummed a dancing tune. Emma's face was thunderous. Sterling rubbed his back. I don't need this, he thought.

The pub began to fill up with early evening drinkers. Mike and Becky managed it all in their courteous, efficient way. Sterling could smell the aroma of cooking. The chef had started up again. He wondered if they'd better eat before their sortie.

Mike approached the silent group, the female half surly. 'I won the toss, so it's me going tonight.' He turned to Sterling and Billy. 'I'm just wondering if you need to be advertising Gravesham Borough Council on this expedition.' He offered a couple of dark jackets.

'Good idea,' said Sterling. 'Quarter to eight. Time to get cracking. See you later, Angie.'

'Hopefully,' she said. 'A full update wouldn't come amiss, either.'

'You shall have it.' Sterling ignored the way Emma spurned eye contact and moved urgently away.

At the van in the back yard, Emma wheeled around to face Sterling. There were little red spots on her cheeks. Sometimes Emma was furious, with language to match, and sometimes it was more a manufactured anger, in the way of a performance. Sterling knew which version this was. 'You don't have to come, Mr PI. There are enough of us. Billy knows where to look. Mike can deal with any rough stuff, if it comes to it. I know the passwords. We've got the full skills set, as they say. Why don't you go back in, put your feet up and do the crossword – and tell her all my confidential business?'

'Now who's being an arse?' said Sterling. 'Without me, you'd still be in Bawdsey Manor. Without me, you'd be pretty much nowhere. You want it both ways, Emma. You want to be independent and disabled, and you want everyone at your beck and call. To help you, other people than me have to know your business. You can't pick and choose which ones. You're lucky that all my friends are trustworthy. So let's just grow up a bit and get on with it.'

Mike and Billy stood to one side. Billy hopped from one leg to the other. In the face of the harsh words, he hunched up as small as possible.

Emma's fingers gripped the hand rims. She moved the wheelchair left and right in little darting movements. She bit her lip. 'Alright,' she said finally. Credit to you, thought Sterling. You're not a sulker.

'So,' called Mike from the front of the van, with Billy tapping away in the seat next to him. Hamworth Place. Directions?'

In the back, Sterling reached out and squeezed Emma's hand. She squeezed back. 'I'm not an arse, Frank. You bastard,' she whispered.

In the gloom, he smiled.

Chapter 26

'Trouble…Big Trouble'

The road behind Hamworth Place was marked as 'unadopted', which was why the van lurched and bumped over poorly distributed gravel and around the deeper potholes. Poor orphaned road, thought Sterling, in his time-honoured irrelevant way. Mike did a slow and unobtrusive pass up and down to check that there were no watchers and drew up at the door built into the two-metre high brick wall. It was a cloudy, misty evening and the two bungalows opposite were spaced apart with long front gardens. Luck was on the side of the expeditionary force. In most other circumstances the white van would only have been marginally more conspicuous if it had had 'Housebreakers Ltd.' stencilled on the side. As it was, it merged to a small degree into the misty darkness. At the door, Billy was fidgeting again.

'What, Billy?' said Emma. She was getting adept at reading the signs.

'It's legal, right? What we're doing.'

'This is my home, Billy. This is where I live. I know the passwords to the lights and the alarms. Look.' She pointed to a brick in the wall and Sterling retrieved a key. Then she swiftly pressed a combination of numbers on the key-pad attached to the door and bumped her wheelchair firmly against the glossy dark wood. The door opened a crack. 'I hereby invite all three of you into my garden and my residence. Good enough for you, Billy-boy?'

Billy did a quick smile that didn't extend to his eyes. 'I'd still prefer for my probation officer not to know. Just in case. She's quick to jump to conclusions. And I can't go back. It would finish me.'

'God, Billy, we keep finding things out about you,' said Emma. 'Well, this bit's fine, I promise.'

Mike pushed the door further open and turned back to the others. 'Right. We could do with some ground rules. No arguing. Unity of purpose – we know why we're here and what we're after. When we're finished we move out in the same careful way. I think we've got the discord out of the way. Agreed, everyone?'

Even in the darkness, Sterling could sense that the back garden was as immaculate as the front had been. The door in the wall swung smoothly and fitted snugly as it closed. Emma pointed to a time delay light switch on the inside wall next to the door. 'Don't press that. I've disabled the floodlights.'

An asphalt path wider than her wheelchair snaked up to the back door of the house. Sterling unlocked it and they were in.

'Let me turn off the alarm,' said Emma. 'OK,' she said. 'We're good.'

Three men stood and a girl in a wheelchair sat in the dark kitchen getting their eyes accustomed to the darkness.

Mike turned on a small pencil torch and pointed the sharp beam at the floor.

'This feels like breaking in,' whispered Billy.

'Shut up, Billy,' said Emma.

'Where's your grandmother's bedroom, Emma? Isn't it right at the top of the stairs and then right again?' Sterling needed to keep things on track.

'You've been here, Frank.'

'Yes. Of course. Standard practice with a MISPER. I think you should wait downstairs. I expect that stairlift is noisy. Billy and Mike can check the writing desk.'

Billy had changed. Before, he moved in a kind of pimp roll, with his skew-whiff rapper cap and half-mast baggies. In the house, he was focused and feline. He padded up the wide staircase two steps at a time and disappeared around the corner.

Mike began a slower trudge. He turned back to Sterling and Emma at the back of the stairs. 'Yup,' he said. 'The boy's done this kind of thing before.'

In the dark hallway, Sterling and Emma waited. Emma's hands fidgeted at the hand rims and her chair jerked back and forth. Sterling wondered what they'd do if Billy was wrong. He could hear stealthy, scuffling sounds from upstairs. A minute elapsed. Two minutes. From somewhere in the hall, Sterling could not remember where, a clock ticked. The house had a complex smell of polish, grease, perhaps from the stairlift, and the aftermath of cooking – garlic and possibly beef. More minutes ticked down.

'What's he doing? It's only a bleeding escritoire, not the Crown Jewels.'

'You didn't even know it was an escritoire,' whispered Sterling.

'Well, I know now. Idiot.'

More minutes passed. 'We're buggered,' said Emma. 'If they haven't found anything, I can't face going back into Grandma's study.'

A shadow appeared at the top of the stairs. Sterling caught the gleam of a large envelope. Billy slipped down the stairs and put it with a flourish and even a slight bow into Emma's hands.

'Brilliant, Billy. I knew you'd find it.'

Sterling shook his head in the dark.

'Cool, eh?' said Billy.

Mike appeared at Sterling's side. 'Now we've got what we came for, we should get out of here as quickly as we can. There's a Range Rover out front, just beyond the gates.'

'No,' said Sterling. 'I've been thinking. What time does your dad come home, Emma?'

'What time is it now?'

'9.30,' said Mike.

'He won't be long. He doesn't do late nights. He'll have dropped off the Scab. Monday's his night off.'

'We can wait in the kitchen in the dark. We can check the envelope with your torch, Mike. The point is, Marcus Whitman-Wood and his goons aren't waiting for your dad. They're waiting for you, Emma. If he comes in and turns the lights on, they're not going to know we're already here. This way, he'll also know that you're safe and sound.'

'That will work,' said Mike.

In the kitchen, the garlic and meat smell was stronger. Sterling's stomach let out a low rumble. He felt for a chair in the dark. He could see vague outlines – a salt cellar and a pepper grinder on the table, a vase of dried flowers. Emma went to a place at the specially adapted kitchen bar that was clearly hers.

'Where's your torch, Mike?' she said.

She eased back the flap of the envelope. There was tension in that kitchen, and an acute sense of anticipation.

Emma laid out a sheet of paper and two more sealed envelopes onto the food surface. The beam of the torch darted over the sheet. 'It's a letter,' she said. 'In German. Mike? Frank?'

'Sorry,' said Mike, 'Dutch, French and Italian are my three.'

'My languages are crap,' said Sterling. 'Just a bit of pidgin French.'

'Billy?'

'I only got Sarf Essex, girl.'

'Angela has German.' Sterling thought of her first class double honours in German and Modern History. He couldn't see Emma's face in the dark, but she said nothing.

'One of the envelopes is addressed to Dad. We'd better wait till he comes.'

The eyes of the whole expeditionary force looked towards the hallway as its ears heard the low purr of a car engine.

'What's that whirring noise?' said Billy.

'The electric gates,' said Emma. 'It's Dad. Good timing for once.'

Sterling leaned over to Mike. 'This is going swimmingly,' he whispered. 'Everything's falling into place.' He watched as Mike tapped the wooden worktop, and found himself automatically doing the same.

It made no difference. The magic was too weak. There were dull sounds, the crunching of gravel and an alarmed shout, suddenly cut off. Sterling and Mike leapt through the hallway to the front door to find it deadlocked. In unison they powered up the stairs three at a time. Through a sliver of the heavy curtain pulled over the large arched window on the landing opposite the top of the staircase, they peered out over the driveway just as a lustrous white half-moon broke from cover and bathed it in a ghostly light.

Sterling recognised Dracula being frogmarched by the Blues Brothers through the rapidly narrowing gap in the electric gates. The snatch had been perfectly timed. The procession, back to the black Range Rover fifty metres away down the road, had a kind of religious look to it, but conducted at a more rapid pace. Marcus Whitman-Wood himself was in the lead, looking for all the world like the priest in charge. Sterling watched his paymaster, the supplier of his beer money, this month's guarantor of his council tax and mortgage, his benefactor at the Co-op and the underwriter of his purchases of tired sandwiches from Spar, recede into the distance.

'Even if we'd got through the front door, the electric gates would have closed. We'd still have been too late,' said Mike. 'CommuniCo has taken out some insurance. What now, Frank?' In matters of tactics, Mike took the lead. Strategy he left to Sterling.

'We'll tell Emma first. But there's no point staying here. They'll still be watching the place, and now that Jameson's gone we won't be able to switch on the lights. It's best for the moment that we stay under the radar.'

'What's going on?' said Emma, back in the kitchen.

Mike looked at Sterling. 'They've taken your father. They must have been waiting, maybe for you, but took him when he came in. It's insurance, Emma,' said Sterling, 'in case we find something to damage them. To prevent anything happening before the flotation. They're pulling out all the stops. There's no doubt about that.'

Sterling had listened to Emma run down her father from Felixstowe Ferry to the Cinque Ports Arms pub. On buses, on trains, in cafes, he'd seen her lip curl when she talked about him and heard the relentless stories criticising his ways. He found it hard to fathom what irritated her so much about him. 'Stupid bugger,' she said, but he caught the quaver in her voice.

Sterling was musing. 'They don't know that we know they've got him. They don't know that we're in the house. They don't know that we've found something. They don't even know where we are and how to contact us. So we should regroup at the pub, see what we've got and take it from there. In the end, this could be when we have to get the police in.'

'No. Not yet,' said Emma. 'These bastards aren't playing by the rules. Why should we?'

'What about your father, Emma?

'He'll be alright. Mike said so.'

'We can't be certain. I still think we should bring in the police.'

'No. We look at the stuff, and then we can decide. Your Angela, Frank. Will she still be in the pub?'

'She isn't "my" Angela,' said Sterling. 'But if she isn't at the pub, we can get her back. Let's go. You'd better do the honours with the security codes, Emma.'

—m—

Angela had been persuaded back to the snug. It didn't take much. She'd learnt that being associated with Frank Sterling meant excitement and variety. She looked through the letter in German. 'This'll take me about half an hour,' she said.

'Get to it, girl,' said Sterling.

The rest of them looked again at the other sealed envelopes, the one addressed to Emma's father, and the other to the chairman of the London Stock Exchange.

'The German letter is the key,' said Mike, 'the one that's already open. Let's get the translation from Angela first, and then we can decide whether or not we're justified in opening the others. And it might get confusing if we don't do things in order.'

'Well, I need the loo anyway,' said Emma. 'Frank, can you....?'

Angela was ready as promised half an hour later. There was a hint of apology in her manner, as if she was sorry to be the first to be in the picture. She looked around the table and set out the translation. 'You'll find this interesting, to say the least. It might be a little rough, but I'm sure I've got the gist.'

Four heads craned over Angela's neat handwriting.

'Dear Mrs Jameson,

My name is Heinz Becker. You don't know me and will never have heard of me, but we are linked together by something that happened almost 70 years ago. Now that I am dying, I must finally put my affairs in order, and more importantly clear my conscience by addressing the biggest source of shame in all my long life.

I asked my granddaughter, a historian here in Dusseldorf, to try and find you and your family. I am glad that her research has given me a chance to contact you, tell you my story and ask for your forgiveness.

I was a captain in military intelligence within the Wehrmacht during the war. It was a rough time of course. I had an early tour of the Eastern Front and was one of the few Germans who escaped from that relatively unscathed. But in 1943 I was seconded to a group guarding a radar station at Cauville in Normandy, with a specific task: to help set a trap.

You will know something of what happened. After the war, there was a lot of talk, on both sides, about the tricks and deceits each got up to. You had your Operation Mincemeat. We had Operation Capture. At the time the Cauville Raid must have been considered a success by you British. But even at the time there should have been doubts. The equipment you captured was out of date. Your paratroopers got in and out with perhaps a surprising lack of resistance. But of course the great advantage to us and disadvantage to you was that we captured your flight lieutenant husband. And that was our plan.

We had a spy in your radar organisation, right from 1936. Your counter-intelligence people probably knew this eventually. Our spy, in Bawdsey Manor, worked with us to set things up. It was he who sent out the photo-reconnaissance planes to Cauville and spotted its 'weaknesses'. He suggested the raid to capture vital equipment. Above all, he engineered your husband's involvement. No one else would do. And Germany had the chance to get one of your best radar scientists. How did we know, in Cauville, which of the raiding party to capture? The answer was in the uniforms. There was only to be one man in the grey of the Royal Air Force and not the camouflage gear of the army – your husband. He was the one we had to target. Our man at Bawdsey arranged this.

Our plan succeeded. You know that because your husband never came home. Even though at first he never went beyond name, rank and serial number I could tell that he was a fine man – a brave man. While he was my prisoner we were almost friends.

Of course, it was war. I had no guilt and still have no guilt about being part of such a successful deception.

No, the guilt came later, when the Gestapo arrived. Then the interrogation changed. Then the Geneva Convention fell by the wayside, and we went beyond anything civilised. Your husband told us many things. No one defies torture. In his case, he did not survive, and it was a terrible death.

I have borne this burden for 70 years. It would be easy to say that if I had resisted the Gestapo I would have gone the same way as your husband – that I had no choice but to do as I did. Perhaps it's true. But after all these years the guilt and betrayal linger on. I can no longer be silent. I ask you to forgive me.

Heinz Becker'

Billy whistled. Mike shook his head. Emma was staring hard at the table. Sterling had come to know her well. She wasn't daydreaming. Her thinking had gone into overdrive.

'Let's move on,' said Sterling. 'We're walking in your grandmother's footsteps, Emma. I'm sure, in the circumstances, that your father is not going to fuss about us reading her letter to him.'

She slit open the letter and placed it over Angela's translation, and they all started reading again.

'My dear Nicholas,

It's easier to write than face you, and it helps me to order my thoughts. There were times when I didn't think that I'd ever need to rake over things that are long gone, and even now there are some things that I will never be able to tell you. We have faced enough challenges in our lives for me to think that the distant past could look after itself, and secrets could be buried forever. Then I received a letter from Germany, from a captain in the Wehrmacht. He had his own demons to face in relation to our family, but hearing from him triggered demons of my own, and I decided that you had to know the truth about a key part of your early life.

Many things you do know. I was twenty-one when the war broke out in 1939, one of the few women in this country to get a degree – in my case, in Modern Languages from King's in London. You know that I was destined for Bletchley and code breaking until the radar people requested my services at Bawdsey Manor in Suffolk. There I met my husband, Richard. Of course, I was young and naïve, but he was a wonderful, talented man, and I knew early on that he was the one for me.

Initially at Bawdsey I was a radar operator, and then I worked in the superintendent's office, where my German was even more useful. Richard was a physicist in the RAF with the rank of flight lieutenant, and no one did more to develop and refine British radar science in the early years. It was wartime, but we married. Not long afterwards, I was pregnant with you. By then, I was too valuable to Bawdsey to be able to give up my work, so when you came along in January 1943, I had to take an agonising decision. None of your grandparents were alive by then, so I sent you out temporarily to foster parents. You were three months old when they arrived in Ipswich and took you back home to Deal. All this you know.

My work at Bawdsey went on, and so did Richard's. Then came the Cauville Raid in June 1943. He was the obvious candidate amongst the scientists to go, and as you know, he never returned.

Dark times. And when this year I received Captain Becker's letter, those dark times returned, together with things I never knew before. To learn that my husband was tortured and betrayed, and died in awful circumstances, was bad enough. But then to realise that a German spy had planned and engineered it, and that I immediately knew the traitor, was even worse. Reading Captain Becker's letter, everything clicked, even the reasons for my misgivings at the time, and even the proof I realised I already had.

There was another scientist at Bawdsey, based in the same superintendent's office as me. He was Richard's close friend, someone who was always there, always with us. Someone who always wanted me. Someone who pestered me when Richard wasn't around – Alan Whitman-Wood. It all makes sense over this long corridor of time. He was the driving force behind getting agreement for the raid. He encouraged Richard to volunteer, saying that he was the only one with the technical expertise and parachute training to join the expedition. He worked with him on the photo-reconnaissance pictures. He did all the organising for the raid. Above all, he was the one who ensured that Richard would jump from the plane in his RAF uniform. I still have all Richard's letters to me from 1942 till his death two years later. In his last one, he told me how Whitman-Wood had 'forgotten' to get him his army uniform.

Of course, as Herr Becker said, it was war. I did not know about Alan Whitman-Wood's act of betrayal. I was not guilty of losing my husband. But in my grief and despair, I turned to Whitman-Wood for consolation, and he took full advantage. Two months after the raid, we were in a miserable affair, lasting to beyond the end of the war, in which I was controlled and belittled, and finally abandoned.

I will make sure that Richard, my beloved Hittite, gets justice for the way he was betrayed, and my beloved country for its betrayal. And I will have my personal revenge on Alan Whitman-Wood. Not for the way he used and discarded me in those black times, but for separating me from you, my son. He never wanted anything to do with you, and he forbade me from any contact. No mother should ever abandon her child, however difficult the circumstances. It was only when I was free from Whitman-Wood that I was able to take you back, three long years from your birth. I ask you to forgive me not only for our long separation but also for the life-long damage it did to our relationship.

Your loving mother.'

The final document was much shorter and was addressed to the chairman of the London Stock Exchange, with a copy intended for the *Times*.

'Dear Lord Jacobsen,

My name is Daphne Jameson. I am a 94-year-old woman who served her country in the Second World War, and what I know matters greatly in your current business. On Wednesday 11 April, the company known as CommuniCo will be publicly floated on the London, New York and Frankfurt Stock Exchanges. This cannot be allowed to take place. This is a British company built on betrayal and British blood. To allow the current owners of the company, and potential shareholders, to profit directly from the death of British forces personnel, no matter how long ago, would be unconscionable.

This is not the ranting of an old woman. I have direct and incontrovertible proof that the founder of the company, Alan Whitman-Wood, not only sent a colleague to his death on a wartime raid in France but was a German spy for the duration of the war and afterwards.

I ask you to suspend the initial public offering of CommuniCo immediately, and contact me for proof of what I am saying.

Yours sincerely,

Daphne Jameson'

'This is all dynamite,' said Emma. 'Bloody dynamite. But there's one thing I still don't understand. 'Fang', in Grandma's project papers – the word that triggered everything. The word that got Grandma killed and me down to Bawdsey. There's no mention of it amongst these letters.'

'Yes there is,' said Angela.

'Really,' said Sterling. 'I didn't see anything.'

'I translated it. If I'd known what Emma just said I'd have put it in brackets after Operation Capture. 'Unternehmen Fang' is 'Operation Capture' in German.

'So it wasn't a tooth. It was a German word. We never thought of that. So 'Unternehmen Fang' was the ruse to capture my grandfather,' said Emma. 'When she got the letter from Captain Becker, Grandma wrote 'Fang' in her papers and I found it. She must have told Alan Whitman-Wood what she was going to do. She must have wanted to make the most of her revenge. So he came up here with Marcus and finished her off. And I just blundered into their clutches. Well, they're not getting away with it.'

'Fair enough,' said Sterling, 'but how do we use all this?'

Emma picked up the letter to the chairman of the London Stock Exchange. 'I think Grandma might have been a bit naïve thinking this bloke would do something. There's a better way. When's this flotation taking place again?'

'1.30 tomorrow, when the US stock market opens,' said Sterling. 'We need to get cracking and sort something out tonight. I could do with another pint.'

At the end of the evening, the last customers had drifted away. Mike and Becky had done the rounds to check that the pub and everything in the immediate vicinity was safe and secure. The group members had pooled their knowledge, their expertise and their contacts. They'd decided who would do what, settled timings and organised contingency strategies.

Sterling looked into the dying embers of the fire. The remains of a log shifted and sent up a crackle of flame and smoke. 'So,' he said. 'We've got ourselves a plan.' He turned to Mike for a dose of reality. 'What are the chances?'

Mike looked into the fire. 'I wouldn't like to say. There are too many variables.'

'Well, I'm off home,' said Angela. 'See me to the door, Frank.' And at the door she said softly, gesturing with a backward glance of her dark eyes and a tip of her head, 'Be careful, Frank. That girl's not after justice. She's after revenge. There's going to be trouble. Big trouble.'

He brushed her cheek with a light kiss. 'Tell me about it,' he replied.

Chapter 27

On the Offensive

Mike's trousers fitted Sterling around the waist but flapped around the ankles. Fortunately, an almost new but newly discarded pair of trainers fitted almost perfectly. Sterling did not like the checked shirt, but a navy blue fleece covered that up. At least he was no longer a Gravesham Borough Council employee. Now he looked like a care-giver who'd overslept and thrown something on. Still, he couldn't have gone home last night. 'Much too dangerous', Mike had said.

Emma had done better. After all, she hadn't been doused in the Thames. She'd borrowed a top and matching cardigan from Becky. 'That pale apricot suits you,' Becky had said. And it did. As she'd wheeled off from the pub down to the Guildhall to catch the bus, apparently fully refreshed, blonde hair with pink stripe gleaming and regime completed, she'd looked as pretty and determined as Sterling could remember. He, on the other hand, had slept badly and had a headache.

He'd dreamt that he was in a completely chaotic school with no kind of physical order or discipline. He was with a colleague he'd never seen before, awake or asleep. Sterling kept shouting for order but none ever came. So they identified a spot in the main hall of the school where they decided to make a stand. Here they would impose order. Sterling had woken up as they'd been clearing the space of rubbish. Do dreams predict or reflect, he wondered. There had been no satisfaction in this one.

He and Emma had been quiet through the streets and alleyways to the bus stop at the Guildhall. As the bus to Deal via Hamworth and the other villages pulled in, she turned her wheelchair to face him. 'Right, Mr PI, are we ready?'

'Yep,' said Sterling. 'Ready as we'll ever be, I suppose. Got the grip bag?'

'Ha ha, funny man. Good of Mike to offer to sponge it down and dry it. Our lucky charm. When this is all over, which of us is going to have it?'

'Me. It's part of my expenses.'

The journey around to Hamworth took ten minutes. Emma fidgeted with the hand rims of her chair. Her eyes were bright. She's relishing this, thought Sterling. He wondered if there were any aspirins at the house.

'Here we go,' said Emma as the bus pulled up outside Hamworth Place. There was a flurry of activity in the black Range Rover parked a few metres up on the other side of the road as they alighted. Emma pressed a combination of buttons in the keypad next to the electric gates and they swung open. Sterling pushed her up the ramp to the front door. She wheeled around and called out to Marcus Whitman-Wood, who had appeared at the gates. 'Come in. I'll put the kettle on. We've been expecting you.'

He stopped, his arms restraining the two men who had appeared hurriedly at each shoulder. Sterling imagined he could almost see the man's thought processes: 'Hang on a moment. This isn't what's supposed to happen. I need to consult.' Emma opened the front door, and she and Sterling went in, leaving the door ajar. Sterling could still smell the beef and garlic from the evening before. In the 10 o'clock spring sunshine, dust motes danced in a beam on the hall table.

It got darker as a large figure filled the doorway. The light behind the figure made the details hard to see, but Sterling realised with a jolt of surprise that it wasn't just one person. Marcus Whitman-Wood was pushing a man in a wheelchair.

'Let's go through to the lounge,' said Emma. To Sterling, she said more softly, 'This is even better. Not just the band – the conductor too.' Then again, more loudly, she did the introductions. 'Frank, I think you met Marcus Whitman-Wood while I was on the ferry to Gravesend. In fact, there might have been an…altercation.'

Sterling nodded. He remembered the filthy water going up his nose. Marcus Whitman-Wood stood impassively.

'And this is Marcus's grandfather, Alan Whitman-Wood, currently chairman of CommuniCo. As you see, he's a wheelchair user like me.'

She's doing well, thought Sterling. Just as we planned. She's in control, and taking advantage of being on her own territory. Afterwards, he described this part of it to Angela as a chess match between Emma and the chair of CommuniCo in which no move was as it seemed.

Away from the bright sunlight in the hallway, he looked at Alan Whitman-Wood more closely. He was very old – of course well over 90 – his skin lined and papery, and pale where it wasn't mottled with age spots. His hair was a grey-white colour and thin, but covered his scalp fully. His chunky black spectacles must have been fashionable circa 1959. Is that what Buddy Holly would have looked like if he had survived? His loose double-breasted grey silk suit was well cut and expensive-looking, but old-fashioned, and the collar of his white shirt too wide for his turkey neck, around which was a plain blue silk tie, loosely knotted. His breathing rasped shallowly. Another wheelchair user, thought Sterling. What were the odds? He nodded at the old man as well.

'I'm surprised my father isn't here. He's always around on Tuesday morning after bridge.'

The old man blinked. 'He was missing you, Emma, so when we invited him to spend some time with us he was happy to come.'

'Right,' said Emma. 'Understandable in the circumstances. Well now, tea. Frank, can you please bring everything through?'

He carried in the tray that Emma had prepared in the kitchen. Tea and biscuits among friends, the acme of innocent conviviality.

'So,' said Emma above the chink of cups and saucers, 'as you see, I'm tired of running. It's good to be home. What now?'

'We wait,' said Alan Whitman-Wood, 'till about 3 o'clock. We do nothing except drink tea, eat biscuits and chat. We let events take their natural course. After that, everything will be fine. In fact, things are going well again at last. No one will get hurt. Nothing unpleasant will happen. You know, we've been very worried about you, Emma. You drop in to visit us, we offer you our most attentive hospitality, and you're whisked off. Poor Marcus was convinced you'd been abducted. Marcus, would you....?'

The stocky man moved to the back of his grandfather's chair and removed a small bag. He handed it to Emma. She took out the iPad and hugged it close.

'Wonderful,' she said. 'It's been weird without this. So, Alan, it was all a silly old misunderstanding. I wasn't banged up at Bawdsey Manor for the duration. Marcus and his security detail weren't chasing me; they were trying to rescue me. That bus driver at Lakeside must have been making the assault up. He was obviously embarrassed to trip over and bash his face in. The cars at Harwich and Basildon. The helicopter. You must indeed have been worried about me. And Frank ended up in the Thames to give me a chance to get away.' She wagged her finger at Sterling. 'You wicked man.' She turned back to the old man. 'All in all, there was no law breaking, attempted kidnapping, assault or intimidation. I reckon I owe you an apology.'

Alan Whitman-Wood spread his mottled hands in front of him. He looked confused. Emma's friendly manner and what she said were jarring and contradictory. He chose to ignore any hint of irony. 'All's well that ends well,' he said. 'We're just glad everything is working out.'

'Well, if everything's OK, can we get Dad in here? I haven't seen him for three days, and I'm sure he'll be glad to know I've turned up safe.'

Alan Whitman-Wood weighed things up. This was surely a gambit he could accept now that control of the situation had passed to him. He nodded to his grandson, and a minute later two CommuniCo men brought Nicholas Jameson into the room and then withdrew. Apart from stubble and slight dishevelment he looked well enough to Sterling. Father and daughter greeted each other awkwardly.

'Emma, I've been really worried. You just upped and went.'

'Yeah, Dad, good to see you too.'

'And then there was last night. What the hell is going on?'

'Sorry, Dad – about everything. I'll explain later. Right now we're just waiting.'

'White cow's just fainting?'

'Dad, for God's sake don't start that now. I-will-explain-everything-later.' Emma looked at her watch. '11.30, Alan. I'm not sure I can wait until 3 o'clock. Actually, I don't think we'll be able to. Frank, can you turn on the television. Sky News, BBC News 24, one of those.' The front door bell sounded. 'I think that will be for me.'

'What's going on?' said Nicholas Jameson plaintively. 'I can't hear a damn thing.'

'Press the subtitles button, Frank, for God's sake,' said Emma.

'Where are you going?' said Alan Whitman-Wood. He gestured to his grandson, who loomed over Emma's chair.

'You'd better tell your…boy to get out of the way, Alan,' Emma sneered. 'All this is pre-arranged, including what happens if I'm not allowed to answer my own bloody front door.'

Marcus Whitman-Wood looked at his grandfather. Sterling could see doubt in his eyes. He and Emma knew all about his inflexibility and knack of antagonising people. Now they knew who took the decisions.

'Let her go,' said the old man. He realised he had no choice. 'You'd better be careful, young lady.'

'Oh, I will, old man,' said Emma. 'I most certainly will.'

As she disappeared into the hallway, Sterling turned to the television. The subtitles across the bottom of the screen were distracting, but then he remembered how quickly he'd got used to pushing a cantankerous wheelchair user around the eastern districts of England.

The newscaster paused and shuffled her papers. 'The founder of a British telecommunications company due to be floated on the stock market today has been accused of being of a wartime traitor. Alan Whitman-Wood, founder of CommuniCo, allegedly colluded with the Wehrmacht during the Second World War and was indirectly responsible for the death of an RAF colleague.

'CommuniCo – formerly Whitman Electronics – is one of the most successful small private firms of the last 70 years, and is being floated simultaneously on the London, New York and Frankfurt stock markets.

'However, we have received reports this morning that may raise questions about that flotation. We now go live to our news correspondent, Nicky Moran, in Hamworth, Kent. Nicky?'

Good man, thought Sterling about his school friend. Nicky had trusted Sterling as he had when they were mates at school. When he'd received the call last night, he'd swung straight into action. Of course, the prospect of a career-bolstering story had also been a motivator.

'Thank you, Sian. Yes, late last night, we were contacted by a local resident who has raised serious concerns about CommuniCo, its officers and the stock market flotation. There are documents that cast doubt on the ethical foundations of the company. I'm currently in Hamworth, a village outside Sandley in East Kent, and am about to speak with Emma Jameson, whose family has links with CommuniCo.'

Sterling watched the television screen as Emma wheeled the Ferrari-chair down from the front door and straight into the newly assembled cluster of TV lighting, busby-style microphones and smaller voice-recorders of the media pack. It turned out that Mike's efforts with his contacts had worked as well, and everyone had turned up at the pre-arranged time. The wheels of Emma's chair glinted as camera flashes popped, but she looked smaller and suddenly more vulnerable than in real life. Sterling noticed how the subtitles didn't keep up with the newscaster's and Nicky's spiel, and how whole phrases were completely missed out or phonetically distorted. But he was still transfixed, and so, he noted, were the other viewers. It seemed strange to be watching on television what was happening just outside the front door.

'I'm going to issue a statement,' said Emma, 'and then I'll take questions.' She's good, thought Sterling. Plucky. Savvy. Determined.

'My name is Emma Jameson. I live in the house behind me. My 94-year-old grandmother, who also lived in this house, served her country as a radar operator and administrator during the Second World War. Recently, she received a letter from Karlheinz Becker, an ex-captain in the German Wehrmacht, about her husband, my grandfather, Richard Jameson. Herr Becker was dying, and there was something on his conscience that he felt compelled to address before he died. My grandfather was a radar scientist in the RAF, who was part of a parachute raid on a German radar station in northern France in 1943. The raid was considered successful at the time. The parachute squadron removed German equipment and managed to return safely via a submarine off the French coast. But Captain Becker was part of the group that captured my grandfather, the only casualty of the raid.

'Herr Becker's letter confirmed what many people in military and scientific circles suspected after the war. The raid was a German ruse. The radar station at Cauville near Dieppe, identified originally by photo-reconnaissance, was deliberately left lightly defended. The equipment captured by Four Para was technologically out of date and had been superseded. My grandfather was captured because he was targeted, the German task made easier because he had been refused an army uniform before the raid. The German operation, known as Unternehmen Fang, or Operation Capture, achieved two ends: it sent British counter-intelligence and radar development down a time-wasting temporary cul-de-sac; and it secured the capture of one of the most talented radar scientists of his generation – the grandfather I never met.

'What have these events all those years ago got to do with CommuniCo? This,' said Emma. 'Herr Becker confirmed that it was a spy in the British radar service who planned the raid and sent my grandfather to his death, a spy embedded in British scientific intelligence since 1936. A man who after the war benefited from his German contacts to build up his company. That man is Alan Whitman-Wood. He might not have pulled the trigger, but he killed my grandfather. Captain Becker apologised to my grandmother for the torture and death of my grandfather that he was unable to prevent.'

In the living room, Sterling and Nicholas Jameson remained mesmerised, but from Alan Whitman-Wood came a low, urgent babble of what sounded like rancorous disagreement. His pale face was now completely drained of colour, and his hands twisted and kneaded themselves in his lap. Sterling glanced at Marcus. He too was distressed, but the source of his upset was his grandfather's discomfort. He's not really listening to what's going on, realised Sterling. He's too busy attending to his grandfather to know what's going wrong. He's too stupid to pay attention.

Emma took a breath and then continued. 'This is not about anti-German sentiment. I am not anti-German. I am pro-German, pro-European. It's about justice, finally, for my grandfather. So, to those individuals, pension fund managers, trust fund managers and anyone else who might consider buying shares this afternoon in CommuniCo: don't. This is a company built on the blood of my grandfather by a man who betrayed his country.'

As she spoke, Emma produced a document from the side of her chair and flourished high above her head. Becky had printed it late the night before. 'The CommuniCo prospectus,' announced Emma. From the same place came a box of extra long, extra thick kitchen matches. Even watching on television, Sterling could see the dark, bulbous tips of phosphorus. This wasn't in the plan. Now she was improvising, embellishing. The first two matches sparked and went out before the papers caught properly, but the flame from the third one did catch, and more flames licked over the pages as she juggled them between her fingers before throwing them to the ground.

The first two failures might have suggested lack of competence. In Emma they combined with the whole performance to show implacable determination. She wheeled her chair back and forth across the glowing paper embers, grinding and crushing them into the gravel of the driveway. Then she looked up into the cameras and microphones and faces of the media pack. 'Questions?' she said.

Nicky Moran was not quite the first, but he'd been primed. Emma turned to face him. 'Ms Jameson, your grandmother was murdered in this house a few weeks ago. Is there any connection between that and CommuniCo's flotation?'

'I believe there is a connection. I think there was a conspiracy to silence my grandmother when she found certain things out.'

'A conspiracy by employees or owners of CommuniCo.'

'I'm not going to say any more than I've said. It's a matter for the police and where they take their enquiries. Naturally, I, my family and my associates will co-operate fully.'

'You've made some very serious allegations against the chairman of a highly successful British company,' said another voice. 'Alan Whitman-Wood and CommuniCo are not going to take this lying down. How will you react to probable legal action?'

Emma sat erect in her chair. 'Bring it on,' she said directly into the camera.

'And is it true that you and an associate had to escape from CommuniCo employees over a period of several days in order to find the evidence you have talked about this morning?' Nicky asked. Good old Nicky, thought Sterling. Mr Reliable.

'I can't comment directly on that at the moment,' said Emma, 'except to say' (she smiled for the first time) 'that we had some adventures. I hope all that will also be looked

into by the police.' She left the implications hanging in the
air like will-o'-the-wisps.

After she had dealt with more questions, all, Sterling
noted, with the same aplomb as at the beginning,
she wheeled around up the ramp and back into the
house. Someone was going to be facing the music, but it
wasn't her.

Chapter 28

Danger, Response...
Airway, Breathing, Circulation

'Thank you, Nicky. We're joined now by our Business Editor with an analysis of these dramatic developments,' said the newscaster. 'Stephanie, these are astonishing allegations, including about events that took place almost seventy years ago. How will this affect activity in the stock market this afternoon?'

'It's an interesting one, Sian. I can't comment on the allegations themselves, although the young woman certainly seemed confident about what she was saying. But situations like this are not completely out of the ordinary. You might remember that sexual harassment suit against the chief executive of Caprico in New York on the eve of their airline flotation. The early release of a profits warning decimated the share price of Prospectis, the Internet search engine company. There have been other instances of disastrous flotations. Potential investors are looking for companies that are sound and have potential. They're looking for profits. But remember, the markets don't operate on emotion. Alleged treason and betrayal by a company chairman all that time ago is not necessarily going to affect his company's public share price today.'

'So the flotation is unlikely to be adversely affected?'

'No, I'm not quite saying that, Sian. We saw how determined and forthright Ms Jameson seemed to be. Flotations are all about timing and confidence. The timing is terrible for CommuniCo. If this had happened a day later, or even a few hours later, after the shares had been bought…What is going to put investors off is any protracted dispute, legal or otherwise, that will divert CommuniCo's strategic team from the very big challenges that becoming a public company will throw up. The last thing its officers need now is a controversy of this sort. Whatever the ins and outs of this young woman's allegations, potential investors will be worried about this turn of events. Just how worried, we'll see' (she looked quickly down at her watch) 'in one and a half hour's time.'

Emma had come back into the room at the start of the interview.

All pretence of politeness and amiability were gone. 'You silly, wicked girl,' said Alan Whitman-Wood. 'Seventy years' work. Seventy years of struggle and risk. Jeopardised by a stupid young hothead. We wanted to avoid this situation at all costs. Do you have any conception of the importance this deal has to the British economy? It would have been better for everyone if you'd stayed with us in Bawdsey.'

'Everyone except my grandparents,' said Emma. 'You killed one in 1943 and the other this year. That's what I care about. I don't give a tuppenny toss for your precious company. Let it rot in hell, like you.'

Alan Whitman-Wood fiddled with his wheelchair. It reminded Sterling of Emma. 'Marcus, I'm getting very hot,' said the old man.' His stocky grandson hurried over and retrieved a face-wipe from a bag behind the wheelchair. With great care and tenderness, he wiped his grandfather's face.

'The situation's retrievable even now,' the old man muttered to himself. He appeared to be retreating into his own decision-making world, not even thinking of Emma's accusations. 'We need to phone Jimmy, issue a denial from the underwriters, contact our solicitors, get out a writ…There's still time. Marcus, where's the mobile?'

The red spots had reappeared on Emma's cheeks. 'Hey,' she said loudly. 'Not here. Not in our house. I want you out. You're trespassing. Dad, make him go. And make him take his damned grandson with him.'

'His tanned bandstand?'

'Dad, don't do this. Not now. I want these bastards gone. Grandma wrote you a letter. I've got it here. It explains everything. Just as soon as they've gone, you can read it and I'll fill in the gaps.'

'We will go now,' said Alan Whitman-Wood. 'How rude of us to have overstayed our welcome, and we have lots to do.' He had fully returned to the polite way of speaking which rationalised his grandson's thuggery. 'But I do need to use your facilities first, Nicholas. Your daughter knows what it's like.'

Weird, thought Sterling. In the movies, bitter enemies didn't use each others' toilets.

'Alright,' said Jameson. 'You'll have to go upstairs. The bathroom is at the end on the left.'

'Dad, no. Let the bastard piss in a ditch after all he's done. He killed your mother, for God's sake.'

'We know nothing for certain, Emma. And if another person is in need, it's our duty to help.'

'Pompous bloody git,' said Emma softly.

That's why they don't get along. Sterling thought about how they were alike and how they were different. They could both be blunt and short-tempered. They both cared deeply about fairness. But Nicholas Jameson seemed to have a forgiving side, whilst his mother's wish to settle scores had skipped him and gone straight to Emma.

'I don't want your scrawny arse in my stairlift,' she said.

Alan Whitman-Wood nodded to his grandson, who went over to him, leaned over the chair and took the old man gently in his arms. An irrelevant thought popped on cue into Sterling's head. He'll get terrible back trouble not bending his legs.

The stocky man passed close to Sterling and Emma on the way to the bathroom. With the old man's face turned away, Emma glared at his grandson. 'You killed my grandmother,' she said softly.

'You know what,' he whispered back. 'I enjoyed it. That old bitch really would have ruined everything. She deserved everything she got. And you know what else? You'll never prove it.' He moved away with his grandfather into the hall.

Nicholas Jameson had heard nothing, but his daughter seethed. 'They're going to get away with it, Frank. You heard what they both said. Money talks. They'll get lawyers and PR people. They'll wriggle and squirm. The police are hopeless. Jon-Jo was right.' She edged back and forth in her wheelchair. 'I've got to have a think. I'm going to my room,' she said abruptly. 'Dad, read this.' She thrust his mother's letter into his hand.

After Marcus Whitman-Wood's heavy footsteps, Sterling could hear the whirr of the stairlift, and as Nicholas Jameson began to read, he settled back in his chair to wait. He'd forgotten to ask Emma for aspirin. His headache was as bad as ever.

'Have you read this?' said Nicholas Jameson, when he had finished.

'Yes, we had to, last night. The Whitman-Woods had taken you – we saw from the landing window. We had to find out what was going on and then decide what we were going to do.'

'That kidnapping, scrawny-arsed bastard is using my bathroom,' said Jameson.

Sterling smiled. He'd been too hasty. Emma had got more from her father than he'd originally assumed.

'Well, Mr Sterling,' said Jameson. 'I really still only have the vaguest idea about what is going on, but obviously I'm relieved and delighted that you've found Emma and brought her safely home. I'm very grateful for that. I'd like you to tell me the whole story when we've cleared the house. But I'm thinking…I really don't know what's going to happen next. Emma has stirred up a hornet's nest and there's going to be a considerable amount of fall-out. I think the police will have to be involved, and of course media interest will remain. It's going to be very messy. Perhaps you'd consider staying on the payroll, as it were, for a little while longer until things settle down. Your immediate next task will be to get the Whitman-Woods out of the house. It doesn't look as though there will be any trouble now things are out in the open and the media is camped outside, but I don't want to take any chances. I suppose I'd better start thinking about lawyers as well, after what Emma has said.'

Sterling nodded. 'Sure,' he said. 'I can help with that.' He remembered how empty his diary was. A bit of extra income for what would essentially be a watching brief would be very welcome, and it would be good to be paid for doing what he would have done for nothing – checking how events unfolded for Emma and CommuniCo.

As he started to brief Jameson on what had happened, there were noises from the bathroom and upstairs: the flush of a cistern; the rumbling of pipes; the scratch of a lock; the creak of a door. There were other shifts and movements that were harder to identify. He basked in Jameson's praise and gratitude, and the prospect of more cash.

Afterwards Sterling remembered how serene Nicholas Jameson had been in his silent deaf world as he himself had leapt up from his chair as if it had suddenly become electrified, prompted by a crash like a wrecking ball on masonry, a loud oath, a reedy scream, and then a more minor but equally intense series of bangs, bumps and scuffles that echoed through to the living room. Just as Jameson sensed some kind of disharmony, Sterling dashed to the hall. Two questions wrestled for ascendancy – an anxious one – what's happened to Emma? – and one that niggled – what's she done now? Surveying the scene, covered in a newly descended silence, and with Emma nowhere in view, he realised with a rush of relief that for the moment he didn't have to concern himself with either.

Instead, a familiar acronym popped unbidden into his head, a stimulus-response reaction to all those hours of first aid training in the job. DR ABC. There was no current danger to Marcus Whitman-Wood – not now that he had completed his fall down the grand staircase of Hamworth Place. On the other hand, there was some unsolicited response – a vague low moaning sound. As for his airway, breathing and circulation, Sterling was too full of antipathy to bring himself to check.

He manoeuvred the stocky body perfunctorily into the recovery position, taking care not to make too much of the leg sticking out at an unnatural angle.

For the old man, the first aid mantra was entirely irrelevant. His frail, 94-year-old frame had been thoroughly crushed by his grandson's heavy body in the downward tumble. His rheumy, bloodshot eyes stared at the ceiling from a head grotesquely twisted from the shrunken body in the baggy suit.

Emma emerged in her wheelchair from her bedroom. 'Bloody hell,' she said from through the banisters on the landing. 'That's a turn up for the books. But did you see how old Marcus bent his back and not his legs when he picked his bastard grandfather up, Frank? Terrible practice.' Emma tutted. 'The idiot must have spasmed, lost his footing and toppled.'

Chapter 29

Pandemonium and Hubbub, Scepticism and Resentment

'Time for the police,' said Sterling as the chairlift whirred and Emma came down the hallway. 'We should have had them in days ago. And an ambulance.'

'Yeah,' said Emma, but her focus was elsewhere. 'While you do that, what's the number of your mate Nicky Moran?'

'What do you need that for?' said Sterling suspiciously.

'We've got a chance to finish the job. Thanks,' she said as she keyed in the number. 'Go on, get the police and ambulance.' Then she turned away as she began her own conversation. 'Nicky, it's Emma Jameson. You need to get back here. There've been some more developments….'

When all the necessary calls had been made, Sterling gathered Emma and her father back into the living room. 'There's one thing we might need to orchestrate – just to avoid any complications down the line when the police interview us all. When the Whitman-Woods fell down the stairs, it would probably be best to say that we were all in here. Right?'

'Why?' said Emma.

Sterling hesitated for a microsecond. His eyes flicked to the floor and back to her.

'Bloody hell, Frank. What are you thinking? That I had something to do with what happened? That I lurked behind my bedroom door, span out of my room, whizzed over the landing to the top of the stairs, smacked them down and went back to my room, all in the time it took for you to get to the hall? That I'm a murderer, for fuck's sake?' She plucked at her hand rims.

'No, I don't think any of that. I know you wouldn't do it, and I know you couldn't have. It's just that I know how these things work. It'd make things much easier for us in the long run.'

'Well, for the record, I'm not sorry about what's happened to those bastards, but I did not push them down the stairs.'

'So we do the easiest thing,' said Jameson. 'We tell the truth. You and I were in the living room when the Whitman-Woods fell down the stairs, Mr Sterling, and Emma was in her room.'

Sterling shrugged. 'OK,' he said. 'But we should be ready for people twisting things.' He resisted the temptation to say 'On your own heads be it' to his stubborn clients.

After that it was pandemonium. There was the media scrum, which had dwindled when Emma had gone indoors after her statement forty minutes earlier but which had swelled again after her conversation with Nicky Moran. There was the luminescent lime and lemon chequered ambulance, the two squad cars and a third, unmarked, police car, all with blue and red lights adding ghostly colour to the scene. There was the white van of the forensics team, and there was a gaggle of villagers in the road outside, at once bewildered and fascinated with the spectacle unfolding before them. The discreet withdrawal of the black Range Rover and its cargo of CommuniCo employees, without the Whitman-Woods, was the only factor not adding to the mayhem.

Sterling was again watching television in the living room at Hamworth Place with Emma and Nicholas Jameson, but the rest of the audience had changed. Now there were the two detectives originally assigned to the murder of Daphne Jameson, Detective Inspector Smithson and Detective Sergeant Murphy. A detective superintendent and another detective whose names Sterling had not caught had also appeared, presumably because of the case's newly reacquired high profile. A young constable, who clearly could not believe his luck to be at the centre of such excitement, completed the gathering.

Smithson was a tall man whose suit hung limply on him, and the moustache in his thin face gave him a lugubrious, hangdog kind of air. Sterling remembered the roly-poly Murphy from the Margate nick, and knew him as a decent man, honest and straight dealing, if occasionally pompous. The superintendent did not look promising – sleek, slim and short – the kind of man who makes up for lack of stature with cockiness and ambition. His manner seemed precise and somehow aggressive. But the other detective was probably even worse. His face was weathered and crinkled with smoke lines, his nails dirty and his fingers stained with nicotine. Scepticism was the default expression on his face and in his watery eyes.

As the group looked on, paramedics were in the process of moving Alan Whitman-Wood to the morgue, whilst his grandson was already on the way to hospital. Forensic officers with all their gear went about their mysterious business. Sterling heard and remembered the rustle the white suits made from when he was on the job.

Nicholas Jameson, and indeed the police officers, had the slightly dazed look of people overwhelmed by a tsunami of events. Emma's eyes shone.

'Back to Hamworth in Kent now for the latest dramatic news in connection with the CommuniCo flotation. Nicky?

'Thank you again, Sian.' Nicky Moran's neat, smooth, well-proportioned face was animated. This can't be doing him any harm at all. Sterling felt a stab of jealousy. He wondered if he still looked as youthful as his school friend. He knew that his own career prospects were far less promising. Behind Moran, the media scrum heaved and surged. 'Well, in the last few minutes we've been receiving reports from inside Hamworth Place that there has been a serious incident. An ambulance has already taken one person to casualty in Margate, but I understand that another man has died at the scene. You can see a body being removed now.' A camera shot panned to the paramedics loading a black bag into their vehicle.

'What's likely to happen next, Nicky?'

'Well, Sian, as you can see, the police have arrived, and they are in the house with Ms Jameson and her father. I understand that an associate of Ms Jameson is also there. Forensic officers have arrived, which is standard practice in the circumstances. Ms Jameson has indicated that she'll talk in more detail exclusively with me as soon as the police give the OK.'

'Nicky, we're going to have to leave it there for the moment. We're getting reports from the City that there's to be a statement from Schredemann, who are underwriting the CommuniCo flotation. I'm joined now by our Chief Business Correspondent, Richard Pelton, at Schredemann.'

'Thank you, Sian. Yes, the Chief Executive of Schredemann, Maggie Feldman, is making a statement to us now.'

At Hamworth Place, the knot of viewers watched on.

'I will make this short statement and then take questions.' The chief executive fumbled with her reading glasses as she worked them one-handed onto her face. One of the arms would not fold back from next to the lenses.

'Get on with it,' muttered Emma.

'As you know,' the woman finally began, 'an initial public offering of CommuniCo shares was scheduled to take place at 1.30 pm GMT in the London, New York and Frankfurt stock markets. Schredemann were appointed as underwriters for the flotation. At all stages of the process, Schredemann acted with honesty and integrity on the basis of information supplied by CommuniCo. An independent audit of the company's finances was supplied by JonesWeekesKline.'

'Rats leaving a sinking ship, and explaining why,' said Emma in her commentary.

'Unfortunately, allegations about the CommuniCo chairman surfaced this morning, and there seem to have been additional developments in the last few minutes. We understand that potential investors need clarity and stability before making major investment decisions, and we cannot now offer such a guarantee. In the light of all the recent events and the inevitable uncertainty they have caused, and in agreement with CommuniCo's CEO, it has been decided to suspend the flotation until further notice. Thank you.'

After a flurry of questions, the news anchor spoke to the Business Editor. 'Stephanie, what now for CommuniCo?'

'Sian, no two ways about it, it's a disaster. Clearly, with this sort of a cloud hanging over the company, not just the alleged treason seventy years ago but the hints of recent criminal behaviour by members of the company, the shares in the open market would not have reached the offer price. The firm would not have received anything like the injection of capital it was asking for. It also looks as though the company may have lost a major creative influence, though we can't confirm that yet. For the current owners, principally the Whitman-Wood family, there will be no windfall. On the other hand, there may well be criminal charges for some company personnel. It's hard to know what CommuniCo's next step will be.'

'Result,' said Emma. She put her fists up and punched the air. Then she swung around and faced the detective superintendent. 'Right,' she said, 'I expect you'll be wanting words. Ask away. I can tell you the whole thing.'

'You'd better start with your grandmother's documents,' said Sterling. He was gloomy. It was going to be a long afternoon. The police officers did not look much more cheerful. They probably feel the same as me, thought Sterling.

'So what have we got?' said the superintendent, leafing briskly through the papers Emma had handed to him. 'A letter, translated from the German; your mother's letter to you, Mr Jameson; and this other one – to the chairman of the London Stock Exchange. Plus a body in the morgue and another at casualty. We'd better take statements separately from each of you. OK, gentlemen,' he said turning to his men, 'let's get going.'

—⁓—

The kitchen still smelled faintly of beef and garlic. Sterling's headache hadn't gone away, though it hadn't got any worse. He sat at the table and rubbed his temples, though it never seemed to help whenever he did it. He knew that a uniform would be discreetly stationed in the living room to keep an eye on Nicholas Jameson as his daughter spoke to one team of detectives in her grandmother's study and Sterling spoke to the other.

'You'd better start from the beginning,' said the superintendent, whose name Sterling had established as Andrews and who had paired himself up with Murphy.

'Right, here goes,' said Sterling. He had nothing to hide and wanted to get it over with. Outside the kitchen, he sensed that pandemonium was becoming mere hubbub. He ordered his thoughts, put his palms down on the table, took a deep breath and began, adopting the flat monotone of reportage that would make his story credible to an audience who in long careers had seen and heard everything.

It took Sterling half an hour, interspersed with occasional questions and requests for clarification from the investigating officers.

He started with the original assignment from Nicholas Jameson, and his discovery that Emma had gone to Bawdsey Manor. He explained the flight and pursuit across East Anglia, the night-time expedition yesterday to the house whose kitchen they were now sitting in, and the discovery of Daphne Jameson's documents. The more matter-of-fact he was, the more he talked, and the more he described all the kind, brave and extraordinary actions of all the ordinary people who had helped, the more ludicrous his story seemed, even to him.

At the end, he sat back. He was tired suddenly after a poor night's sleep and all the following drama.

Murphy whistled. 'Well,' he said. 'I've known you for a long time, mate. You'd be hard pushed to make that up.'

'We'll see, sergeant,' said Detective Superintendent Andrews.

Oh God, thought Sterling. There's always some idiot to muddy the waters. He remembered why he'd left the job and why he knew he'd done the right thing.

'Let's see if I can summarise. Three weeks ago, Daphne Jameson is found murdered in this house. Smithson and Murphy are the investigating officers, but they and their team find little evidence at the scene and in particular no sign of a break in. The daughter, Emma, and her father Nicholas, are not in the house at the time and have solid alibis. The girl apparently discovers something amongst her grandmother's papers that she thinks is connected with her murder. Instead of informing us, which she obviously should have done straight away, she contacts the chairman of the firm CommuniCo, whose name has come up, to ask him about her grandmother. According to your version of events, alarm bells allegedly ring for Alan Whitman-Wood, and he invites the girl down to his base at Bawdsey Manor, ostensibly to help clear up her queries but actually to keep her quiet and out of the way before this afternoon's planned flotation.

'You track her down, "rescue" her and together you work your way back to Kent, at a snail's pace, by ferry, bus and train etc, allegedly pursued by Alan Whitman-Wood's grandson, who holds the job of head of security at

CommuniCo, and his colleagues. You get back to Sandley last night, mount an expedition to the house here, led by a convicted South Essex burglar, and unearth the documents Daphne Jameson has hidden away. Taken all together, they purport to reveal that Alan Whitman-Wood was a spy who betrayed her husband, and for whatever reason this 90-odd-year-old woman threatens to blow the whistle. That's why, the girl alleges, the Whitman-Woods, grandfather and grandson, come down and silence the old woman three weeks ago by beating her to death. The girl takes over the job of revenge from her grandmother and on behalf of both grandparents, and wrecks the flotation.'

'Very effectively too, as it turns out,' added Murphy.

'An excellent summary,' said Sterling, 'apart from the "allegeds" and "apparentlys" and "your versions".'

'Thank you,' said Andrews, smiling except for his eyes and ignoring the gibes. 'Now we need to consider all the instances of law breaking. That's going to be difficult to untangle. I think we can leave out what allegedly happened 70 years ago, so…Daphne Jameson's murder. The girl will be saying that Marcus and Alan Whitman-Wood did it.'

'Yes,' said Sterling. 'And remember I heard Marcus Whitman-Wood say to Emma that he enjoyed doing it.'

'And you're prepared to testify to that in court?'

'Certainly.'

Andrews pursed his lips. 'It's a bit weak. What else is there? The Whitman-Woods allegedly kidnapping the girl. The assault on the bus driver at Lakeside. You and your mate getting tossed in the Thames. The Whitman-Woods apparently abducting old man Jameson. We could work with our Suffolk and Essex colleagues, but you were in the job, Mr Sterling. It's all a bit flimsy, isn't it? All a bit "he said, she said". You can see what we'll be up against when the CommuniCo PR office gets going and the Whitman-Wood family gives their version.

'Then there's the girl. She's withheld information, so she's impeded a police investigation. Maybe there's something about obstruction of justice in there. I suppose the denunciation of the dead man is libel. Wrecking the flotation is probably a civil matter rather than one for us.'

Sterling stared and shook his head. Who was this jumped-up idiot who'd risen to the top in the Kent police? He wasn't even playing devil's advocate. He seemed to believe what he was saying. His warped approach reminded Sterling of Alan Whitman-Wood's outlandish explanations for all that had happened. An uncomfortable thought struck him: Andrews had been bought. Sterling fought to dismiss the notion.

'Let's move on to today. Tell me again about the incident in the house an hour ago. The alleged accident.'

'I don't believe this, Detective Superintendent Andrews. The girl and I are chased for our lives, right across eastern England and Kent by a bunch of maniacs, two of whom end up in this house, and you take their side. Astonishing.'

'Well, what happened?' Andrews was persistent.

'As I said, we heard a crash, went into the hall and found the Whitman-Woods, one dead and one with a broken leg.'

'And where was the girl?'

'In her bedroom upstairs.'

'So she could have....'

'What? Leapt out of her chair and done for the old man? Snapped the other one's leg like a twig? A stocky bloke like that? From her wheelchair?'

'We'll be speaking to Mr Whitman-Wood when he comes out of surgery – as he was the only other person on the scene.'

There was a sudden eruption of noise and commotion from Daphne Jameson's study, where Emma was being interviewed by the other detective team. Clearly, both teams had been taking the same misguided line.

Emma burst into the kitchen. 'Frank, these muppets are really irking me. They're making all kinds of insinuations. They're even suggesting – well, I can't even bloody well say it. Dad and I are the victims here. It was his mother and my grandmother who was murdered and I'm the one getting a grilling. Talk about the Establishment closing ranks.'

Nicholas Jameson came in. He might be deaf, thought Sterling, but he's developed a sixth sense. He knows which way the wind is blowing.

'Unless you're going to make any arrests or press any charges, officers, I'd like you all to leave my house. My daughter and Mr Sterling are exhausted, and your attitude has lost you any right to co-operation. If you have any further questions, communicate through my solicitor. Here are her details. Gentlemen?' He opened the kitchen door and swept his hand towards the front door.

Smithson and Murphy had the grace to look sheepish as they left, but Emma was implacable. 'That's why I did what I did. Plods. No bloody help at all. The opposite.' She flicked her wheelchair to face her father. 'Thanks, Dad,' she said clearly and slowly. 'I appreciate the support.'

Jameson reddened. He wasn't used to that. 'I'll put the kettle on.'

'Yeah, Dad,' said Emma. A mischievous look, one from an array of expressions Sterling had come to recognise so well, flitted across her face. 'Bop the cattle yon.'

Chapter 30
Jimmy Comes Negotiating

Sterling sprayed the furniture polish over the windowsill of his office and wiped it with a duster. A fortnight had passed since the drama at Hamworth Place and a spring clean was overdue. After days of 'police enquiries' and relentless media pressure, things had gradually quietened down. Emma had given her exclusive interview to Nicky Moran, and Sterling was convinced that he was in line for more than a 'thank you' pint. His school friend's previously erratic career had taken off with a loud whoosh.

He looked out over the square. The grass in the churchyard had spurted in the warm weather over the last couple of days and was now a luxurious, shiny downland green. An elderly woman and her son, who looked as though he had Down's syndrome, drifted into Jack's café for morning coffee. Jack, thought Sterling. He'd have loved the latest shenanigans. He'd have gossiped all night in The Cinque Ports Arms. He shouldn't have double-crossed me on the Etchingham thing. Now he'll only get it all third-hand, with lots of inaccuracies.

Then he caught the glitter of Emma's Ferrari-chair as it came into his peripheral vision from around the corner leading down to the Guildhall. It was ten o'clock. She was right on time and looked up at his window from in front of the library door.

'I'll be right down,' mouthed Sterling, and Emma put her thumb up in a little acknowledging gesture. He checked his hair and face, feeling a mixture of complex emotions. When Emma had scuppered the CommuniCo flotation and Alan Whitman-Wood had died from his topple down the stairs, he'd thought it was all over. They, as well as Billy and their other supporters, had felt a sense of anticlimax. The days had got emptier and emptier. Now it seemed that things were moving again. But it wasn't just that. He'd been with Emma Jameson for hours and days on end. I've missed her, he thought. There's been a void there as well.

Angela, zealous about inclusion, had managed a year ago to get an automatic sliding door fitted to the library, with wheelchair access. Sterling met Emma just inside the small vestibule.

'This is good,' said Emma, as the doors whispered closed behind her. 'I need to rejoin. I'd been putting it off. This'll prompt me.'

'Yeah, it's good – till we get to my stairs. You didn't give me enough notice to get a stairlift installed.'

Emma peered up the stairs. 'They're too narrow.'

'I know. So my reasonable adjustment, for you and you only, is our usual LNB gig. But if I'm going to expand my customer base to include disabled people, maybe I should shift offices.'

Sterling's comment was lighthearted, but Emma gave it serious consideration. 'Maybe. But what if you're really attached to your office? You don't need to move. Reasonable adjustments under the legislation don't have to cost a fortune, or even be about money, particularly for a small business like yours. We talked about this before. Mindset is what's important, and yours is pretty good. So if someone can't get up the stairs, maybe you could have an arrangement with your pal down here for a cubicle or side room.'

'Good thinking,' said Sterling. 'Reassuring too. Well, I can't carry you bride-and-groom style up the stairs. It will have to be Landguard Fort method.'

'OK,' said Emma as she flopped forward onto his back and put her arms around his neck.

He'd forgotten how much eight stone was and wished he'd taken his jacket off before the long manoeuvre upstairs. But the Chloe perfume that filled his nostrils and the press of Emma's chest against his back felt good. He eased her into the client's chair and sank into his own behind the desk.

'Mmm…Mr Sheen. Nice office.' said Emma. She took in his old desk in front of the window with its telephone and computer, the two-drawer filing cabinet, his high-backed office chair, the chair and sofa for clients, the green-shaded editor's lamp and the scenes from rural Kentish life on the walls. Then she turned to Sterling.

'Danger, pursuit, kidnapping, attempted drowning, housebreaking and the like must suit you, Frank. You're looking good. Dapper's the word, actually. That tie. The suit. The shoes. I'm honoured.'

'As you should be, girl. Obviously I should be pulling out all the stops.' He fingered his favourite, little-worn tie – a skinny affair with a piano keyboard running from top to squared bottom. He rarely got out his light grey Josef Siebel shoes or indeed the White Stuff shirt and Daniel Hechter two-piece. Everything fitted too, gratifyingly. 'You're looking good yourself. Beautiful top. Nice tan.'

'I'm honouring you as well, Frank.' Her hair was immaculately cut, and the blonde colour sharp and fresh. The pink strip from the side parting above her forehead had been touched up and was as distinctive as ever. The top came from the shop in Dovercourt, newly laundered and precisely ironed. There was still a glittery whirl of colour from the design on the front. Her upper body was muscled and curved generously in all the right places and her jeans hugged her more slender legs.

Behind his desk, Sterling felt the same stirring he'd felt when he'd bathed her at Lily's flat in Socketts Heath. He shuffled uncomfortably. They'd spoken on the phone virtually every day, but now they were face to face and it was different.

'OK, time for an update. Spill the beans,' said Sterling.

'We did a good job on CommuniCo. The flotation's been abandoned till further notice – so no change there. I'd be spitting if there had been. The police have come round to our version of events, thank God. I couldn't believe that stupid detective superintendent. What was his name? Andrews. Alan Whitman-Wood's post-mortem has been done. Cause of death was accidental – a broken neck falling down my staircase. Good,' she said. 'Fully deserved. We'll find out more in a bit. Marcus Whitman-Wood's leg has been set, but I'm told it was a multiple fracture, so with luck there will be complications. He had severe concussion too. I didn't know that at the time. All good.

'He's going to get done for Cedric at Lakeside bus station. The relevant members of CommuniCo's security team have caved in on that, and Cedric's identified them all. The police have found the couple in the SUV at Tilbury Dock who witnessed your ducking in the Thames, and Billy can also testify. You and Mike witnessed Dad's abduction from the landing window and Dad's willing to see it through. Even if it was really just keeping him out of the way for a few hours, you just can't go around doing that willy-nilly, can you? That family thought it could do as it pleased. And then there's the big one: Grandma's murder.'

Sterling leaned forward.

'Yesss,' said Emma. 'The Crown Prosecution Service looks as though it is going ahead, despite that incompetent prat Andrews. Marcus is going to be charged. There's no forensic evidence, but plenty of circumstantial stuff, and as we all know, loads of motivation. And of course there's us – saying that we heard Marcus admitting it – that's what clinched it. The police are also searching for CCTV from Suffolk to Kent on the day of the murder. As they so pompously say, 'enquiries are continuing'.'

'Good news indeed,' said Sterling, and he was pleased, but inside he was also thinking, the girl's relentless. 'So, why are we meeting Jimmy Whitman-Wood, and why here in my office?'

'The second question's easy, Mr PI. I wanted to see where you worked. Learn a bit more about you. Whitman-Wood offered the Schredemann offices next to St Paul's Cathedral, all expenses paid, but why would I go into the lion's den? If the bastard wants to see me, let him make the effort. Also, I wanted you present, and where more convenient for you than your office? Why does he want to meet? I honestly have no idea, but it's no skin off my nose. Let's hear what he's got to say. And I'll get the chance to have a gloat.'

'OK,' said Sterling. He looked at his watch. 'We've got 15 minutes. I'll bop the cattle yon.'

'Do that,' said Emma.

—⟩⟩⟩—

Sterling looked down into the square, wondering what it was that caused parking spaces to open up for everyone except himself. Gloria Etchingham, when he had been involved in her case in Flanders, had had the knack of arriving to an empty space. Now the familiar black CommuniCo Range Rover pulled in just as a Renault pulled out. He looked back at Emma. 'Ready?' he said. He watched as Jimmy Whitman-Wood emerged from the back of the SUV and looked up at the sign the way clients and other interested parties always did. Sterling listened to him come up the stairs. It wasn't brisk and brusque, two-at-a-time, like Nicholas Jameson all those weeks ago, or a despairing plod like some of his visitors. This seemed more like a scamper.

There was a rap on the thin door. Sterling waited. He put his forefinger to his lip. There was another rap, louder, impatient. Sterling winked at Emma. 'Come in,' he called out.

The small man entered. As usual, Sterling was assailed by irrelevant thoughts. This time they were about Christina Van de Velde at the Hotel Sultan in Ypres and her mother during the Flanders case. They could have been twins but for the 25 years or so between their ages. Jimmy Whitman-Wood, too, looked like the much younger twin of his father. He must have been in his sixties, but already his skin was pale and papery, and his black-framed glasses were simply a more fashionable version of his father's. His Savile Row suit still managed to hang from his slight frame, no matter how accurately it had been cut, and his collar was too wide for his thin neck.

Sterling had known a family of four daughters – feuders, he remembered – when he had lived in Ramsgate. The first and the third had the slender, wiry frame of their father, whilst the second and fourth were solid and large-boned like their mother. Marcus Whitman-Wood was stocky and slow, unlike his father and grandfather. Did that mean he was like his mother?

Sterling pointed to the sofa as he half got up from his chair. Emma swung around in the client chair. Whitman-Wood made to offer his hand but decided better of it. He perched in the middle of the sofa and pressed his palms together. Even perching didn't get him level with Sterling and Emma, who looked down on him from different angles, Sterling protected additionally by the desk. Good, he thought. Just as planned. He'll be used to proposing and disposing. Let him do some begging for a change.

Sterling and Emma stayed silent, waiting.

'Thank you for meeting me. I'm sorry circumstances have been so difficult. What I'm hoping to get from this is some clarification and perhaps to see how we can make progress on things that will be of mutual benefit.' Jimmy Whitman-Wood looked from Sterling to Emma.

Emma stared at him. She's good at this as well, thought Sterling, just as she was a natural with the media.

Whitman-Wood looked at his praying hands. 'We won't be floating CommuniCo. You'll know that already. I strongly refute the allegations you made against my father, but we won't be taking any action on that either. The rights or wrongs of it all won't affect the fortunes of our private company and it would turn out to be an expensive legal diversion.'

'That's a relief. Thank you so much,' said Emma. 'I've been quaking in my boots.'

Jimmy Whitman-Wood didn't appear to have heard. 'I acknowledge too that things have not been easy for you, Emma – losing your grandmother and so on. I know you're angry. I think we can set CommuniCo aside for the minute. I want to talk about Marcus. He was very much influenced by his grandfather and they had a strong bond. It's a strange thing to say, but I was often excluded. And that's why things got a little' – he stared up at the ceiling – 'out of hand. Marcus lacks his grandfather's creative genius and my entrepreneurial skills. He's limited. There's not much in the way of social skills. Doing the security at CommuniCo was about the right role for him. But I'm afraid my father wielded a rather bad influence. He'd put so much into the company for so long – well past anyone's usual retirement age – that his perspective got a little warped. And Marcus wanted only to please his grandfather.'

Emma stared. Sterling swivelled in his chair and listened to the faint rhythmic squeak it caused. If he swivelled slowly, the noise disappeared.

'He's not well. He's not as robust as he looks. He's still getting headaches from the concussion and he's going to have a permanent limp.'

'Boohoo,' said Emma. If she was in her wheelchair, she'd be gripping the hand-rims and doing those little jerks, thought Sterling.

'Don't get me wrong. Marcus has done some bad things. I know the evidence is solid for the assault on the bus driver. And throwing you in the river, Mr. Sterling. And the other things. We're preparing for him to go to prison. But your grandmother, Emma. We can't let him go down for that.'

The familiar red spots flared up in Emma's cheeks. 'That's the biggest crock of shit I've ever heard. That big bullying lunkhead murdered my grandmother and went on a criminal rampage across East Anglia and Kent. And you're trying to say that he was just following his grandfather's orders. I don't think so.'

Whitman-Wood sighed. 'I was hoping we'd come to some kind of accommodation. You see, Emma, Marcus told me what happened at your house on the morning of the flotation. How he carried his grandfather upstairs to the bathroom. How they were at the top of the stairs, about to descend, when he glimpsed you coming out of your bedroom....' He looked up again at the ceiling, and let the words hang in the air. Sterling swore he could see his mouth formed into a little 'o', as if he was whistling. 'Marcus is going to be punished – no doubt about that – but if the charge to do with your grandmother could go away – maybe you and Mr Sterling could cast doubt on what you heard Marcus actually say – then the complications of a charge against you for my father's death can be avoided. A neat symmetry in fact.'

Sterling sprang forward. Now it was his turn. He was trying to work out why he was so furiously angry. Of course he was protective of Emma. Having to run with her from Marcus Whitman-Wood and his thugs all over eastern England had seen to that. But that wasn't it – not principally. No, he was disgusted at the abuse of power. Even at the nadir of CommuniCo's fortunes, even with his father dead of a broken neck and his son charged with murder, assault and a range of other offences, even with the weakest possible set of bargaining chips, the man on the sofa was trying to cut a deal. And Jon-Jo pushing his cleaning trolley in the mall at Gravesend was right too. You had to take every chance to stick it to the Man.

'You and your son are living in fairyland, Mr Whitman-Wood,' said Sterling. 'Emma wasn't even on the landing. I saw that myself, and that's what I'll testify. The forensics will back it all up. Your son was concussed anyway, so who knows what he remembers and what he makes up? But even without any of that a jury will see an accusation of Emma for what it is. A pathetic attempt to slip off the hook. You know what? This meeting's over.' Sterling strode to the door and swung it open. 'Get out.'

Jimmy Whitman-Wood looked shocked. He was not used to getting anything other than his own way. He rose awkwardly and stumbled to the tiny landing. Sterling slammed the door.

'The brass neck of the man. He had nothing and he tried to negotiate.'

'Yeah. Bastard. But I'm glad you were with me, Frank. It made it easier. Thanks,' said Emma. 'In fact, while I'm about it, thank you for everything.'

'Well, I don't like to say "I told you so",' said Sterling. He cocked his head, weighing things up. 'Actually, I do quite like it.'

'Get to the point for goodness sake, Frank,' said Emma.

'Well, I still think we should have done what I originally suggested, and said we were all in the living room when the Whitman-Woods fell down the stairs. Then we wouldn't have left that little chink of daylight for Jimmy to work on. But we can't do anything about it now and hopefully it won't come to anything. Right, I reckon it's time for another pick-me-up cup of tea.'

He put up his traffic policeman hand. 'Please, no... what are they called again?... mondegreens.'

—◆—

'So Frank, you really think he's bluffing, do you?' They were sipping their tea, easy in each other's company. The office could be cosy at times, and this was one of them.

'It's all bluff, girl. The last throw of the dice, and it came up with a "one". Marcus Whitman-Wood is going away for a long time, even if it's going to take a while to get to the guilty verdict.'

Emma looked into her cup. 'There's another thing, Frank. That time when we were coming back from Bawdsey.' Her gaze was usually strong, but now she was avoiding eye contact. 'All those adventures...We got close. I saw how you felt about me, and it might not have been obvious at the time, but I really enjoyed your company. It was pretty scary, but you made me feel safe. And we had fun, didn't we?' Her eyes were fixed downwards. 'I know I can be difficult. I know I'm prickly. I know I fly off the handle, but I was thinking...maybe we could go out together.'

This is confusing, thought Sterling. 'You mean, as in, be an item,' he said.

'Yeah, go out. Be an item. Bump pelvises. Well, you'd have to do the bumping, obviously, but there are different ways to skin a cat.'

Sterling took advantage of Emma's lack of eye contact to swivel around and look out of the window. 'I can't,' he said.

Emma raised her eyes. 'I shouldn't have said anything. I knew what you'd say. I must be mad.' She flapped her hands vaguely around her legs. 'It's because of this, isn't it? Me being a cripple.'

'No,' he lied. The pelvis bumping, as she put it, and proposed related activities, the different ways to skin a cat, were intriguing. Of course they were. And she was beautiful and passionate. But he knew he was no caregiver long term – recent experience had taught him that. Then there was the procession of abandonment, as Andy Nolan called it, a much more significant factor, starting with his mother when he was a baby and continuing through school and the police. His wife had gone. Even his father had gone. He couldn't risk it.

'No, it's certainly not that, Emma. And it's nothing to do with you neglecting the grip bag duties, turning the air blue from Felixstowe Ferry to Hamworth Place, and being a general, attention-seeking pain in the neck.'

'You cheeky bastard,' said Emma.

'The bond is there of course, and always will be. It's just that,' he gave her one of the sly sideways looks he'd seen her use so often, 'it would be too dangerous. The first row, and it wouldn't be long coming, let's face it, you'd bash me down the stairs with your wheelchair. Now that someone's given you the idea.'

Emma laughed. She'd always been quick to bounce back. 'You've got me there, Mr PI. OK, no mad wild fling. Your loss. You had your chance and spurned it.' Then she looked vulnerable again. 'But you are coming to the pub tonight for a bit of a celebration, as planned. Billy will be there 'cos he's staying with us. Dad will be, but not the Scab, so that's good. Becky and Mike. Your pal from downstairs.'

'Of course, girl. I wouldn't miss it for anything. Let's get you back downstairs.'

On the tiny landing, Sterling worked himself so he was facing the stairs going down, with Emma clinging in the usual manner to his back. He could still smell the Chloe perfume as he took one laborious step at a time, hands and feet on the stairs, and feel her warm breath and the press of her breasts, inducing a sense of dismay and loss. And something damp on his neck. And the vibration caused by a tremble. 'Hell's bells, Emma, are you really only eight stone? You seem heavier going down than up.'

'Shut up, Frank,' said Emma, laughing and sobbing. 'Just get me down, stick me in my chair and let me get out of here.'

Chapter 31

Bathsheba

The West African queen and the smartest private investigator currently operating in the East Kent area strolled arm in arm from their almost neighbouring homes through the breezy, early evening, late spring streets of Sandley on the way to the pub. Through the Guildhall the regal procession passed, up No Name Street, into the churchyard, across St Peter's Street and into Holy Ghost Alley, arriving at the pub in the High Street from a shallow, jagged rightward curve.

Sterling drew up outside the door, causing Angela to stop next to him. 'There's talk of a party to commemorate the triumph of the little people over the rich and powerful, getting all our helpers together from Suffolk to Sandley. Emma's mentioned Basildon, as it's the half way point, or the pub in Harwich, The Union Flag, as possible venues. Just giving you the heads-up in case it's mentioned.'

'Thanks. I'm not that keen on parties,' said Angela.

'Me neither,' said Sterling gloomily.

'Anyway, would I be invited?'

'Well, you're not her best pal, and vice versa, but one thing about Emma is that she's straight as a die.

You helped a lot, so you meet the criteria. So of course you'd get an invite.'

At the bar, Sterling ordered his pint and Angela's gin and tonic. Mike and Becky had got someone new in to help out so they were free to join the celebration. The girl pulled the pint expertly. Sterling heard Emma's voice as it drifted up from the snug. He chinked glasses with Angela, leaned with his back to the bar, resting his elbows, and listened. He wasn't quite ready for Emma yet, especially as she was in evangelical mode.

'You can get experts in for an audit,' the girl was saying. 'I could tell you some things, like how I could get to the bar and be the same height as other customers, and why I don't want to have to come in the pub by a ramp at the back, like a thief in the night, rather than on one at the front like everyone else. Dad could tell you about the deaf stuff, like having Quiz Night questions projected on a screen as well as being called out. But there are disabled professionals who'd be able to cover the whole spectrum of impairments and the adjustments available. It's really subtle these days. Your nondisabled customers wouldn't even notice, or, if they did, it would soon seem perfectly natural.' There was passion in her voice.

'So they'd look at it step by step, area by area, and do us a report,' said Becky.

'Yes. Including costings. I'll do some research for you and come up with the best choices.'

'Thanks,' said Mike. 'It will be good for business.'

'No,' said Emma. It was like a whiplash echoing through the pub.

'Uh oh,' whispered Sterling to Angela. 'There's a faux pas in there somewhere.'

'Sorry, Mike,' said Emma. 'I get a bad reaction to some things, and that's one of them. Actually, it will be good for business. If The Cinque Port Arms is fully accessible, disabled people from all over will come to eat and drink here, and that's good. But lots of disabled people, including me and Dad, hate the 'business case' as a motive for companies and businesses to make changes. Why should 'the business case' be a reason for us having what is ours by right – the same opportunities and access as everyone else? It's about equality.'

'I get it,' said Mike.

Angela and Sterling drifted over to the snug. 'Don't worry about it, Mike,' said Sterling. 'It's all gobbledegook. She makes it up as she goes along.'

'Sod off, Frank,' said Emma. 'You can joke about some things, but not that.'

'You're right. Sorry. Yo, Billy,' said Sterling. 'He went through the finger touch and fist bump routine.

'Yo, bro. Where did you learn to do that?'

'I've been practising with Angela.'

At eight o'clock, the small party was complete with the arrival of Nicholas Jameson, looking like the same Count Dracula as a few weeks ago. The pub had filled out with regulars, and everywhere Sterling looked, people's glasses were full. He glanced over at Nicholas Jameson across the table. He had a small notepad and a pen on the surface in front of him, but for all his positioning in the middle of the party, he was as isolated as if he'd been in the middle of an empty field in Hamworth. Sterling was about to call over when Emma banged on the table. Billy, rapidly assuming the role of second-in-command, or possibly lackey, called out 'Order, order'.

David R Ewens

'Frank,' said Emma in front of the assembled company, with the rest of the pub also falling quiet – perhaps this was a birthday announcement – 'we've been through a lot together. You looked after me, and, let's face it, you put up with a lot. We shared a guardianship.' (Eh? thought Frank. What "guardianship"?). 'So as a token of both my thanks and my esteem, I've got you a little present – or rather, resurrected a little present.' She nodded to Billy and he produced a large package in bright red shiny wrapping paper from under his seat, giving it to Emma to hand over.

'Thanks, Frank.' She leaned over and kissed him on the cheek.

Sterling took the package. It had a familiar bulk and weight, and when he had torn away the paper, there it was, the fully sponged down, cleaned and dried, olive drab grip bag.

'Thank you, Emma. I promise to look after it to the very best of my ability.'

'It doesn't stop there. Check inside, bro,' said Billy.

Sterling unzipped the bag and rummaged through. There was a pair of dark navy trousers, a matching V-neck cashmere sweater, two white shirts in his favoured style, socks and underwear, a pair of taupe desert boots and a full sponge bag.

He looked around and nodded. Words were difficult. 'Thanks,' he said. 'Thank you very much.'

'Grip,' Emma called out. Billy took up the chant. 'Grip, grip, grip.' Even regal Angela smiled, started clapping her hands in rhythm and joined in. The rest of the pub – the regulars on the bar stools, the diners and their children in the restaurant area, the lovers at the side tables, the casual trade up from the boats at the quayside – weren't sure what was going on, but knew it

300

was a kind of celebration. They started chanting too, until the whole pub echoed. 'Grip, grip, grip....' Faster and faster, and more and more loudly, until Sterling stood up and sheepishly brandished the bag one-handed like a budget day chancellor.

As the chant turned to cheers and died away, Jameson wrote something on his pad and pushed it over. 'Why was everyone shouting 'Shit, shit, shit....?' He and Sterling locked eyes and laughed.

When the noise had turned to a buzz, and everyone had turned their attention back to their own groups, Emma turned to Sterling. 'Billy helped me choose everything – not as handy as you might imagine. His tastes are wacky. But I've got all the receipts if you want to change anything.' She gestured for him to lean closer, and whispered in his ear. 'Everything's there for a dirty weekend, if you change your mind, Frank. All designed for us to leave at a moment's notice. Make sure you look after it.'

He smiled and toasted her, while Emma threw back her head and laughed. She doesn't sulk, thought Sterling, and she doesn't bear a grudge except when she sees wrong – but then she's like a ferret.

Her father tapped his arm. 'I gather you and Emma met James Whitman-Wood.'

'Yes. He was trying to wriggle out of everything and do some bargaining for his son. Emma will have told you. She gave him short shrift. I wanted to kick him down the stairs.'

'What? You wanted to pick him pounds of pears?'

Sterling wrote on the pad 'I wanted to kick him down the stairs.' He knew he'd be using the pad for this whole conversation.

'I'm glad you didn't do that, Frank.' Jameson scored heavily through the sentence so that it could no longer be seen. 'The trouble with the pad is it leaves evidence,' he said as an aside. 'We don't want to have to explain to the powers-that-be yet another accident to yet another person from the same family. That would be too much of a coincidence with you and Emma around.' He handed over an envelope. 'Thanks for your invoice.'

Sterling looked at the amount on the cheque. 'This is really generous, Nicholas.'

'You did exactly what it says on the tin, Frank. Actually, you did that and more. You got Emma back, but she and I would not have got through all the rest of it without you. I've said it before, but still…I am very grateful.' Business transacted, Jameson motioned to Angela to come and sit next to him. 'There are a couple of things that I still don't quite understand,' he said to them both. 'Maybe you'll be able to help sort them out, Angela. Maybe they're connected. The first thing is my poor mother's last words. In one of our earlier conversations, Frank, you said that you reckoned they were 'Bawdsey Manor''.

'Yes. That's how I came to go down there. I saw a book in a bookshop in Woodbridge about radar and Bawdsey Manor. I knew Emma had gone down to Woodbridge. It all clicked. It was a mixture of luck and maybe a bit of good detective work.'

'But the thing is, 'Bawdsey Manor' is four syllables. Whatever my mother said, the paramedic who treated her heard phrases or words amounting to three syllables. I can tell you from my own deaf experience that that is a big difference.'

Sterling shrugged. 'We got the result though, didn't we?' He felt a little niggle. After all they'd been through, including Jameson's own abduction, who cared about a syllable?

Angela felt his irritation. 'What was the second thing, Nicholas?'

Jameson was still focused on Sterling's reaction. 'I wasn't criticising your work or your instincts, Frank. You did brilliantly. It's just something that doesn't add up.' He turned to Angela. 'The other thing was something in my mother's letter to me. I don't mind that you read it by the way – of course you had to, in the circumstances – but there was a phrase when she referred to my poor father as 'my beloved Hittite'. I've done a bit of research on the Hittites and I'm none the wiser.'

Angela drained her gin and tonic. Sterling could tell she was having a good time because she hadn't stopped at the second one. Her fingers drummed on the tabletop. 'Frank, I need a top up. I reckon you both will as well. I think I'm going to kill two birds with one stone here.'

She had a gulp of her next drink and took a breath. Now the whole table was listening. 'Your mother was using a biblical reference. I think I'm right in saying that it was in the Old Testament, in the Book of Samuel. The King of the Israelites, David, saw and took a fancy to the wife of one of his soldiers, whose name was Uriah the Hittite. If I remember it correctly, and it's a complicated story, in the end David sent Uriah off to fight, arranged for him to be in the front line and in effect engineered his death on the battlefield. Then he married Uriah's widow.'

'So my father was my mother's 'beloved Hittite', and Alan Whitman-Wood was David. What was the wife called?'

'Bathsheba,' said Angela. 'Three syllables. Your mother didn't say 'Bawdsey Manor'. She said Bathsheba.'

'Damn,' said Sterling. 'How was I so right and so wrong? Everything I did in Suffolk – going down to Bawdsey and all that – was based on a wrong assumption.'

'Don't worry about it, Frank,' said Jameson. 'As things turn out, it's not important. I just wanted them resolved in my head. My mother's going to get justice thanks to Emma. I don't want my cheque back.'

'Thank goodness for that.'

It was nearing 11 p.m. Mike began the long routine of closing up the pub. Emma and Billy were in raucous competition, downing the Jagerbombs they had graduated to earlier in the evening, and Becky and Nicholas Jameson were communicating intensely using the notepad and pen. Angela sat looking at the dregs of her last drink.

'What?' said Sterling.

Angela looked up at him. 'Are you ready to go, Frank? I wouldn't mind you walking me home.'

Sterling surveyed the table. Everything would be breaking up in a few minutes anyway, and there was something in Angela's manner. 'Sure,' he said.

'See you all soon,' he said to the stragglers.

'Got the grip?' called out Emma.

He held it aloft with thumbs up. In the dank streets, Angela took his arm. 'Come in for a coffee or a nightcap, Frank. I was thinking just now – I told you the story of David and Bathsheba, and Uriah the Hittite – but I left some things out.'

Chapter 32

Sleeping Dogs

Sterling clasped the tumbler of Scotch at Angela's kitchen table. All the houses in the terrace were the same shape and design, so it was always a strange feeling being in a room that was so familiar and yet so different.

'OK, Angie. Shoot.'

Angela sipped her own drink. 'Did you get the feeling in the old woman's letter to her son that she was holding something back? I only read it a couple of times, and I'd need to look at it again, but it didn't all add up.'

Sterling listened.

'I don't think it was just about a guilty old woman asking for forgiveness for deserting her son for three years, and for being so difficult with him throughout their lives. There was a phrase in the letter when she confessed that there were some things she'd never be able to reveal – something like that. If I've got this right, she always referred to 'my husband' or 'my loving husband' or 'Richard'.

'Rather than....?' Sterling wasn't sure where this was going.

'Rather than 'your father' or 'your dear father'.

'So what are you saying here, Angie?' said Sterling, though he was beginning to think he had an inkling.

'I didn't tell the whole story about King David, Bathsheba and Uriah the Hittite, just an abridged version. The fuller version goes something like this. Uriah was one of David's soldiers, and while he was away, David saw Bathsheba bathing and wanted her. He made her pregnant. Uriah came back from a campaign, and David wanted him to sleep at home with Bathsheba so that Uriah would think that it was he who had done it. But Uriah, following a convention of the time and place, wouldn't sleep at home but stayed with his fellow soldiers away from the palace at the barracks. To get out of his difficulty, David sent Uriah on another campaign and arranged for him to be killed on the frontline. After Uriah's death, David married Bathsheba. Maybe, just maybe, Richard Jameson wasn't Nicholas Jameson's father.'

'So,' said Sterling, 'you're saying that Alan Whitman-Wood and Daphne Jameson might already have already slept together before Richard Jameson went to Cauville. Maybe he forced himself on her. Maybe it was a silly fling. Things like that happened all the time during the war. Alan Whitman-Wood got Daphne pregnant and got rid of Richard.' He sipped his Scotch. 'There's so much we don't know.'

'Perhaps Nicholas's relationship with his mother was difficult because he reminded her of his real father – Alan Whitman-Wood,' said Angela.

'Perhaps,' said Sterling. 'Thinking it all through, if Daphne was this modern-day Bathsheba, Alan Whitman-Wood David and Richard Jameson Uriah the Hittite, then that would make Nicholas Jameson....'

'....Alan Whitman-Wood's son,' said Angela, 'and Jimmy Whitman-Wood's half brother....'

'....and Emma....'

'Alan Whitman-Wood's granddaughter, and Marcus Whitman-Wood's step-cousin.'

'....And Richard Jameson....'

'....would not actually be related to Nicholas and Emma at all.'

'If this theorising is accurate, Emma wrecked the CommuniCo flotation on behalf of a man, Richard Jameson, she was not related to and ruined a man who turns out to be her grandfather and a war spy who died in her house.'

Angela blinked. 'Hell's bells,' said the woman who never swore. 'I never thought of that.'

She and Sterling sat in silence. It was a small, friendly kitchen. Sterling stared at a beach scene in Trinidad on the wall above the worktop. He listened to the hum of the fridge. There was a vague aroma of spices – perhaps the Cajun chicken he loved when they had an occasional supper together. He rubbed his fingers on the table, feeling the smooth top. It sometimes helped him think.

'What are we going to do, Frank?'

He looked at his watch. It was 1.30 am. 'We're going to drain our drinks. I'm going home. We'll sleep on it. I'll call in to the library tomorrow, either before or after I've been to the bank.'

Sterling had slept unexpectedly well – a long and dreamless sleep unencumbered by angst or tension. Angela would already have opened up the library as he walked through the Guildhall and up No Name Street into the square. Sure enough, the library door was open and he could see the teacups in the small office behind the counter. Angela appeared from behind one of the shelves.

'Morning, Frank,' she said cheerfully. She must have slept well too, he thought. 'I'll just put the kettle on.' She handed over a sheet of paper. 'Have a look at this.'

Sterling took the sheet to the table. 'Bathsheba 1918-2013' was the heading. Everything they'd discussed late last night was set out in perfect mind map form, with a beautiful genealogical table centred on Emma Jameson and working backwards presented as an inset in the top left hand quarter of the page. In Angela's neat, precise lettering, it was a perfect work of art.

'I thought you'd do something like this,' said Sterling. 'It's brilliant.'

Angela poured the tea. 'I had to get it down on paper. It would have driven me mad otherwise. So, what next, Frank?'

'This case is going to run and run. Emma, Nicholas and I are going to be witnesses at Marcus Whitman-Wood's trial. There will be plenty of argy-bargy with his various employees as well. They're all invoking the concentration camp guard defence.'

'What on earth....?' said Angela.

'I-was-just-following-orders....'

'Oh. Right.'

'Anyway, it's all far from over. You and I could stir things up even more – discuss it all with Nicholas and Emma, explain the situation, look at Daphne's letter again, suggest some DNA testing to establish the accuracy of this family tree....'

'All on the basis of supposition,' said Angela. 'Febrile hypothesising based on a biblical story after a night in the pub.'

'Exactly. The way things are moving at the moment, Emma is achieving justice. The guilty have been punished or will be punished, and those wronged have or will have some redress. There's no point in upsetting Emma and Nicholas about their family origins, and it's pretty clear that the Whitman-Woods don't know the whole story either. Sleeping dogs, eh?'

'Sleeping dogs,' she said. She took the sheet of paper and went over to a machine in the corner.

'What are you doing, Angie?' said Sterling.

'Shredder,' she replied.

'That beautiful effort,' said Sterling.

'It doesn't matter,' she said. 'It's not something I'm ever likely to forget.'

The whir of the machine grated in Sterling's ears.

Lightning Source UK Ltd.
Milton Keynes UK
UKOW02f0006051216

289177UK00001B/10/P